The Face

in the

Bathroom Floor

Portland Jones

To the family who have shaped my past and my future, and who I love so much.

The bathroom

When I first saw the face in the bathroom floor, I asked Fey, the local witch, to come and take a look, see what advice she could give me.

We both stood there, too close together for comfort, but that's how it had to be given the amount of space in my small, downstairs bathroom. Fey's head was down, red hair fading to white draping past her shoulders, obscuring her face. She tucked her hair behind her ear, raising her startlingly blue eyes to look into mine.

'Do you know who it is, Erica?' she asked.

'Not a clue,' I replied, shaking my head. How on earth would I know a face that's just appeared on my bathroom floor?

Fey nodded sagely. 'Spirits often surface where there's water. It's the fluidity that attracts them. The element of water has a strong attraction for the spirit world, it lets them flow peacefully, lets them surface to make contact.'

Sounded a bit mumbo-jumbo to me, but then again, she is a witch, and I did ask her opinion.

'But the bathroom? You mean the water in my toilet?'

'Be gentle with her,' said Fey, ignoring my comment. 'Let yourself reach out to her. You may find that she has things to tell you, lessons for you to learn, something you need to know.'

And with that she was gone, leaving my house with not another word. Oh well, I suppose that might be normal behaviour for a witch.

I sat on the loo and stared at the face on my bathroom floor. A young woman, with a jaunty hat placed on top of her abundance of hair, smiling, eyes sparkling. Someone you might like to know, but not of this generation. There was the feel of looking at an old photo.

She had appeared shortly after I had taken up the linoleum. Mother was coming for one of her frequent, welcomed, but stressful visits. Last time, she had commented on how long it had been since I had decorated the bathroom, and how it desperately needed doing. I'd scarcely noticed; after all, it's the smallest room in the house, somewhere the kids dash in and out of when they're playing out with their friends, where David goes to wash his hands after he's been doing the gardening, where I wash my hands after taking the dog for a walk. And of course, where we all go if the upstairs bathroom is taken!

So after Mother had left, I took a good look at it and yes, she was right. It was a bit of a state. I really needed to get it sorted. Bother. But on the bright side, it was only a small room, so it wouldn't take long. I ripped off the paper, tore up the lino to reveal the concrete floor, spattered with multi colours of paint I had   used previously, pale lemon from when we first moved in, bright pink from that phase when I'd been watching too many home makeover programmes on TV, and grown up oatmeal from the latest reincarnation.

And a few days later, the face appeared.

One night the floor had been clear and the only thought in my head was to get on with it before Mother came to visit. The next day, all I could think of was this smiling face, staring at me, holding my gaze every time I went in there.

After staring smiling at this young woman for a couple of hours, I realised that I needed to do something. I could already feel this becoming a bit of an obsession. I'm like that. I get a thought in my head and I can't put it to one side till I've looked at it from all angles, done my research. I just can't let go. I could feel it coming on quickly so that's when I decided to contact Fey. We all know she's a witch. You wouldn't know from just looking at her, well, not really. She didn't have warts or walk round in flowing robes or anything like that. But she had this long, long straggly hair which would look just right blowing back from her face on a windy night. And she had this way of looking at you that made you feel distinctly uncomfortable.

She had a shop where she sold animal food, dog beds, balls of wool in a range of colours and textures, packets of sequins, glue for any occasion and myriad items that nowhere else sells. The shop hadn't been open long, but I'd soon fallen in love with it. I went there often. It fed my love for making things – special birthday cards, advent calendars, projects with the boys in the school holidays. She also stocked candles, incense, little statues of strange voluptuous women and stranger male faces with leaves curling round their heads. She kept this stock to one side, laid out stylishly on black velvet, a complete contrast to the rest of the shop. And the customers who went to buy these items were a total contrast to the rest of her customers. Dressed in black, many of them, or in long floaty skirts. Usually polite and friendly but not quite the same as the rest of us. I found them interesting but my other half, David, was very scathing.

'What a bunch of weirdos. That shop just encourages this new age clap trap. Should be stopped, if you ask me.'

I hadn't asked him, so I ignored his hostility. He would rant and rave, then watch the latest silly video clips on the TV, rapt in someone else's misfortune, and forget what the problem was.

David didn't know who the woman was on the bathroom floor. At first, he outright denied he could see anyone, but then he relented and admitted he could. I asked Annie to have a look. She said she felt pretty stupid doing it, but as she'd known me for so long, she would have a quick look. Annie didn't recognise my face either. Jackie had a look when she popped in for coffee; she doesn't pop in anymore. Debbie from the chip shop said she didn't recognise the face either.

I even called my sister Eileen. I can't stand her really but thought it might be someone in the family, and as she knows everything there is to know about our family – or so she claims – it was worth asking her over. Eileen was quite enthusiastic, given the circumstances, but became rapidly bored when she realised she couldn't put a name to the face.

'Probably just a damp patch in the concrete. After all, you don't have a radiator in there, and it feels cold to me.'

She had a point. I waved her off quite happily and sat down to give this some deep thought. It had been over a week now. I'd asked everyone I knew well enough to have a look. No one knew the woman. Some of them said they thought I was barking. Debbie was quite forthright about this. Almost rude, actually. I might drop her off my Christmas card list.

Mother was due any day now, and I still hadn't finished the bathroom. I had to pull myself together, forget the face, and get on with it. I picked up my latest copy of Home and Garden and started leafing through it, looking for inspiration. The phone rang.

'Hello, Mother. How are you?' I felt that familiar sinking in the pit of my stomach and once again felt angry with myself. How could someone have that effect on you when you're my age? Nearly forty for heaven's sake, and I still felt like a child caught with my fingers in the cookie jar whenever she phoned.

'You're coming on Friday? That's only two days away.'

'No, no problem at all. It's just that I was hoping to have finished decorating before you came, so there's nothing to do when you're here.'

'Oh, you know about the face on the floor? Who told you?' Of course, Jacob, at the age of ten, could not keep a secret. He'd told Mother all about it when she phoned to speak to me but obviously he'd forgotten to tell me she'd phoned.

'Well, I'll see you Friday then. And you can see what all the fuss is about.'

I was not looking forward to this at all. I wasn't so bothered about the face, but that Mother would want to get involved with the decorating. It would take ages choosing the colour scheme and buying the paper and exactly the right shade of paint. And the floor covering. Mother would hardly settle for lino. And what's more, she would see the mess on the concrete floor, all those colours of paint I'd spilled in the past and not bothered to clean up. Now that really would upset her.

I flicked the pages of my magazine furiously. David walked in.

'Let me guess, your mother's due.' It really was that obvious.

By Friday, I was worn out. The house gleamed from top to bottom, especially the box room, which we grandly call the guest room, where Mother would be ensconced for the duration. Freshly ironed sheets (I never do my own), fresh flowers in a vase, and Febreze in large quantities on the ageing carpet – otherwise you can tell that Bruno likes to spend his spare time in there, asleep in the patch of sun that glares through the window late afternoon, leaving his black and tan hairs, and pervasive doggy smell, everywhere.

The kitchen was also strangely gleaming. Mother took a keen interest in cooking, always cooking to Delia's standards, and expecting all kitchens to be ready to be seen on TV at any time. My attempt at baking stood rather lopsidedly on the cake stand. I had just decided it would look less like a disaster if I sliced it before she arrived, when the doorbell rang, meaning I had no time to cut the cake. I prayed it tasted good enough to make up for its shortcomings in appearance.

'Mwah.' I air kissed Mother's cheek. Then followed it up with a sturdy hug. Despite everything I say about her, I love to see her. If only I could live up to her expectations of me. Or perhaps I mean my expectations of me on her behalf.

The boys proudly fetched her bags from the car, Jacob struggling manfully with her case, packed, it seemed, for a month, and little Joe carried her toiletries case, almost as heavy. Mother believed in taking care of her skin, and it showed. Her skin glistened with more youth than mine. Tesco's face cream just doesn't seem to do it as well as Clarins.

Bags and coat away, cup of tea on a tray with a crumbly slice of cake later, Mother asked the question.

'What exactly is all this fuss about the face on the bathroom floor?'

I explained how the face came to be here, not that I knew that much about it, and told her what Fey Witch had said. I told her of my fruitless search for the identity of the pretty young woman, my reluctance to cover her up, despite the need to make the bathroom usable once more.

'Let me see,' said Mother. I let her go in first. Immediately she looked at the spilled paint from years ago.

'You know, if you mop it up straight away with a damp cloth, it's much easier to get up.' Mother was just about to get into full flow when she stopped in her tracks.

'Good lord, it's Dorothy.'

'Dorothy who?' The only Dorothy I knew was my aunty, a plump little woman, with round red cheeks and a shock of red hair that she could never contain properly. She had passed away a good few years back. All I could remember of her was her wonderful cheery nature; she loved children and spoiled us rotten when we were kids - bags of goodies for me and my sister whenever we went to visit. The last time I'd seen her, I was still just a child. The face on the floor wasn't the Dorothy I knew.

'Not as she was when she passed on. This is Dorothy when she was a young woman, not long after the war ended. You can tell by the hair and that smile.' The smile was familiar when I thought about it. 'Of course, she wasn't actually your aunt. She was my cousin. It was just polite to call her aunty.

'And look at the hat! Dorothy loved her clothes. We had so little during the war and we all had to go without. But soon after, Dorothy took up with Jeremy whose father owned a clothing factory. He made sure that Dorothy had all the clothes she wanted. And that was ok for me too, as when she finished with stuff, she passed it on to me.' I'd often wondered about the fashionable clothes in the old photos. She'd told me that they were really poor, but I'd doubted how poor they were based on the clothes. That explained it.

We both looked at each other with one single thought in mind.

'So what would Dorothy be doing on the bathroom floor?'

Mother's visit went quite well, all things considered. We shopped for paper, delicate green leaves on pale beige background. Paint perfectly matched to the leaves to enhance their colour. And vinyl flooring, soft to walk on, with a pattern: swirls of beige, darker brown with just a scattering of green flecks, guaranteed to disguise even the dog's muddy footprints. Jacob and little Joe had new coats, smart navy blue to see them through the winter. We cooked magnificent meals which, strangely enough, the family really enjoyed. They never showed the same relish for my daily offerings.

David returned from the pub where he had hidden most of the week.

"So can we finish the decorating?" he asked. I accepted this as an offer of help, and we managed to paper three walls in one evening.

A couple of days after Mother's departure, an envelope arrived in the post. Pictures of Aunty Dorothy. There was no mistaking it. The woman in my bathroom floor was definitely Dorothy, in her early twenties.

On Saturday morning, David and I laid the vinyl floor and thought we had laid Dorothy to rest.

The bathroom looked really good. You have to hand it to Mother, she understands how to make a room look like a photo in a magazine. I proudly sat on the loo, wondering how long it would remain so pristine and new.

And then there were two

'David,' I screamed.

David came running.

'What's the matter?' I never scream, so he knew instantly there was a major problem. He followed my gaze, down to the floor.

There, in the same spot, was Aunty Dorothy, still smiling up at us, hair piled on high, hat perched at the exact angle to make it jaunty.

Aghast, David and I left the bathroom, closed the door, and headed to the booze cupboard in the kitchen. David poured himself a whisky and vodka for me.

'Do you want anything in it?' he asked. I ignored his question, downed the glass in one, then topped it up again.

'David, is she haunting us?'

'I don't think you can call it haunting, can you? She isn't doing any harm; it's not like she's being horrible or scary, is it?'

'Well, it's certainly not nice to have your dead aunty smiling at you when you're sitting on the loo.'

David glanced at me, and I could see the start of a smirk on his face. I matched it with a smile, and suddenly we were both rolling around the floor laughing. Could have been relief, could have been the alcohol but whatever it was, we felt much better for it.

We slept well that night, too well, and I woke up late. Mad rush to get the boys off to school, David grumpy as he hates being rushed in the mornings, and I almost forgot about Aunty Dorothy.

But it wasn't something I could forget for long, so when I got back from walking the boys to school, and taking Bruno for his obligatory race round the park, I stepped into the bathroom to take a look.

She was definitely there, smiling up at me. I have to say, she wasn't scary in herself, but the fact that she was there at all was scary. I had to take this seriously now. I decided to visit Fey Witch again.

The little shop was fairly quiet, and she'd had a new delivery of handmade papers which were ideal for the card I was thinking of making for Mother. I was almost side-tracked, but I forced myself to speak to Fey.

'There is a reason she is visiting you,' said Fey wisely, blue eyes looking directly into mine. 'You need to discover this reason. Did she die with unfinished business? Perhaps she wants you to contact someone for her, to straighten things out.'

'But how do I find out?' I had no idea how to communicate with the gone and departed.

'Make quiet time. Meditate to prepare yourself. Light a candle. Clear your mind and focus only on the woman. She will come to you when you are ready to receive her.'

Fey walked off at this point to re-arrange some items on her witchy display, so I presumed my audience with her was over. I left the shop, then realised I needed a candle so went back in. Fey was holding a candle in her hand, fat and white, and a little bottle of some sort.

'Anoint the candle with this oil.'

I headed home.

I looked up the word anoint in the dictionary and it meant to apply the oil. You can anoint people apparently, a bit biblical. However, I had a cup of tea, turned off the radio and sat on the loo. I put the candle on the floor just behind Aunty Dorothy, having anointed it with the said oil. It was a bit slippery and I nearly dropped it.

It was quite difficult to sit and think of nothing else but what you were supposed to be thinking of. I heard a leaflet being pushed through the letterbox. Next door were cutting the lawn; that meant ours needed doing. I wondered what to cook for dinner, and remembered I needed to fetch something tasty for the boys' lunch boxes for tomorrow – school trip – and I sighed at the amount of washing waiting to be done.

'This is ridiculous,' I thought out loud and took on a new strategy. I looked Dorothy full in the eye and started to talk to her.

'What are you doing here? Why now? What do you want me to know? How am I going to find out?' and then I felt much closer to her. I told her my memories of her, how I loved to visit her house, the excitement of being spoiled and the goody bags to take home with us. I told her how I fondly remembered her cheery smile and red cheeks, and that mass of red hair.

This seemed to be working for I felt extraordinarily peaceful and close to Dorothy, a warm glow inside. And then I knew. Dorothy was going to show me. Show me what, or how, I still didn't know but I just knew with certainty that she was going to show me something.

I blew out the candle and left the bathroom to get on with my daily business, washing, cooking, cleaning as usual. The house felt different. I felt different. At least till it was time to collect the boys, and then it all returned to the usual state of bedlam and chaos.

I checked on Dorothy several times that evening but everything looked exactly the same. I was disappointed. I thought there was going to be some magical sign or something.

'You really must grow up,' I told myself. 'David is right, that Fey just encourages this nonsense.'

Wednesday morning dawned dry and clear, great weather for the school trip. Wellies for the pond dipping, lunch box with oodles of food to keep them topped up, waterproof coat just in case. The boys went even more happily than usual. I took Bruno for an extra-long walk – he told me himself it was time to go back. He stood there and refused to walk another step further away from home.

I went to the bathroom to wash my hands. I know it's the done thing to poop scoop but there is really something quite distasteful about the whole process.

And then I saw it, or rather, her. Now I didn't have one face on my bathroom floor, I had two.

This face was in total contrast to Dorothy. She was a stern older woman with hair scraped back off her face in a high topknot. Not a single hair escaped to soften the outline. Her eyebrows arched high as if she was looking at you in disdain. No trace of a smile played on her lips, her head perched atop a high stiff collar with a hint of lace, framed against the plain dark fabric of her dress.

This was a different feeling from Dorothy. Dorothy invited you to like her. This woman wanted you, forced you, to respect her.

I couldn't bring myself to speak to her in the same way I'd spoken to Dorothy. It seemed almost too forward to use that approach. I left the bathroom and went into the garden to ponder.

'Well,' I said aloud, 'now I know that there really is something going on.' One shadowy face in the lino could be a damp patch. That same face appearing through the new flooring could also be explained as damp seeping through. But a new face in a different place – there is no way that could be coincidence.

Pleased with my logic, I went to make a cup of tea. I decided to phone Mother.

'A rather stern lady, with arched eyebrows.'

'Do you have any photos of Granny Cooper? So I can check if it's her.' Mother promised to put the photo in the post. Apparently she only had one photo, very fragile, from the days when you went to a special studio to have your photo taken. Granny, that is, my mother's granny, had only consented to have one photo taken, and was so disturbed by the whole performance that she had never gone again.

Mother phoned back within minutes. She would come to see me, and she would come tomorrow. She didn't trust the postal service to deliver Granny's photo intact. I understood her feelings and was really glad that she was prepared to come over so quickly. She must be as intrigued as I was. Then I remembered I needed to get her room ready, so hastily downed my tea and took the vacuum to the guest room.

I collected two tired but excited boys from school, muddy wellies in plastic carrier bags, empty lunch boxes rattling in their bags. Cleverly, I had secreted a couple of chocolate bars in my pocket to buy myself some time to purchase sirloin steak and a bottle of wine to make a special meal for David and me for tonight. I had to bring him round somehow to the news that Mother was visiting again so soon.

Mother duly arrived with her bags and the precious photo. We compared the stern face in the floor with the stern face in the photo. We were indeed looking at Granny Cooper.

We sat down with a fresh cup of tea. You could see that Mother was somewhat shocked by all this. Gently, I asked Mother what she remembered about her grandmother.

'A proud woman, so Mum said. Seemed to think herself better than her neighbours. Cleaned her front step every day, black-leaded the grate every week without fail. Her bed linen was beautiful. I remember Mum showing me a sheet that she had kept for years. Plain white cotton with hand embroidered flowers and leaves all over the turnback.

'Mum said that she had come from a rich family who had disowned her when she fell in love with Grandfather. He was a farm worker who broke in the young horses, got them ready for riding. She spotted him when she was on an outing to the farm, tackling a feisty young horse, who had reared up on him, Grandfather's long red hair tousled by the wind.'

'If she came from a posh family, does that explain why you had us call you Mum rather than Mom, like everyone else in Birmingham? David and I had a battle about that when the boys were little. I'm afraid he won that one.'

Mother chuckled. 'You may be right. My mother always insisted on it. I never really thought of it. Anyway, Grandfather went away to travel the world, went to Canada, was a lumberjack for a while, walking the logs as they floated on the river. She'd waited for him to come home, married him, well beneath her, and spent much of her life in the back-to-back housing in Nechells. But she loved him, from what I'm told.'

'That's so interesting, you've never told me that before. But what does that tell me about why Dorothy is in the floor? Or why Granny Cooper is in the floor! What else do you remember about her?'

'Not a great deal, to be honest. I wasn't very old when she died. Mind you, I do remember Mum saying that the neighbours had a healthy respect for her. They called her when anyone passed away to lay out the dead, and whenever anyone was ill they came to her for herbal remedies.'

Mother paused, deep in thought, a little crease in her otherwise perfectly smooth forehead.

'Mum once said that Granny saw a ghost; she saw her mother walk through the wall in her bedroom. That was the only way she found out her mother had died. Her parents would have nothing to do with her.'

'Now that is strange. Granny seems a little different, doesn't she? Second sight and all that. I wonder if she saw just the one ghost, or if she saw them all the time. And laying out the dead. I'm glad we have undertakers to do that nowadays.'

'We're too far removed from death,' said Mother, surprisingly. 'We are sheltered from realities. Death isn't frightening; it's part of life.'

Now I felt a little concerned. It wasn't like Mother at all to be so philosophical; she always focused on the practical, the here and now.

Fortunately, it was time to collect the boys, so the strange mood passed.

That night, I dreamed. I saw my Great Grandfather, only he wasn't Grandfather, he was Jack, my Jack.

Jack

I saw the horse rearing up on him, with Jack clinging onto its back, only I didn't know his name was Jack, not yet. I let out a squeal, fearing he would fall. Luckily, no one else heard me. I watched his long red hair streaming out behind him, so strange for a man to have long hair like that. I felt my stomach churning in fear, then I realised he was laughing, enjoying the challenge. I marvelled at such a man. I looked more closely as my fear subsided and saw that he was scarcely a man, a beautiful young boy, not much older than I was myself.

'Catherine!' called my tutor, reminding me wordlessly to lower my eyes and not be so brazen.

Immediately I turned my head back to the other girls, with their pretty bonnets and ribbons, decked out for our harvest outing to the farm. We were helped from the cart by a farm labourer, supervised by Miss Trounce of course, then the farmer himself showed us round the farm. We wrinkled our noses at the unfamiliar and unpleasant smells.

I heard someone calling his name. Jack. How wonderful. I stole glances at him whenever I could manage it under the watchful eyes of Miss Trounce. He knew that I was watching him.

We clambered not quite as ladylike as we should back into the cart as the visit came to an end. Jack stopped what he was doing to watch us leave. He raised his hand to wave farewell to all us girls as did the other workers, but his eyes remained on me.

I smiled shyly to myself. Miss Trounce noticed.

****

I woke up, wondering what had disturbed me. I was sure I had heard a noise.

'David, wake up. I can hear something.'

David sat up groggily, heard what I was hearing, and became alert. He went to the window and looked out. Then he laughed.

'Nothing to worry about. Only a cat sat on the fence singing to the moon. It's really bright out there; must be a full moon.'

David was asleep again within minutes. I spent the rest of the night recalling my dream. So this was it. This was how Dorothy was going to show me – through my dreams.

Jack and Catherine must have been in their mid-teens; I hadn't seen what Catherine looked like as I was Catherine, but the other girls seemed to range from thirteen to fifteen, although I felt more grown up than the others with their constant chatter and giggling. Their finely made dresses showed them to be from wealthy families – too much lace and fine cloth to be poor people.

Jack was a good-looking lad, and so much in control. He was wiry but you could tell he was strong and would probably grow even taller as he finished growing. The contrast was interesting. Catherine still a child just on the verge of becoming a woman; Jack doing a grown man's work yet holding on to the last vestiges of childhood, still joyful with his lot.

Hmm, this felt a bit odd, feeling this way about my great-grandfather. But I couldn't help it. I had definitely been Catherine.

The early morning sun poked its face into my window. I decided to start taking notes so that I would remember my dream. I also decided to share it with Mother. She would be interested.

'My mother did always say Granny was a little different from the other women where they lived. Looked down on the others, made the girls stay away from the other 'rough' children. They lived in a really poor area, shared the brew house where they did the washing with lots of other families, had a communal privy. Granny fought a constant battle with the bugs that shared their house and their beds, and Mum scared me with tales of how they combed the kids' hair with paraffin to kill off the head lice.'

'How dangerous,' I marvelled, thinking of what people would say if you did that nowadays.

'If she really was from a wealthy family, it must have been awful for her, living like that.'

We both paused and thought about it for a while. Mother fetched down the rest of the photos she had brought with her, and we spent the afternoon piecing together our family tree from the old black and white photos and even older sepia tones, some hand coloured with too bright colours that looked oddly out of place.

Steak with button mushrooms and leaf salad, plus a bottle of Lambrusco later, the house settled down for the night. I was a bit apprehensive but excited at the same time. Would I dream again tonight?

****

I lay in my high warm bed, soft covers pulled up to my chin.

'It's time to get up, Miss.'

I still lay there and rather rudely ignored her. I didn't want to move but to carry on dreaming about Jack. Was it foolish to be so infatuated with someone I'd not even spoken to? But then again, I was young and ready for romance.

'Miss,' said Mary again, gently.

I fairly danced out of bed and drifted towards the window where I looked towards the farm, though I knew it was too far away to even glimpse distant figures.

'You're in a strange mood this morning, Miss, if I may say so. Is there something on your mind?'

Mary was as much a friend as a maid, and I could sense her smiling at me.

'Or should I say, someone?'

'How do you know?' I asked but Mary always seemed to know everything. It was not worth trying to keep secrets from her.

Mary smiled her strange smile but said nothing.

'He's wonderful, Mary. So brave, and so handsome.' I dropped my eyes, realising I'd said too much.

'You would be best not to think about him, Catherine. Your parents would never permit it. He's not from a suitable family.'

'It's so unfair, Mary. Why must I marry someone my father says? I want to marry for love.' I swirled round the room, then remembered my mother would be waiting for me to go to church with her. I would have to go without breakfast if I didn't hurry.

The weather was still fine for early autumn, bright, crisp though cold, and we decided to walk the short distance to the small square church where our pew would be empty, waiting for us. I heard the distant sound of horses' hooves and for a moment, my heart raced, hoping it was Jack on his newly mastered horse. 'Don't be silly,' I told myself sternly.

A carriage clattered past us, taking more worthy souls to church. I recognised the carriage; it belonged to the Worth family. I spotted the youngest son staring at me through the small window, Justin Worth, a young man my father thought would make a suitable suitor when the time came. I shuddered. His pudgy loose-lipped face revolted me. Especially in contrast to my Jack.

I heard horses again, this time coming slowly, and there was my Jack, seated on a towering black horse, leading another on a long rein. His hat was pulled down low over his brow, but I knew, just knew, that he was looking at me. When he was almost level with my mother and me, he lifted his head, looked me in the eye and smiled, then swiftly averted his gaze and carried on.

'Did, did he just sm..?' She stopped mid-sentence.

'What, Mother?' I asked politely, as if I didn't know.

She ignored me and carried on walking, with a thoughtful expression on her face.

I knew now that Jack liked me in return. The sermon passed much quicker than its usual slow rendition permitted. My mind journeyed on its own, miles away in time and in space, to a world where I could be with Jack without any criticism.

Days passed where all I could do was think of how to see Jack again. Mary's eyes were on me all the time, as if she knew what I was thinking. My tutor reprimanded me frequently as I failed to answer her questions, exclaiming that I was becoming slow to learn. In truth, I wasn't listening to learn in the first place.

On Friday morning, Mother called me.

'I need you to run an errand for me this afternoon. One of the parishioners is unwell and I agreed with the vicar to send her some wholesome food and one of Mary's poultices to apply to her chest. I don't have time to go myself, as I am waiting for the dress maker. She's putting the final touches to the dress for tomorrow night. Mary will go with you.'

This was exciting. The first time that Mother had considered me old enough to take on some of her duties to the parish, as befitting a young woman. It would also excuse me from lessons for a while. I looked for Mary to ask her advice on what to wear but she was nowhere to be found.

At 2pm, Mary arrived, ready for us to leave with the food and poultice packed in her basket. It wasn't far to old Mrs Bracebridge's cottage, though we did have to walk through a wooded area, away from the main road. She was a widow with no children to care for her in her old age. Usually she was hale and hearty, like most of the villagers round here though not well at the moment.

As we left the road and entered the shade of the trees, Mary seemed to be finding it difficult to keep up with me. I was impatient, my head wanting my feet to move as quickly as my thoughts.

'You go on ahead. I'll catch up with you.'

I must admit, I forgot to be ladylike and ran through the trees till I was breathless. I stopped, laughing, to regain my breath and to place my hat firmly back on my head. And then I saw him, leaning against a tall, sweeping oak tree, his back against the rough bark.

He stood up straight as I saw him, hat now in his hand, the long red hair smoothed and pushed back to lie in small curls round his neck.

'Hello, Catherine,' he said shyly.

'Hello.' I could think of nothing intelligent to say, nothing friendly or encouraging, so I smiled at him, to show I wasn't upset by him being there.

We stood there for a while, not knowing what to do or say.

'I think you are beautiful,' he blurted out at last. My smile grew even broader and I lifted my face towards his, so that I could clearly see his dark brown eyes framed with lashes so long they belonged on a girl.

I reached up and touched his face, still soft though his features were hardening, becoming more defined, as he reached early manhood. I couldn't believe how forward I was being. It was a good job that Mary was on her way to us.

He took my hand in his and pulled it to his mouth, placing a gentle kiss on my palm and folding my fingers over it. I heard Mary cough as she approached; Jack turned on his heel and left, leaving me dizzy with delight.

****

David woke me with a cup of tea.

'You've slept straight through your alarm,' he said, waiting for me to sit up and take the hot drink. I smiled at him lazily; I felt totally relaxed and for some reason, really happy for a Tuesday morning.

'You were talking in your sleep last night. Who's Jack?'

My dream came flooding back to me and I knew why I was so happy this morning. Jack's kiss!

'No one for you to worry about. Jack's my great grandfather. Mother was telling me about him yesterday.'

Mother came with me to walk the children to school and on the way back we stopped at Fey Witch's shop, to browse the card-making supplies, and so Mother could meet Fey, or at least, get a look at her. Fey walked over to us.

'Hello Fey, this is my mother Jocelyn.'

'Is she still there?' asked Fey abruptly, ignoring my introductions.

'Yes,' I answered, 'and another woman has joined her.'

'So, you made contact with her; she knew she could bring others.'

I was about to reply when she walked away to deal with a customer, a man in a long black leather coat, black jeans, black T shirt, and a leather hat with a brim that covered much of his face. On top of that, he was wearing sunglasses. Definitely a bit of overkill going on. He was holding a star, as if intending to buy it, a five-pointed star enclosed in a circle.

Mother was watching him closely.

'What's that he's holding?'

'It's a pentacle, a symbol of witchcraft.'

'How do you know that?' asked Mother surprised. I was surprised myself. I had no idea how I knew that.

I purchased some sheets of handmade paper, textured, with spring flowers embedded in its pale blue. It reminded me of a fresh new day.

After we had left the shop, Mother asked me if I had overheard the conversation between Fey Witch and the man dressed in black.

'That woman definitely said, 'I knew she was powerful' to him, and I'm certain she was referring to you.'

I laughed.

'You're getting carried away, Mother. I may have faces in my bathroom floor, but I'm definitely not powerful.'

City of a thousand trades

Mother wanted to try a new recipe she had seen in Country Kitchen magazine, so we bought chicken, free range of course, aubergines, spring onions and ginger. We stopped for a coffee and watched the world go by for an hour, then we headed home.

While Mother went to the kitchen to play with her recipe, I started arranging the photos we'd sorted yesterday. I was planning to make an album with them, a story board of our family. The sun was warm coming through the window and I lay my head back against the comfy cushions on the settee.

****

'It will never happen,' said Jack. "Your father would never allow us to marry. I'm not good enough for you. I'm from the wrong family."

'We could run away together, Jack. We can go where no one will know us.'

'We will not,' said Jack furiously. 'You don't know what it's like, being poor. I won't do that to you.'

I didn't cry. I knew it was futile. Our situation was hopeless. We couldn't be together. My father would never accept Jack. Jack wouldn't let me suffer, as he saw it, by leaving my family. My heart was breaking every time I saw Jack as we went about our daily business.

One day, Jack left. A note found its way to my room.

'I have to go. I can't stand being so close to you, knowing that I can never be with you. And I believe you feel the same. It will be better for both of us for me to go away. Forget me, Catherine; move on with your life. I will always carry a part of you in my heart. Jack'

I threw myself into my life, studied furiously with my tutor, ran errands for my mother, took up my place as carer for the poor and weak. I came out, attending balls and celebrations, my mother decking me out in all sorts of fineries and fripperies, to make me attractive to the 'right' sort of man. But for all the activity and apparent acceptance of my parents' plans, inside my heart was still and cold. I wanted only Jack.

Occasionally Mary would let me know how Jack was getting on. He was in Canada, a lumberjack of all things. But of course, that would appeal to his love of excitement. I bet he's forgotten me, carried away with his new life.

Mary watched me with enquiring eyes.

'You still love him, don't you?'

'Yes, how could I not?'

'Then do something about it.'

'What can I do?' I asked hopelessly. I could see no way to make this right.

'Listen to your heart. You know what to do. What your mother and your grandmother have done before you. Draw on what lies within you.' And with that Mary was gone, leaving me bewildered.

As I paced my room, wondering what she meant, I found a cloth bag on my dresser, pulled tight at the neck. In it were candles and herbs I didn't recognise. Mary must have left them there. I smelled the herbs, trying to decide what they were. I breathed in the richness of their odour.

I needed to be outdoors, away from this feeling of being trapped, the walls that surrounded me, the family bonds that tightened round me. I ran to the front door and out on to the lane; I ran towards Alice Bracebridge's cottage, to the oak tree where Jack had given me his kiss, so gentle on my palm.

I found a large flat stone where I placed the candles, their flickering dancing flames commanding the focus of my eyes. I sprinkled the herbs on the flames and breathed in deeply, the aroma reaching deep within in me and drawing out something I never suspected dwelt there.

My love for Jack filled me, pulsing till I felt I would burst. My whole body pulsed with my heart, louder and louder, stronger and stronger. I felt my body grow and expand but even this could not contain my love and longing. At last, it escaped, leaving my body. I could see my love, a writhing, beating tangible being, strands of light reaching away from me.

'Jack, come back to me.' And I watched as my living love went on its journey, to find Jack and bring him back to me.

****

I woke with a start, wringing wet with sweat, my body tingling and breathless as if I'd been on a run in the park on a frosty day. I went to the kitchen to get a drink where I found Mother still labouring away with our evening meal. How anyone could invest this much time and effort into a meal that is devoured within minutes, I would never know.

I took my glass of water outside, to cool down. So Jack came back because somehow Catherine had made him. What had she done? Whatever it was, it wasn't natural. What good would come of it? I wanted to know more but I was scared to see. Then I reminded myself that I already knew the outcome. They lived happily ever after – didn't they?

That evening, Mother announced that she would have to go home, the garden needed attention, and she was giving a talk on caring for fragrant roses at the Women's Institute monthly meeting next week. I had to admit, her meal was wonderful, and I appreciated the effort she had put into it, even if I could never do that myself. David was coming round to Mother being here – he also appreciated regular meals to her high standard, although the regular consumption of alcohol was a little too much.

That night, by the time my head hit the pillow, I was Catherine again.

****

It was Tuesday, my turn to use the brew house. I'd been working all day, poshing the sheets in the copper, wringing them out and hanging them on the line to dry. The wooden handle on the poshing stick had rubbed the skin on my hand. The sheets always come in covered in bits and smudges, the air round here thick with dirt from the thousands of small workshops that sprawled across Birmingham. City of a thousand trades, the workshop of the world; that's what they call it. I shouted at the lads to go play elsewhere with their ball before my sheets were covered in mud as well.

My back ached; my hair was falling around my face. I glanced at myself in the small scrap of mirror that I guarded preciously in my kitchen. Where had the years gone? What had happened to that pretty young girl I used to see smiling back at me? I stirred the stew simmering in the pot on the grate, nothing much, a bit of knuckle end of lamb with some potatoes, but at least it was hot.

Where were Lily and Edna? They were taking a long time. I'd sent them to the market. I knew it was late but as the market is closing, you can sometimes get things cheap. They were old enough to be trusted to do it.

I heard the latch go and I got up to greet the girls, see what they had come back with. Only it wasn't the girls; it was Jack. Not this early, not again. What had he done this time?

Jack's angry face said it all.

'I told him what he could do with his job. I'm a man, not an idiot, nor someone's servant.'

City of a thousand trades, and Jack was working his way through all of them. He would never settle in the city; I knew that now. But we had nowhere else to go. We lived hand to mouth as it was, and each year, each month, became a little harder as Jack's reputation for being a hothead grew, and he earned less and less with each job he took.

I did what I could. The knowledge of herbs I'd gained from Mary stood me in good stead with these city dwellers who'd never learned those ways themselves. I made simples and possets when they were ill, usually for the children. And I would sit with the women in childbirth, as they brought another mouth into the world to feed, easing their pains, helping the babe to take its first breath, and just as often wrapping the ones that didn't make it, ready for the churchyard. Often they had no money to pay me – life was hard for everyone here – so I accepted what they had to offer, usually food, or a bit of coal.

I made a few pennies laying out the dead. I had no fear of the dead. They're just part of living, part of being on this world. I knew they were nothing to be feared; I'd seen them sometimes, disorientated as they left their bodies, realising they were free to go, to leave this harsh world behind them.

The girls arrived home with a windfall; they'd found some carrots and a swede that had fallen to the floor and been forgotten about. I could use those well.

Jack called Lily and Edna to him, and they sat with his arms round them on the settee that sat low on the floor, its springs too old to offer the sitter any comfort.

So there was Jack, my wonderful gentle Jack, so brave and fearless, so in love with life. I'd brought him back to me, called his spirit to me, made him do my bidding, bound him to me. I thought I knew what I wanted but this trapped haunted man wasn't my Jack. He hated the city and with every lost job, with every new trade he tried, with every breath of the sulphur filled air, a part of him died. He was gentle with me, and was full of love for the girls but I knew something was coming. He couldn't go on like this. He needed the open air and clear skies like I needed his love.

Be wary what you wish for

David nudged me in the ribs.

'You're dreaming again. Keep the noise down! Some of us are trying to sleep.' I could tell that David was joking, not angry. I rolled over without speaking to him, and settled straight back into sleep.

****

I watched Jack as he as he sat on the settee, barely holding together anymore. I'd fixed it with bits of wood as well as I could, and stuffed it with newspaper but you may just as well be sitting on the hard, tiled floor. Jack was looking at his watch, turning it over and over in his hands, hands no longer work hardened. The red was fading out of his hair, white at his temples, his rugged face deeply lined, his lips loose.

His mind was no longer sharp. His happy memories of open skies and fresh, fresh air were keen and clear, but this life, our life, held nothing for him. He forgot it as soon as it happened.

I know I will always care for Jack. He's a good man. He's my man. He's how I made him. I owe it to him to be there for him, no matter what.

****

I woke with tears streaming down my face. How could it have gone so wrong for Catherine? She thought she knew what she wanted and somehow, what she wanted was so strong that it made it happen, and yet she was wrong. Catherine had put her own needs ahead of Jack's, and this is what it came to.

Sadly, I told Mother the rest of Catherine's tale. We both sat dejected for a while, with a cup of tea and a slice of fruit cake – that it was Mother's offering was apparent by the lack of lop-sidedness.

'That is so sad,' said Mother. 'And I always thought they had a wonderful life together. But I can't see why she's on the bathroom floor. There's nothing you can do to help her now, is there?'

'I don't know what to think. Really sad. But you're right, I can't see that there is anything I'm meant to do for her. I don't know if Fey is right when she says it's for us to do something to put things right.'

'Perhaps there's more story to come. Perhaps you will dream about her again tonight.'

'Might do; but I could really do with some rest. It's quite exhausting how intense these dreams are.'

Mother left that day with a promise to take the boys for a few days during their half-term holiday. I would look forward to that. Good as the boys were, a break was always welcome. Pity she couldn't take David as well...

I slept soundly for the first time in days. I stretched out my lazy limbs and curled up in a ball. This felt good. Saturday morning, so I could have a lie in. Downstairs, I could hear cartoons blaring on the TV. The boys were up.

The bedroom door nudged open. Bruno had come to see what'd happened to his early morning walk. Obviously, David hasn't thought to do that for me. I dressed in joggers and sweatshirt, good enough to take the dog out in the fields but not to worry about the mud. It was always muddy in the fields, even in the middle of summer.

A mug of tea, and I was ready to go. Jacob and Joe were waiting at the door, vying for first position with the dog. We burst out of the house like an explosion, and fairly ran to the entrance to the fields.

'Steady on, boy. I'm not awake enough for this.'

Another dry, sunny day tried to hide the changing weather, but autumn was well on its way. The boys searched for conkers under acorn trees, and looked for blackberries on every bush, fought over every stick they found on the floor.

Still, after half an hour, they were getting quieter, carrying home their swag, although I made it clear that they were not taking the big black beetle home with them.

I scooped up the dog's morning offering, and we headed for home. I hoped the boys would settle down after all that exercise.

'Into the bathroom, wash your hands, please.'

I kept an eye on them to make they did actually wash their hands, rather than just play in the water. Then I washed my hands and wiped round the sink to clean off the muddy fingerprints the boys had left. I glanced down at the floor.

Catherine had gone. I smiled at Dorothy, who beamed back at me.

'So I didn't have to do anything for Catherine. Was it something I needed to learn, something I need to know?'

I left the bathroom deep in thought. I was intrigued by the story, and happy to hear it, but when I stopped to think about it in detail, I didn't know what to think. If this was real, that Dorothy and Catherine were speaking to me from my bathroom floor, then this was something supernatural, from a world I knew little about. I had to admit Fey Witch fascinated me, and Medium was one of my favourite TV programmes, especially as I knew it was based on a real person. But if you asked me if I believed in ghosts and the supernatural, I'd have probably said 'no'; until now.

Now I'm not sure. If I said I didn't believe, then what was happening? Was I imagining things? Was I going mad? I didn't feel as if I was. And I'm sure David would have mentioned it if he thought I was. Mother certainly would tell me in no uncertain terms. Yet she seemed to be urging me on, although as such a practical, no nonsense person, I would have expected her to tell me I was being silly.

I wrapped my arms around David and gave him an uncharacteristic hug.

'Fancy leaving the grass to grow for another week, and let's go out somewhere nice for the afternoon?'

David was easily encouraged to forsake the gardening. The boys dropped what they were doing, pulling on coats and wellies, grabbing Buzz Lightyear and big ted on the way. I picked up my bag and off we went.

Lying in bed that night, David reached for me, and I responded, a closeness we hadn't experienced for a long time. Too busy, too tired, too settled with each other. Tonight, we had time, we were happy, we just enjoyed each other, as Catherine must have longed to be with her Jack.

'When do you think this will end, David? When will Dorothy go away?'

' I don't know, love. We just have to wait and see. Don't fret over it. I don't think any harm will come of it. All seems ok so far, just interesting.'

I lay there, wrapped tight in his arms, and realised he was right. All I needed to do was to wait and see.

I didn't have to wait long. The next afternoon, I found not one new face, but two new faces on my bathroom floor. An elegant woman, with her hair piled on high revealing a graceful neck, high cheek bones and petite bowed mouth. Her bare shoulders rose from a sheath of frills decorated with tiny bows; her arm wrapped around a little girl with a head of red curls that nearly obscured her face. They seemed to be looking at something together, perhaps a book, yet their clothes suggested they were going somewhere special, a party or grand dinner perhaps. These were happy smiling people, a total contrast to stern, unhappy Catherine.

I watched them for a while, drawn by their closeness. This was mother and daughter, sharing one of many happy moments. What were they looking at? Where were they going? I drew myself away from the glowing image and went to rummage in the photo box that Mother had brought with her. I didn't remember seeing these two before, but perhaps we had photos of when they were older.

There were no photos that showed any resemblance to these two; not a photo of mother and daughter with any resemblance, no young girls with red hair or curls of any colour. (Straight hair obviously runs through our family – I don't even need to straighten my hair. It hangs in long straight locks that won't bend or curl for long, even when savaged with curling tongs.) I felt dejected. How was I supposed to find out about someone with just an image to go on? I realised how little I knew about my own family. I determined to write things down about my life, even routine things, so that my children and their children would know their history, their roots, in a way that was becoming obvious I didn't. Perhaps that's what this was all about. Perhaps the faces were there for me to learn my family history, to know where I had come from.

I looked forward to sleep that night, even though I wasn't tired, glancing at the clock to see if I could claim it was time for bed. I wanted to dream; I wanted to find out who these newcomers to my house were.

At half past nine, I started to yawn, rubbing my eyes. David glanced over at me.

'What have you been up to today? You look exhausted.'

'I made a start on the Christmas shopping. Seemed a good idea at the time.'

'You look done in. Why don't you get an early night?' I felt a bit guilty as I walked upstairs, until I heard David switch the TV on to the sports channel. I chuckled; he'd probably be up to bed later than usual, revelling in the unexpected opportunity to watch football without the usual squabble.

My oyster satin pyjamas felt cool on my skin as I slipped between the sheets. My well-worn T-shirt seemed hardly fitting for the elegant people I was hoping to meet; I thought I would put on this present from Mother that I seldom wore. Although I didn't feel that they could see me – that would have been weird.

I drifted into sleep.

******

I heard music playing in the distance, strings – violins, cello – and piano. Dancing music, it set my feet tapping. Impatiently, I waited for my maid to finish my hair. It must look special for tonight; I want to be the belle of the ball. The hot iron hissed on my hair as the final curl emerged. Lucy gently placed the shining tiara on my head, careful not to disturb any of the myriad curls.

I pinched my cheeks to add some colour to my carefully white skin, always shaded from the sun with wide brimmed hats and parasol. My pale blue dress highlighted the blue of my eyes. I stared at myself in the full length gilt framed mirror. I was beautiful. How could anyone resist me? Certainly not Justin Worth. Tonight he would realise he loved me. I would make sure of that.

At last it was time for me to make my grand entrance. I walked with Mother to the ball room, where the orchestra was seated to one side, screened from the dancing couples.

'Ladies and gentlemen, Mr and Mrs Archibald Addington and Miss Eugenie.'

Faces turned towards us as we walked into the grand, spacious room, brightly lit with hundreds of candles and flowering as though it was a garden with beautiful, scented flowers. I curtsied to the many elderly ladies I was introduced to, graciously giving my hand to gentlemen of all ages. Everyone seemed eager to make my acquaintance. I smiled sweetly at the other young ladies, those of my own age, my competitors. None of them made me fearful. Tonight I could take my choice, and that would be Justin. Now Catherine was no longer in the frame, who else would he choose but me?

My dance card rapidly filled, and I danced and twirled around the room, dizzy with the dance, dizzy with the thrill of being the centre of admiration, dizzy with the little bit too much wine I had drank. Justin asked me to dance, and we made an elegant couple, making our way around the floor, each movement as perfect as we could make it, showing off to each other. We finished, breathless, and Justin took me for refreshment on the terrace, still in sight of our watchful elders but out of hearing.

'You look beautiful tonight,' said Justin, looking at me with appreciation.

'Why, thank you.' I didn't know what else to say. On our own, all the clever things I had rehearsed went out of my head.

'You dance wonderfully.' I was flattered to receive his compliments, though I felt a little awkward under his scrutiny. His eyes travelled from my face to my bosom, plumped up on display in my new dress, and stayed there for a good while. As he lifted his head, I boldly met his gaze, just for a few seconds, glancing away under my lashes, before it could be considered brazen. His fair hair glowed in the candlelight. Catherine had always hated his pale complexion, but I found it fascinating, with his full, inviting lips. How I longed to feel them against my skin, on my neck, on my lips. I was embarrassing myself with my wanton thoughts.

Justin coughed.

'Eugenie, there is something I want to ask you. I would like very much to speak to your father. I know that our fathers have discussed this between themselves already.'

My heart faltered. What was he asking? Did he mean what I fervently hoped he did?

'Eugenie,' Justin continued. 'I have watched you grow into a beautiful and accomplished young woman. I feel that you would be a fitting companion. I trust that you will have no objections to me asking for your hand in marriage.'

He waited impatiently for my answer but surely he must have known it already. As if anyone would turn him down.

'That would be most acceptable,' I said shyly.

'Then I will speak to your father as soon as an appropriate opportunity presents itself.' With that, he led me back indoors. I hoped we would dance again, and I would find myself in his arms. He left me in my mother's care before heading towards his friends.

He must have been excited to tell them of the success of his proposal. They filled their glasses and raised a toast to him, their laughter carrying across the dance floor. I did not see him again that night, except at a distance.

The music gathered the evening to a close; I said my farewells, and left the company, carried on little lifts of cloud beneath my feet. I undressed with my head full of images, of the sparkling ball room, of the fineness and colours of the ladies' dresses, of how handsome the men looked in their dark suits, of my own lovely image reflected in the darkening windows and mirrors as I passed them, of Justin's shining hair. I smelled again his faint aroma when I breathed in as he held me.

I thought I wouldn't be able to sleep with all the bustle in my thoughts, but I soon was deep in my safe haven, asleep and perchance to dream.

****

I woke to David landing heavily on the bed.

'Good match?' I asked.

'No, we lost,' he said, with a tell-tale slur in his voice. Obviously, he'd had more than a few lagers while watching the match. He would be asleep very soon. The rhythmic snoring settled into a pattern, proving me right. I lay in the dark, in my unnoticed satin pyjamas, feeling slightly resentful, and wide awake, but the regular rhythm hypnotised me back into sleep.

****

I looked eagerly through the window. The day was dry and sunny. What a wonderful day for my wedding!

The household was busy, despite the early hour. I knew there would be people at the church already, decorating the pews with swathes of flowers. This would be important for our small village. Family and friends were coming from across the counties, and Father had invited many local dignitaries who potentially could help with his business. Justin's family would be present, gracing the event and adding that touch of class. Although they didn't quite accept me – after all, my family was in trade, whereas they had land – they were happy to welcome me as their daughter. I was impatient for this day to be over. I wanted more than just my married name and a ring on my finger. I wanted Justin.

The villagers had gathered in force outside the church to wave us off as the carriage took us away from the crowd, Mr and Mrs Justin Worth. We headed off to our new home together. Lansdowne Farm, our house settled in landscaped grounds away from the farm buildings. Justin was no farmer, but he knew how to manage men.

The farm hands, their wives and numerous children were lined up on the driveway, waiting to welcome us. The children were waving and cheering, dancing around in the unaccustomed merriment. I waved back, smiling and revelling in their excitement. A man's voice shouted a gruff warning, a woman screamed, the happy crowd fell silent. I didn't understand.

'What's happening?' I cried.

I heard a man's voice, urgent, clear. 'Woah. Stop the carriage. The child is trapped.'

'Get the damned child from under the wheels.' Justin was shouting at the men. I could hear angry voices, the low rumble of the workers, and the higher grief of the women.

'What's happening? Someone please tell me.' I could feel tightness in my chest, my breaths coming quicker as panic started to take over.

'That 'damned child' is my son. He has a name – Robert. Robert Underhill.' The pain and fear in his voice sunk behind menace, his dark hair falling over his eyes, shielding the anguish in them from public view.

'I don't care who he is. Get him moved. Distressing my wife like this.'

'To hell with your wife.' The retort cut Justin short. 'The child's injured bad.'

'Step aside, William.' A strong, commanding voice stepped in to sooth the situation. 'If you can just bear with me Sir, we'll soon have the lad out of your way.'

'See to it Wright.'

'William, steady.' People held his arms, dragged him back. 'Leave it to John. He will get the boy free.'

Instead, William surged forward, towards the carriage, towards Justin. 'Bastard.'

Justin snatched the whip from the driver and lashed out at the angry man, then lashed the horse.

The crowd's angry murmuring increased to a roar, a hostile wave of noise washed over me; the carriage sprung forward, bouncing madly as if something impeded its progress.

****

I woke gasping for breath, my chest tight and constricted, my hands flailing in front of me. David was awake instantly, catching my hands, calling my name, calming me down. He flicked on the lamp; I looked round for the people, the angry faces, and realised I wasn't there. I was here, and it was now. Slowly, I returned to normal, I became me again.

'Another dream?' asked David, gently. He rubbed my shoulders protectively. 'It's all getting too much, isn't it, the faces and the dreams. I think you need to give it a rest, forget it all. I'll take up that damn vinyl and put proper tiles down, plain ones without any trace of a pattern.'

'Please don't. I need to know what happens next. A few bad dreams won't hurt me.'

I did as many people do when they want reassuring – I phoned Mother.

'I've seen them, Mum, but I've no idea who they are. What I do know is that the young woman married Justin Worth. Isn't that the one who Catherine was supposed to marry? I haven't seen the little girl yet.'

'Mum didn't know much about Catherine's family, said she never spoke about them. I think that she was so hurt when they disowned her after she married that she determined never to talk about them again. So I can't really help you there.'

I told Mother all about the dream. We agreed it didn't look good for the relationship, Justin being so hot tempered and so careless of other people.

'No matter how big the man, he can't just trample over people. Such bad breeding.' Trust Mother to shed a different light on matters.

I was beginning to think that David was right – and that doesn't happen often, so I decided to give this some serious thought.

I felt exhausted, struggling to do even the basics. The boys had clean uniform for school and food on their plates but that was more likely to be frozen pizza rather than anything remotely healthy. David had taken to bringing in take-aways for me and him, Chinese, Balti, even good old fish and chips. Much as I enjoyed these, my waistline was suffering. Although my body was lethargic, my mind on the other hand was in hyperdrive, mulling over what I had learned so far, trying to fathom out what was happening, desperate to know what was going to happen next.

I decided to go and see Fey Witch.

The shop was fairly quiet, just an elderly lady in a purple knitted hat buying treats for her dog, a fat little thing which huffed round her feet, and a young woman I recognised from the school run buying hamster food. I looked at card blanks and toppers while I hoped for them to leave. Fey Witch came over to me, stood next to me for a while.

'I'm shutting the shop for lunch soon. Would you like to join me for a cup of tea? I feel that you need to talk.' Without waiting for a response, she said goodbye to the leaving customers, shut the door with the tinkling bells, turned the sign to 'closed'.

Over a cup of surprisingly drinkable lemongrass tea, Fey told me how to ground myself, so that I didn't get swept away in this tide of information.

'Take time out, place your bare feet on the earth, feel the energies of the earth flowing through you to the sky above. Sink the roots of your being deep in the earth, your branches reaching upwards.'

Fey suggested that I write down my experiences in a journal, keep a detailed record of what I had seen and heard, and to record anything else happening in my life that I felt was unusual. She asked how I felt before a dream, did I know when I was going to get one, and did I know when I was going to get the next one. So many questions. And all questions I couldn't answer.

I looked at the collection of writing books in the witchy section of her shop. I fell in love with a large leather-bound book with handmade paper, soft, scattered with hints of petals. The leather was warm to the touch, the tooled patterns inviting me to run my hands over them. The price tag made me wince. Could I justify spending this much? Probably not, but I wanted it, so I paid for it and carried it self-consciously from this odd little shop. The tiny fat dog yapped at my ankles, the old lady in the purple hat standing on the corner watching me.

'Come here Loki. Leave our lady alone.'

This shop certainly attracts some odd people! I smiled at her as I walked past, just to be on the safe side.

Back home, I worked out that I had an hour before I had to pick up the boys from school. That was enough time to have a go at this grounding thing. I thought about going into the fields to do it but wasn't too sure about walking barefoot where all sorts of people walked their dogs. I decided to have a go in our back garden, so overgrown at the moment that I could easily pretend I was somewhere wild and untended. I removed my trainers and socks and planted my feet in the grass. It was damp from yesterday's rain and felt squishy as I shifted my balance. My initial revulsion soon changed into a comfortable feeling as grass tickled my toes and mud pushed cold round my naked feet. I thought of myself as a tree. Hmphh. This wasn't that easy. What had Fey said? Feel the energy flowing. I could feel my heart racing at this unexpected activity, pumping away, pulsing, pushing blood round, and as I listened to my roaring heart, I felt the energy, actually felt a tingling surging round my body. I pushed it into the ground, into the squishy earth, felt it bound back to me. I raised my hands to the soft blue sky above and the energy raised from my feet to the sky.

Oh my word, I had done it. Made a connection with heaven only knows what. I felt alive, yet more settled than I had done since the face first appeared on my bathroom floor.

I lingered, enjoying the sensation, a breeze that had sprang up from nowhere pushing my hair back from my face. Then I remembered the children and ran, grabbing the tea towel to hurriedly wipe the mud from my feet on my way out.

I stopped at the shops on the way home, bought minced beef, chilli beans, salad, and, for the first time in a while, cooked a pretty good meal, even though I said it myself. The clean white plates confirmed my thoughts.

My new mood continued to the bedroom, David and I renewing our acquaintance, and I slept soundly with no dreams to disturb my slumber.

Evaporating dreams

The book sat on the dining room table waiting for me to turn its pages, stroke its patterns. I picked up a biro from by the phone, sat down at the table. It was no good, a biro was an insult to this beautiful book. I couldn't soil its pages with a blotchy, bitten biro. I crept into the study where David pretended to 'work' but more often than not was just looking for peace and quiet to read the latest crime novel. I had bought David a fountain pen for Christmas last year, but I felt certain he had never used it. I rifled the drawers of his desk and sure enough, there it was still in the packaging, complete with a glass bottle of ink.

I practiced writing with ink. This was a good pen, worth the money I paid for it. No blotches, no rush. I was ready to write in my beautiful book. But what? Where to start? I decided to start at the beginning so that's what I wrote on the first page – The face on the bathroom floor. The ink spread a little on the handmade paper, making the words soft, as if they were afraid of upsetting you, unearthly. I wrote for what seemed like hours, though it flashed by in minutes. I was lost in the writing, the telling of my story.

I realised I probably needed to set an alarm to remind me to pick up the boys, if I kept on with this. I lost track of time, too engrossed in the story that sounded unbelievable even to me, who was living it.

Tonight, I wanted to dream. I was ready to find out more, to discover who this poor woman was, married to such an obnoxious man.

******

The carriage pulled up outside the house where I was to live. The horses were steaming from being hard driven, Justin was angry, his face red, his eyes protruding, his soft lips twisted.

'Stop your crying, Eugenie. Show some dignity.' I wiped my eyes, bit on my tongue to silence my tears. The coachman opened the door, Justin leapt down, leaving me to struggle out, alone. I followed Justin in through the door. A kindly woman took my arm and guided me into a small room. I realised this must be a room for use by the servants, it was nowhere near grand enough to be a room Justin would use.

'If you would prefer to go to the drawing room, I can take you straight there Miss, but I just thought..'

Thank you, this will be fine for the moment.'

Lucy arrived with the things to make tea, prettily laid out on a large tray. Without speaking, she poured tea then gestured to the biscuits on a fine white plate patterned with flowers. 'Hot strong tea, and something sweet. Good for shock, Miss. You'll feel better soon.' I had never been so glad to see her, happy that she had come with me to this new place. A familiar face in the turmoil.

And sure enough, I started to feel stronger as I sorted out in my head what had just happened. The day had started out so well, my wedding day, my beautiful dress, the best wishes of everyone in the pretty little church, dressed in flowers. Then more well-wishers, their good mood changing to hatred and hostility. That poor boy, how severe were his injuries? Twisted and ruined under the wheels of the carriage, that stomach churning lurch as we rolled over him. Then Justin, my wonderful, gentle Justin – where was he now? I had seen a side of him I didn't know existed. And I was scared.

I went to my marriage bed that night, hoping to find my gentle Justin had returned. He hadn't. I think now that he had left for good, the moment our marriage became finalised, when I had no escape. I woke the following morning, sore, humiliated. My dreams evaporated, hopes shredded, scattering like the confetti they sprinkled over us as we left the church. I hoped Catherine found greater happiness with Jack that I had with Justin.

****

I woke in overwhelming sadness. Poor Eugenie, so young, so naïve. Justin seemed to be an awful person, not just to Eugenie but to everyone. And the dream told us that Eugenie was Catherine's sister. Catherine had a lucky escape. At least Jack truly loved her, and she him. I knew there was more to come of this tale.

I phoned Mother to give her an update.

'This is becoming quite exciting, isn't it?' she said. 'I think it's time I contacted Patricia; she may remember something about that side of the family. I'll invite her out for lunch somewhere tasteful, a couple of G and T's, that should do the trick, get her talking.'

That made me chuckle. Mother and Aunt Patricia didn't exactly get on. They were civil to each other but only tolerated each other in small doses. This was a great sacrifice my mother was making, to volunteer to spend time with Patricia. Mother must have found this really interesting.

'Thanks, Mum. Anything you can find out about the family history would be helpful.'

I felt a bit out of sorts. The boys went off to school happily enough. It was animal man day. They love that, playing with the little animals he brings into school. They would have lots to tell me on the way home that afternoon. Bruno was padding round, hoping for a walk.

'This is your lucky day, Bruno. Come on then, extra walk,' and we burst out of the door at a fair pace for the fields. As we turned into the entrance to the fields, I heard a yapping that sounded distinctly familiar. Looking up, I recognised the fat little dog and not far behind it, the woman in the purple hat. Strange that. I didn't remember seeing this woman before, yet now I'd seen her three times in as many days. I put my head down and kept walking quickly – not that I had any choice as far as Bruno was concerned. I wasn't sure why I didn't want to engage with this woman. A little old lady with a fat annoying dog should be harmless enough but something told me to stay clear.

The sun was bright even though it wasn't that warm. It shone through the tree branches that were almost bare, with just a straggle of leaves clinging grimly to their length. I felt a rush of happiness, like I was coated in sunshine, warming me, hugging me. I smiled to myself, picked up speed and broke into a run, admittedly not a very quick run, but Bruno enjoyed it, pulling me along, urging me faster. I hadn't felt this alive since I was a small girl.

Back at home with a cup of tea, I thought about this. What had made the change? The grounding exercise Fey recommended had made me feel good. Had it opened me up to a deeper contact with the earth and its energies? I sat down to write more in my lovely book and added these thoughts alongside the details from last night's dream.

****

The alarm clock had brought me back to reality with its tinny ring, reminding me to fetch the boys from school. They were so excited, chattering ceaselessly about the animals, the snake that wasn't slimy at all, the big owl with its big round eyes that watched you everywhere you went, the spiky hedgehogs. It was exhausting keeping up with their chitter chatter, switching from one to the other.

We had cheesy baked beans on toast for tea – their favourite. The boys wore off some of their excitement playing football in the garden.

I would love an evening to myself, I thought. A bit selfish I know. I have all this time at home while the boys are at school but there is something different about evenings, as it gets darker and you feel like snuggling up with a good book – or a good dream. Never mind, I thought, let's see what I can cook for dinner for when David gets home. As I disappeared into the freezer searching for vegetables to go with the meat pie I was planning, the phone rang.

'Hi love. Look, I met up with an old schoolfriend while I was walking to the car park. Mike, do you remember him?'

'I think so. He came to our wedding didn't he?'

'well, he's asked if I could join him for dinner. He's only in town for one night. Going home tomorrow. Would that be ok with you?'

'That's fine,' I said,' but if you have a couple of pints, get a taxi. Please. Have a lovely time, you'll have a lot to catch up.'

David seemed happy. And the boys came in, settled down on the settee, much calmer now, sleepy almost. I sent them for a bath and bed and for once they went quite happily and soon the house was quiet.

****

I lit the log burner. This was a special treat, usually we rely on the central heating. I turned off the overhead light, flicking on soft lights in the arches either side of the fireplace, Christmas tree lights running through their sequence of colour. I changed into cosy pyjamas and grabbed a soft throw to wrap round me, stretching out on the sofa with all the cushions plumped up at one end. The flames were fascinating, dragging my eyes back to them again and again, dancing, weaving, flickering. I was awake, I'm sure I was.

*****

Justin came to my bed frequently, usually after he had been sharing a bottle of red wine or golden whisky with his friends who often lingered in the house. I could hear them talking, braying rather, like a herd of animals, getting louder as the night went on. In the early hours, it would go quiet. That's when my stomach would churn. Would he be incapable tonight? Or would he come for me? I could not say no. I had no right to say no, he told me. I was his, he owned me. He was careful to hit me where the bruises wouldn't show, so the servants didn't know, but I was sure they had guessed. Their kind eyes averted when I winced in pain trying to do some simple task.

My courses were late. At first I was merely relieved to be free of the discomfort. What a child I was. My maid, Lucy, asked how I was feeling. Had I experienced any nausea? Yes, I had. My usually healthy appetite told me that breakfast was the best meal of the day but for a few days I had not eaten much at all. I could see that Lucy wanted to say more but didn't know how to start.

'What is it Lucy?'

'Miss, do you think you may be with child?'

My hand flew to my face. How could I be so silly?

'Thank you, Lucy. I feel you may be right. I have missed three times.'

'You must take extra care of yourself Miss.' She touched my hand, her eyes rimmed with tears.

That night, Justin came to my bed. I told him that I was expecting, hoping he would be considerate.

'That doesn't stop me taking what is my right,' he shouted, forcing himself on me, if anything rougher than usual, as if the thought of a baby depriving him had angered him greatly.

I woke up in the morning, my stomach cramping. As I rose from the bed, I saw the blood, bright red against the pure white of the crisp sheets, felt it trickling down my legs. I sat down, waiting for the inevitable, waiting for my baby to leave my body. My baby. How strange it should become real to me as it was about to leave me. I couldn't cry, I was too shocked, too angry. Lucy came to my room to perform her usual morning functions for me. Instead she became a friend as she held my hand, put her arm round me when I did not object to the physical contact. I welcomed the warmth that spread from her into me. We waited together till it was all over. Then Lucy cleaned up the mess, cleaned up me, and I carried on with my life.

I informed Justin of the loss of our child, walking away swiftly without waiting for his response. He stayed away from me for two whole weeks. Then his frequent visits continued, no longer with any trace of tenderness, just contempt and hatred. 'You can't even carry a child to fruition. Why did I marry you? You are useless. At least you are cheaper than a whore though nowhere near as accommodating.' I was to find out years later that whores would not accommodate him, no matter how much he offered them. He treated them too badly. With them, he did not attempt to conceal their bruises which left them out of work till they were healed.

Six months later, I realised that I was again with child. I was in despair. What if I was to lose another child to Justin's malicious need of me? Lucy knew of course and she also sensed my fears.

'I can help you Miss. If you are willing.'

'What could you possibly do that would save this child from Justin? He listens to no-one.' Tears slipped from my eyes.

'There is a woman. She lives in the woods. A very exceptional woman, skilled in the old ways. She's good with herbs and… and other things.'

'What? She would poison him?'

'No, no Ma'am. Nothing like that. But she could stop him from doing harm to you.'

'Bring her to me. Let me hear of this for myself.'

'She won't come here Ma'am. You will need to go to her.'

What was I doing? Clutching at straws, that was what I was doing. I agreed to go to see this mysterious woman. Fortunately, Justin was away a great deal during the day, visiting bankers, making business deals, making money, dining in fine manner in town. I left the estate early one morning with Lucy leading the way. Lucy carried a wicker basket over her arm – our ruse if anyone should question where we were off to – we were collecting elderberries to make a cough syrup ready to treat the children of the estate in the coming winter. Lucy also had some packets concealed under a cloth though I had no idea what they contained.

Lucy led us from the well-formed paths of the estate onto the wilder overgrown paths of the woodland. We walked for a while, then Lucy insisted I rest before continuing our journey; we sat on the grass beside a small stream rushing on its way. We started our progress through the trees, the wood becoming dark as the trees met overhead, forming a canopy that kept out the light. Lucy pushed whippy branches aside to let us through and suddenly, as though out of nowhere, there was a cottage in front of us. Quaint, tiny, like the illustrations in children's books. The door opened and a woman walked out, her hand raised in greeting. She was younger than I expected, and I felt that I knew her.

'Welcome Eugenie, please come in.'

That voice, I recognised it. I recognised her. This was Mary, Catherine's maid. She had been dismissed as no longer needed when Catherine ran away, accused of influencing the unforgiveable behaviour.

'Mary, how come you are living here? How have you been?' I was so pleased to see a friendly face that I filled with tears. Mary put her arms round me.

'Come now. None of this. Let's sort out the problem so you can relax and smile again.'

We sat inside the rustic but clean and comfortable cottage with a cup of tea in a crock mug. Mary explained that when she left employment at my parents' house, she came to live with old Alice Bracebridge, looked after her in her last years. Mary knew Alice had no children nor other family but had been touched to find that Alice had left the cottage to her. She had somewhere to live and carried on Alice's work, making remedies, giving advice, tending to labouring women and laying out the dead. She often didn't get paid in money but in kind - food, cloth, coal. Mary managed well enough.

'You can find an awful lot of useful things in the wood, once you know what to look for. I collect things and barter for what I can't find for myself.'

Lucy gently reminded us of our need to get back before we were missed.

'All this talk about me, Miss Eugenie! Let's talk about what I can do for you.'

It was as I feared. Mary had learned much from Alice. The local community accepted her even if they were wary of her. Others kept well away from that witch in the woods.

'Eugenie, we can bind Justin so that he will not harm you. He will leave you and thus the baby alone till the baby is born.'

I was frightened of what I was about to do but I had no other choice.

Lucy produced from her basket one of Justin's gloves and some hair. She had taken this from his hairbrush.

'Place the hair inside the glove, Eugenie.' I did this and then I rolled the glove up and wrapped it in some wool to hold it closed.

'Repeat after me:

I bind thee from harming me
This hair from your head will guide ropes to you
I bind thee from harming me
This glove is from your evil hand that will not hit me again.
I bind thee from harming me
You will not reach for me again till my baby is safe
I bind thee from harm
I bind thee from harm
I bind thee from harm.

Now go to the stream, throw the glove into the running water, and watch it drift out of your life. You will not be molested; your baby will be safe.

Lucy and I made our way home; my heart lighter than it had felt since my ignominious marriage.

Are witches real?

David arrived home later than I expected. I heard a car pull up outside, not ours, and a door slam, then a key fumbling in the lock. He's had a drink I thought. Good man, getting a taxi back. I listened to him clattering down the hall. Good job it was Friday. He wouldn't be in any state for much in the morning. I went to the kitchen, thought I'd be kind to him, made him a coffee, glass of water and paracetamol, to ward off tomorrow's hangover.

As I waited for the kettle to boil, I thought about my strange evening. I hadn't been asleep if I heard the car outside. What was it then that I was seeing? Not a dream obviously. Was it a vision? Things were becoming stranger by the day. It wasn't normal. These stories I was hearing, seeing, taking part in – was I under stress? Was I unwell? It didn't feel like I was; my day to day life was carrying on as normal, and the stories weren't a jumble of nonsense – it was like I was reading a book from the point of view of a character.

David drank his coffee, telling me where he had been, not always making much sense. I chuckled – it wasn't often he had a night out like this. He wrapped his arms round me, dropping his weight unsteadily on my shoulders. He was a good man, loved me, loved the boys, such a contrast to Eugenie's beast of a husband. This was my reality, my normality. I helped him upstairs to bed and we both slept soundly.

****

'Mum, could you come over? I've learned a lot; it's quite sad.'

'Of course I will. I've a lot to tell you as well. I met with Patricia and she remembers much that I didn't know. I can come on Monday if that's alright with you and David.'

'That would be lovely Mum. See you soon.'

It would be great to see Mother. She felt like my partner in crime but of course, the house needed a thorough clean. David wouldn't want to go out, I suspected he would have a massive hangover to nurse. The boys were playing happily in the garden, the grass dry enough for football, so I started on my mission. It was a bit mean to start with the vacuuming given the state of David's head, so I tidied toys, dusted, polished. I even groomed Bruno. He likes being brushed till it comes to his big furry tail – that's a bit of a battle. The kitchen gleamed, at least till the boys came in looking for snacks which I provided, then started cleaning again, removing muddy footprints and bits of grass. The sky clouding over, the boys settled down to watch Stewart Little on DVD, their current favourite. I took advantage of the coming hour and half undisturbed to update my book. I couldn't resist running my hands over the intriguing patterns on the cover, the leather smooth under my fingertips. I recorded Eugenie's story, and how I was wide awake when I received the story. I added how I had wanted an evening to myself and unexpectedly got one.

The film finished; I could tell by the sudden increase in volume from the boys. David tumbled downstairs, looking rather sheepish and worse for wear. I smiled, gave him a hug. 'Paracetamol?'

I didn't wait for an answer, put the kettle on, fetched the tablets. After fishfingers, beans and chips for the boys, and plain toast for David, we all ventured out to take Bruno for a walk, a bit of fresh air to clear his head. As we reached the entrance to the fields,

David nudged me. 'Is that someone you know? She's looking this way.'

Again the lady in the purple hat. 'I can't say that I know her, but I have seen her several times. She uses that shop with the pet stuff.'

'Oh, an oddball then,' laughed David, wincing as the noise echoed round his head.

'Serves you right' I said. 'I use that shop and I'm not an oddball.' I stopped to think about that. The events of the last few weeks would suggest that I definitely was.

David must have realised what I was thinking as he slipped his hand into mine and didn't speak for a while, just letting a comfortable silence sit between us as we walked among the trees.

****

Mother arrived promptly on Monday morning with her usual array of luggage, and a cake box.

'Save you the trouble of making one,' she said. I felt a bit sheepish; I hadn't thought to make one, not after the last lop-sided effort.

'How was your lunch with Patricia? Did it go to plan?'

'Actually, we got on well. It's been ages since I've seen her. Perhaps we have both mellowed with age.' Mother must have mellowed, admitting that she is getting older.

'Patricia remembered Mummy telling her about Great Aunt Eugenie, or rather about her husband. You were right, Eugenie married that Justin who wanted to marry Catherine before she ran off with Jack. Granny Catherine seldom talked about her sister, but

Patricia said that one day Granny was sad, and was talking to Mummy about Eugenie, or rather about Justin. Said he wasn't a nice man, an ogre, and Eugenie was terrified of him. This made Patricia giggle as she thought Granny meant like the ogre in Puss in Boots, which is why she remembers it. Mummy told her to be quiet or leave the room, and Granny raised her eyebrow at her, with that terrible look she gave people. He lost his life in a riding accident, and Granny said that this was a blessed relief for Eugenie. Which seems an odd thing to say. And Granny never spoke of it again. What do you think of that?'

I had a sinking feeling as I digested what Mother had told me. Did Justin die because of what Eugenie had done? That would be terrible.

'Mum, I think Eugenie was tinkering with witchcraft. She did a spell on Justin.' Her reaction was not what I expected. She didn't seem in the slightest surprised, or if she was, it didn't show on her face.

'Tell me what you found out. Was it another dream?' Her voice was gentle, sympathetic.

I told her the sad tale of Eugenie, how violent Justin was, how she lost the baby. I confess I cried; telling Mum made it seem so real. I told her how Eugenie visited Mary in the cottage, how Mary was Catherine's maid.

'Mary was the one who told Catherine how to get Jack back, wasn't she?'

'Yes, and Alice Bracebridge left her cottage to Mary, and Mary carried on where Alice left off. They were witches, Mum, witches.'

'Remember dear, people were quick to label spinster women as witches, especially if they lived on their own, in the woods, and if they had healing skills. It doesn't mean they were really witches.'

'But Mum, they did a spell, a binding spell, on Justin, to make him leave Eugenie alone till after the baby was born.'

'So you think it was the spell that killed Justin?'

'Well, it's possible isn't it? They did a spell and he died.'

'Slow down, Erica. You don't know the dates or anything. And do you really believe in magic?'

I put the kettle on, and we had a slice or two of Mother's cream and jam filled Victoria sponge.

'Mum, this also means that Catherine used magic to get Jack to come back.'

'Hmm, certainly something to ponder on, but I suspect there will be a much more rational explanation.'

It was that time of day to pick up the boys.

'You stay here and relax a little. I'll pick up the boys and take them for an ice-cream in the park. We'll all enjoy that.'

'Thanks Mum,' I said, barely noticing her leave, my mind still horrified that Eugenie had killed Justin.

The puppy

Justin barged into my room, slamming the door behind him. I could see he had been drinking, and that he was angry. I shied away from him. This irritated him further. He grabbed my arm.

'Justin, please, I am with child. I couldn't bear it if I lost another baby. Please leave me in peace till after the baby arrives.'

'What? You would use a child as an excuse to avoid your wifely duties? No wife of mine will do such a thing.'

He ripped my dress in his eagerness. He lowered himself on me and I waited for the pain I knew I would feel as he entered my unwilling body. I still waited. Justin cursed, touched himself, then heaving himself to his feet, he slapped my face, hard, blood bursting from my lower lip. Even the sight of my blood couldn't arouse him. He backed away from me, left my room, and I slept in peace.

That was the last time he came near me during my pregnancy. Red haired Constance arrived healthy.

****

'**She hadn't killed him** with her magic spell. It did exactly what she'd wanted – it stopped him raping her while she was pregnant. How terrible that she had to resort to such lengths. That man was an absolute pig, and no recourse to law back then. A woman a mere chattel. It's a good job the world has changed.'

'Totally agree, dear. By the way, when we were at the park an old woman tried to speak to the boys, funny little person in a hideous purple hat. They said hello to her but not much else, fussed the dog, and we carried on. To be quite honest, she didn't seem the type of person you would be friends with, so I asked the boys how they knew her. They said they didn't really but had seen her around several times with her dog. Thought I had better tell you, just in case.'

'In case of what Mum?' I sat up straight instead of sprawling on the sofa. 'What do you mean?'

'Don't panic! I just thought, well you know, young boys and cute dogs and strange people. It's not a good combination, now is it? You hear such terrible things.'

'Oh, I see what you mean but it's ok, Mum. No need to worry, the boys are never out on their own.'

The next day, Mother and I walked to the witchy shop, as we had jokingly taken to calling it. I bought some dental chews for Bruno. He was definitely in need of some. My stomach churned when he jumped up for his morning lick of my face. Mother found some ribbon that would be ideal for the flower arrangement she was planning for the WI competition. She chatted for some time to Fey Witch, who seemed to be knowledgeable on just about everything. I stayed well away from the mystery of design for flower arrangements. I loved flowers but just shoved them in a vase, kept them in my kitchen where I could see them while I worked, not these carefully crafted displays taking pride of place on the polished sideboard – not that I would ever say that to Mother.

Fey came over to me as I was leafing through knitting patterns. 'How are you doing with your Book of Shadows?'

I looked at her blank, thinking I had misheard. 'Book of what?'

'Shadows,' said Fey. 'A witch's record of spiritual learning and study.'

I spluttered, choking back indignation, or was that a laugh?

'I am most definitely not a witch.'

'Yet you have faces appearing to you, they commune with you, you have dreams of the past and find them true. You know things.'

'That doesn't make me a witch.'

'Or does it make you a witch who hasn't realised it yet?' Fey smiled gently at me and walked away to deal with Mother who had finally reached a decision on exactly which ribbon she wanted to buy.

'Come on Mum. Time to go. We have to pick up something for dinner before we collect the boys from school.' I think Mother thought I was being a bit rude, but I needed to get out of there. As I marched towards the door, I bumped into a man who was just about to enter. He wore a black leather coat, reaching almost to his ankles. I had seen him there before. He turned his face to me, his eyes hidden behind dark glasses. I hastily apologised and moved aside, feeling chastened. His demeanour didn't match his clothing. I was angry at myself, realising how judgmental that was. And added to what Mother said about the woman in the purple hat not being the type of woman I would be friends with, I felt shaken. I didn't know what had upset me more – valuing the way a person dressed more than who they were, or the accusation of being a witch.

While Mother bought steak from the butchers, I headed to the off-licence for a bottle of wine. Actually, I bought two.

Christmas was finally well and truly over, the children back at school and David at work. I revelled in the quiet. Even Mother was occupied. She would be a while in the bathroom completing her beauty routine. I went to my book on the dining room table. I stared at it, scared to touch it. Was this really a Book of Shadows? I was just recording what I was finding out from my dreams and more recent waking dreams though more correctly these were visions, weren't they? Oh, and of course I had started recording those odd moments when things seemed too coincidental.

I wrote carefully Eugenie's story, how effective her spell was, how it kept little Constance safe.

'I am not a witch,' I said out loud to no one in particular. 'I just write down what I find out about people who happen to be witches.'

Almost sadly, I realised I would probably not hear any more of Eugenie and Constance but although this was the logical thought, something also told me that their story wasn't finished. What an idiot! I had forgotten to check the bathroom floor. Catherine had faded after she had told her story. I sat on the loo and studied the posh vinyl. Eugenie and Constance were still there. I sat there for a while, pondering.

'Are you alright Erica? You don't have an upset stomach or anything do you?'

'No Mum. I'm fine.' I pulled the door open. 'Look Mum, Eugenie and Constance are still here. There is more to their story.'

Mother stepped into our tiny bathroom to take a closer look at the floor. She shuddered, her carefully styled curls bouncing on her shoulders.

'How long will this go on for, Erica? What is it all about?'

I sensed her distress, although I couldn't see why she was quite so upset. It was me going through it after all.

'Come on Mum. Let's have a cup of tea.' I awkwardly put my arm around her and gave her a hug. We walked to the kitchen still holding on to each other. A cup of tea puts anything right.

That night, I dreamed of Eugenie. Constance, or Connie as they called her fondly, had grown to a bonny child, about 7 years old. Everyone loved her for her sweet ways, talkative, a ready smile. Everyone that is but Justin. He detested the child, her chatter, her existence; he hadn't forgiven his humiliation before she arrived on this earth.

****

John was walking towards the farm offices at the back of the house. I saw him often, getting the workers' instructions for the day. His eyes roved backwards and forwards, almost furtive, but I knew he was watching out for Justin. Justin had made it clear that John was under intense scrutiny since the day when the little lad was injured under the wheels of the carriage, when John called on Justin to stop. I felt sure that Justin wouldn't get rid of him, no matter how much he disliked him. John was a man who commanded respect. He walked tall and upright; when he spoke it was considered, delivered with confidence and surety. The farm labourers did as he asked, and under his guidance they did it well.

I had little to do that day, so continued my lazy gaze through the open window. John came back into view, walking alongside Thomas Walton, the estate manager.

'Right, we'll start harvesting the wheat in the top field. With this good weather we should get it done soon enough,' John said. He reached inside his coat and then stooped down to the ground. A tiny flurry of brown and white scuttled round his legs. A puppy. Someone else had spotted it too.

Connie flew across the grass from the path, where she had been taking exercise with her nanny. Her squeals of excitement brought a smile to my face. It was always such joy to see her happy. Fortunately, Justin was away on a business trip, so Constance was enjoying her freedom to run round, be a child, rather than always checking she wasn't within Justin's earshot.

John let her pick up the puppy, cuddle it. I went outside; I wanted to join in this happiness.

'Mummy, Mummy, look at the puppy. He's gorgeous. Can I have a puppy Mummy? I would love one so much.'

Her blue eyes shone in the sunlight as they filled with tears of longing, of anticipated disappointment. John approached me, respectful but nervous. He stood there, waiting till Connie had run after the puppy, both gambolling on the dry grass.

'Madam, I would be happy to let Miss Constance keep this puppy, if that would be acceptable to you.'

'That would be wonderful but.' I stopped not knowing how to tell this kind man that my husband would not allow Constance to have a pet. After all, it might make her happy.

'I understand that dogs can be a nuisance, especially in the fine surroundings of your elegant home. Perhaps the puppy could stay on the farm with me, and Miss Constance could come and visit with her nanny.'

I didn't reply. I was thinking this through. There was so much risk here, yet perhaps Nanny could vary the route of their morning walk.

'Pardon me Ma'am. I've been presumptuous.'

'Not at all. It would be wonderful. Would you like to tell her?'

Constance was the happiest I had seen her. Laughing, singing, dancing round. This mood persisted, fuelled every day by her visit to play with the puppy she named Mr Bouncy. Bouncy was descriptive of both of them.

'Constance, calm yourself down, your behaviour is not appropriate for a girl of your age.' Chastened, she became still and silent, contrite. 'Connie, when your father returns you must control yourself. You do not want him to become angry with you. You have to remain quiet and not draw attention to yourself.'

Constance knew what I meant. If Justin became aware of her presence in the house, she would be banished to her room to remain there.

'Connie, my love, your father must never learn of your puppy.' His spite would not let her keep something that made her so happy. 'Do you understand me Connie?'

'Yes Mummy.' She sobbed, her curls falling over her face, hiding her tears. I knew that she would take care. For a child, she was very aware of the need to be discreet in everything she did. Perhaps underhand, deceitful would describe it better. I was saddened by this knowledge.

*****

'Why is that wretched girl going out in this weather? The mud will ruin her dress. Does she have no thought for the cost of her clothes? No respect for those who provide them?'

'She is with Nanny at my request. Dr Elstone recommends exercise for children, especially girls. It calms their natural tendency for hysteria.' I was now also reduced to lying, uncomfortable but necessary to protect my angel.

Justin accepted my explanation though grudgingly. Over the coming days I noticed Justin watching Constance, keeping track of when she went out and when she returned, a distasteful eye when she came back damp or muddy, more so if she returned laughing, having enjoyed her time out of the house.

We maintained an uneasy truce over Connie's outings throughout the summer and autumn. Winter became more contentious. Nanny, though dedicated to Connie, began to be distressed by wading through inches of snow. Justin insisted that these walks should be restricted to the immediate grounds till more clement weather. I had to concur.

'Connie, I understand that you wish to see Mr Bouncy but if you defy your father, you may well not be allowed out of the grounds even when the weather improves. Surely you can see this?'

She did but it was wrenching her heart to be away from Mr Bouncy. The cold snow-filled weather lasted for several weeks and Connie's mood deteriorated. It hurt me to see her sad eyes, her uncharacteristic sullenness.

The next time John came to see the estate manager, he had a companion. Mr Bouncy who was now no longer a little puppy tripping over his own feet but taller, fuller, with huge paws that were out of place with his frame. Constance appeared as if from nowhere, running towards the dog. Mr Bouncy ran towards her. It seemed he had missed her as much as she missed him.

'That was kind of you John. Thank you.'

'Not at all Ma'am. Glad to oblige.' His face crinkled into a smile, giving him a much less serious appearance.

This became a regular occurrence. At least once a week, John would bring Mr Bouncy to the grounds, Connie would magically appear to play with him, while John conducted his business with the estate manager. Justin became aware of this.

'A dog Eugenie? A dog is not suitable for a girl. Too boisterous. She becomes silly when it is here. I will ensure that John does not bring that wretched animal with him.'

Justin went to talk to John who was standing patiently while Connie fussed Mr Bouncy.

'Constance, get away from that animal.' Justin stared at Connie, her dress covered with muddy pawprints. 'Just look at the state of you. You look like a peasant, as if you run with the hired hands' children. '

'John, get that animal away from here. If I see it here again, I will have it shot. Do you understand?'

'Very clearly, Sir.' John called Mr Bouncy to him and left the grounds without another word.

Constance fell to her knees on the damp grass. 'Please Father, no. I love Mr Bouncy. Don't stop me seeing him.'

'You will not see that animal again.'

'You are mean father. I hate you.'

I hurried towards them, fearful of how Justin would respond to this insolence. He moved towards her, raised his hand to strike her. I put myself in between them, took the blow that would have knocked her slight frame to the floor.

A weekend away

'This can only end badly,' I said to David. 'I so desperately want to know how their story ended but I'm almost frightened to hear it. I know it's all in the past, but it seems so real to me, as if they are people I know, can reach out and touch.' He put his arm round me as I wept damp patches on to his chest.

'I know you can't stop this. You won't be satisfied till you know, and I truly understand that. But this is getting stressful for you. I think we need to get away for a bit, have a break somewhere so you can relax.'

I wanted to say no, I didn't want to go anywhere, but I couldn't hurt his feelings like that. He was only taking care of me. The contrast between my husband and Eugenie's made me want to hold him tight.

'That would be lovely David. Thank you.' Apart from that, surely I could dream anywhere.

'It's Whitsun break in a couple of weeks. I'll see if I can book somewhere. How about a long weekend in Harlech? Beautiful beaches, lots of space for Bruno, and the lads would love the castle.'

'Sounds wonderful David.'

Mum agreed it was a good idea and promptly started planning my packing. I would have left it a bit but she, as usual, was quite right. It took a long time getting the dust off the suitcases which had been left in the loft – uncovered as Mother pointed out.

Leaving several lists of things I needed to do in readiness for our weekend break, and in a flurry of bags and packages, Mother left on Wednesday afternoon so she would be home in time for her WI meeting. I promised faithfully to relax, and also to update her immediately on anything else I found out. I suspected these two would be mutually exclusive. Perhaps I needed to make more time for that grounding Fey witch told me about.

Saturday rolled round and I took the boys out shopping for new waterproof jackets. Holidays in Wales guaranteed rain. I added new wellies. Joe wanted ones with frog eyes and a big smile on the toe. Jacob chose bright red but plain much to my surprise. Sometimes I forget he is growing up fast. We went into Waterstones. After the bedlam of shoppers charging round as if this was the last shopping day before Christmas, I welcomed the peace of the bookshop. The boys loved books and it was always a treat for them to get a new book. Jacob opted for the suitably spooky Coraline while Joe chose The Worst Witch. I tried to dissuade him, but he was adamant he wanted it.

'While we're here,' I thought, 'I could just pop to the next floor, see if there is anything that might explain what is going on in my head.' I wasn't certain if I needed books on witchcraft or psychology for beginners. I decided on the former and headed for the religion department. I found them under alternative beliefs. I was amazed how many were on the shelves. They were right there next to highly respectable books, so I settled down to browse. Jacob and Joe made themselves comfortable on the floor to read their new acquisitions. I came away with two books, one a comprehensive but basic introduction to witchcraft, so it assured me. The other looked like more intense reading, explaining things like clairvoyance, clairsentience – whatever that was – and second sight, contacting the dead. That sort of thing. I paid at the desk without anyone commenting on my strange reading choice and headed off with two tired boys who were more than ready to go home. Joe fell asleep on the bus and slept soundly till we reached home, when I had to wake one grumpy boy for the short walk home.

The next week was busy getting ready for our break. David had found us a chalet close to the beach. We were setting out Friday night as soon as David got home from work and coming back Tuesday. I packed plenty of things for the boys to do on the journey; bank holiday traffic would be a nightmare.

For two whole weeks I had not a vision nor a single dream. That was the only thing I had to update in my book. People said I needed a break from all this drama, I agreed, and I got a break. Was that me controlling it? Or was something else at work? I couldn't say, but I felt lonely, a deep separation from Eugenie and Constance, as if I was letting them down.

We set off on Friday early evening. David driving, me in the front passenger seat, where I could keep an eye on the boys and enjoy the scenery once we had got out of Birmingham and off the M54. By 9 o'clock, the boys were drifting off to sleep with the steady hum of the car, and I must confess I joined them.

****

Justin was returning from his ride around the estate, checking on the progress of the harvest, reminding the labourers who was in charge. His horse was a magnificent specimen, a full seventeen hands, glossy brown coat, groomed to a shine by the stable hand, though a bit temperamental as Justin liked to tell people. 'But that's no problem to an experienced rider like myself. Just have to let the brute know who's in charge.'

Mr Bouncy must have escaped from his home with John, missing his little mistress. He raced up the lane, ran onto the gravel drive, under the proud horse's hooves. The horse shied, reared up, threw Justin to the floor. He lurched to his feet. I could see from my safe distance in the window that he was fuming, not just angry but red in the face, spitting angry. He grabbed Mr bouncy by the scruff of its neck, raised his arm holding his riding crop and flashed it down on Mr Bouncy's flank. The dog screeched in pain, an agonised scream that pierced the glass in the window and reached into my heart. Justin hit the dog again, and again; blood splattered with each cut of the crop. I was ashamed. I should have gone down to intervene, to protect the animal. Constance would be sorely grieved, but I was frightened. I knew that Justin could just have easily turned the crop to me. I stayed by the window, sickened but unable to turn away.

My heart stopped. Constance ran across the drive. I had thought she was in the library with her tutor.

'Stop it Father. Leave Mr Bouncy alone. You are killing him.' She ran up to Justin, tried to grab his arm. I watched as Justin let go of the dog and turned to Constance. I saw him raise his arm, crop still in hand. I was too far away to help. I couldn't watch him do this to Constance, not my daughter, the only joy in my life.

I called to the spirits that had helped me to save her life once before. My body trembled as I made my plea. Energy rushed through me, through my feet, through my head, meeting at my heart then surging through my arms, through my hands. I pushed this power, this living, vital feeling that understood my heart, aimed it at the hateful scene unfolding on the drive. 'Save my daughter, save my daughter.'

The horse that had settled down once the dog was subdued shook his head, twitched his ears, snorted. Steam rose from his body as if he had just finished a wild run. The stallion reared tall on his hind legs, hooves flailing in the air. Justin didn't stand a chance, so intent was he on venting his hatred of Constance, of me. He didn't realise till too late. Huge hooves ringed with iron flashed through the air, smashed Justin's skull. The sickening blow floored him. Blood patterned the gravel.

Its task done, the horse settled, trotted away. Constance ran into my open arms as I raced across the grass to her. I hugged her, clung to her as we both sobbed. Mr Bouncy lay still, hot blood cooling on the grass beneath him. His pitiful whimpers faded. Connie's tears fell like rain, washing the blood away.

****

I woke up, looking around drowsily. 'Far to go?' I asked David.

'We're not far off now. You've had a good sleep. It's doing you good to get away from it all already.'

I didn't like to tell him about my dream. I reached for a mint from the bag sat in the well between us. This could preclude conversation for a while, so I sucked noisily while I thought over what I had just seen. Apart from that, my mouth tasted awful so a couple of mints would be a good thing for everyone.

Justin had died. Eugenie thought she had caused it. I knew what she had put into it. I felt that energy surge through my body as she did. Yet she hadn't zapped Justin. He died because of the horse, who may have been startled by the dog's cries. Nothing to prove it wasn't an accident but a huge coincidence. Yet this magic, if that was what it was, wasn't for her own benefit, not really. It was to protect her child. I thought about this for some time, turned round awkwardly in my seat to gaze at my boys, both now asleep, their faces sweet and pure, a reflection of my love for them. Would I kill to save my children? At that moment, I knew that I would.

The last of the light left the sky as we pulled up at the chalet. David punched the code into the key safe, let us in, switching lights on as we went. I went with the boys to explore the chalet, decide who was sleeping where, while David carried in the bags. It was clean and smelt fresh. The boys tried hard to get the double bed, but I told them firmly that was Mommy and Daddy's room, and they had the single beds in the room next door. Jacob and Joe were excited and tired, a bad combination, which meant they were getting somewhat grumpy. David huffed in with the last of the luggage as I retrieved the cool bag with emergency rations. I made hot chocolate, produced peanut butter and jam sandwiches, and less exotic ham and tomato, rounded off with cheese and onion crisps. I warned the boys that they were going straight to bed as soon as they finished but they didn't need to be told. They asked if they could read their new books which they had brought with them. They were asleep, books discarded open on the duvet, when I checked on them five minutes later. David and I lingered over the sandwiches and I produced a doughnut and a bar of chocolate which we ate while watching the TV before bed, Bruno curled up on the carpet by our feet.

Saturday morning, the boys bounced out of bed almost as the sun rose. David and I took a little longer to move. The sun was bright, a very unusual occurrence – a dry, fine Welsh bank holiday. We headed for the beach, walking in deep, soft sand, following the path through the dunes onto the wide expanse of golden beach. We went to the water's edge so the boys could paddle in the shallow waves, while Bruno chased round them, scattering water droplets that sparkled in the sun. The boys collected shells which they put in David's upturned hat. We hadn't bought a bucket yet. We spent most of the morning at the rock pools, water captured by the rugged stones. Tiny crabs, minute fishes, the excitement on finding a star fish and staring back at the anemone kept the boys fascinated. Jacob could well be a future marine biologist.

It's amazing how much food children can put away after a morning on the beach although David and I also made a good attempt on the contents of the picnic boxes. The boys played quietly making patterns in the sand, interspersed with sudden shouting when one or the other kicked the patterns away.

'Stop kicking sand; it'll get in your eyes.' It was starting to get irritating.

'Come on lads, get your trunks on and we'll go down to the sea.'

'Stay here Bruno.' I thought Bruno might have trouble with that command, but the lazy dog curled up by my feet and did a good impression of being asleep.

'Thanks David,' I said, stretching out and making myself comfy on the picnic blanket, discreetly sliding my book out of my handbag.

Introduction to witchcraft. It certainly was. I didn't know what I expected but this wasn't it. I hadn't given witchcraft much thought till all this strange stuff started. I'd watched a couple of episodes of Charmed on TV, but it was just a lightweight programme to while away an evening. I knew Fey was a witch but only because of the books in her shop, The Hedge Witch, the Green Man, the Power of the Crone, titles like that. But even that didn't mean she was really a witch; she just looked like it. I must make more of an effort to stop being judgmental. I had never called her witch to her face; I wasn't brave enough.

Thinking about it, I didn't really have a religion. Mother never took us to church or sent us to Sunday School although we sang carols at Christmas and gorged on chocolate at Easter. I know I wasn't Christened as we had a bit of trouble with that when I came to get married to David and we ended up in a register office. Mother wasn't too concerned nor apologetic which surprised me at the time. Given Mother's knack for planning perfect events, I would have thought that a pretty church setting would have been an essential starting point. When I thought about it, I didn't believe in God although I paid him lip service.

I read of the wheel of the year, the celebrations that marked the turning, strange names like Samhain and Lunasagh, ones that I recognised like summer and winter solstices. It was fascinating putting this into context of what I had learned about my distant relatives. The wise women who healed with herbs, tended to others, who cast spells to bend the world to their will. This sounded just like Catherine and Eugenie. I carried on reading, lazing in the sun.

****

I was now a wealthy woman. Justin had no brothers nor sisters; his parents had died some years earlier. The estate and everything that entailed came to me. I had not thought before how lucky I was not to want for material goods. My concern had been to be loved by my husband, at the very least not abused and for my child to grow up safely in a loving home. Justin's death had now removed the threat. Instead of hiding to avoid his anger, I found that I needed to become visible, to take control of this building – my home – and the land that surrounded it. The staff in the house and the labourers on the farm depended on me to keep things in good order and productive.

Despite my innermost joy at achieving safety, I deemed it best to pursue an appearance of mourning, dressing in black, weeping gently when people were there to observe. I could not risk anyone making any connection, any suggestion of my involvement in Justin's death. I could not permit anything that would let people make accusations against me, raise suspicion that could lead to me losing my newfound freedom and security.

Staff from the house and farm hands lined up to watch the funeral carriage go past, their heads respectfully lowered, hats removed. I stood at the graveside, little Constance drawn but brave, standing close to me.

My parents dutifully attended the funeral, but they left as soon as they respectfully could. I could never replace Catherine.

She was the favourite daughter, clever, obedient, willing to learn and take her place in the life of the house. They had such high hopes for her, wickedly dashed when Catherine ran away with that farm boy. They were left with me, vain, spoiled, lazy. How I missed my sister. I doubted I would ever see her again. I had no knowledge of her whereabouts. Even if I found her, would she want to see me? Perhaps I received what I deserved, taking Justin from her. Yes, I can admit it to myself if never to others, I had flirted with Justin attracting his attention while he was yet courting Catherine. She could have been living in comfort rather than shamed and in poverty. I doubt that Justin would have dared lay a hand on Catherine.

Thomas Walton, the estate manager, met with me to discuss the running of the farm.

'It's all in hand Ma'am. I've been running this farm many a year now. The seasons come and go, the weather can be good one year and bad the next, but we always get through. The biggest problem we are facing is this war. Many of our brave young lads have gone to fight, volunteered. They said this war would be over by Christmas. They got that wrong.'

I sensed anger in his voice. 'Do you have anyone gone to war Thomas?'

'My youngest, Albert. Volunteered as soon as he could. Lied about his age. Just 16, he was.'

'You must be proud of him.'

'Proud? The fool. He should have stayed here working on the farm. We needed him. Enough work for those left behind as it is.'

'I'm sorry.'

'Ar well. The problem is going to get worse with this here new law they're bringing in. Military Service Act, they call it. Not enough to take those who wish to fight their bloody war, they're forcing people to join up whether they want to or not.'

He stopped for a moment, whether to gather his breath or his thoughts, I didn't know.

'We'll have to be ready to fight it, stand by the lads. They can go to tribunal for exemption. We've got to stand our ground – we need our lads to keep bringing the harvest home.'

'How many workers do we have on the farm, Thomas?'

'We have fifteen men who live on the estate in the cottages. And of course their women and children who help out when needed, at harvest time and lambing when we need to keep an eye on the ewes overnight, feed the rejected lambs and suchlike.'

'So we have thirty adults and their children dependent on the farm?'

'That'd be right, plus the labourers who live in the village.'

Thomas took me to see the cottages, bouncing around on a cart designed with no thought for comfort. I had seen the cottages briefly before, in a row down one side of a lane. They looked quaint from a distance but closer up you could see the dilapidation. Windows with cracks in the glass covered over with faded newspaper. Rooves which even I could tell had slates missing. An unpleasant air hung like a mist. I wrinkled my nose. Thomas noticed, his lips curving in a smile, quickly aborted.

'It's farm life Ma'am. No proper cess pit.'

'Where is everyone Thomas?

'Out working Ma'am.'

'Even the children?'

Ar, them as well.'

I gazed at the hovels my workers were living in, the unsanitary conditions. They had to fetch water from a spring a good distance away. I had to do something.

'Thomas, what can I do to improve the conditions here? Where do I start?'

Thomas looked at me, a long stare as a genuine smile slowly spread across his face.

'Do you mean that Ma'am? Cos if you do, you'd do best to speak to John Wright. He has all the ideas round here. He'll tell you what needs doing and how to do it.'

We found Mary

I woke up with a comfortable feeling relaxing me, seeping into muscles I hadn't realised were tense. Just in time, as I could see David and the boys coming up the beach. I pulled towels out of the bag ready. I was so proud of Eugenie, putting right the deprivation Justin had caused with his attitude to people, just rubble heaped at the bottom to help him climb the wall.

Although the sun was bright, the water had been chilly and little Joe was cold, his teeth chattering. I wrapped him in the biggest towel, rubbed him vigorously to dry him off and warm him up. Jacob, independent as ever, dressed quickly, remembering to empty the sand out of his shoes before putting them on.

We were all ready for dinner. I happily agreed with the boys' pleas to go to the chip shop. I fancied chips myself. We drove past a pub advertising music on that night, children welcome. We came back after eating chips with little wooden forks, sat in the garden where we could still hear the band playing but the boys could run around without disturbing people. The band was good, old stuff that people were soon singing along to, the Beatles, Abba, even some Bon Jovi. Today had been a good day.

'You look much better already,' said David, pushing stray hairs off my face, running his fingers gently down my cheek, under my chin. 'I recognise that smile. Was beginning to wonder where my wife had gone.'

'I love you David, but.'

He put a finger to my lips. 'I know love. This is something you have to do.'

****

Wednesday morning, 8am, Mother phoned. 'I need to speak to you today. Are you staying at home today or taking the boys out anywhere?'

'Hi Mum, I suspect I'll be in all day. Lots to do today, what with the washing'

'And the packing. Are they coming tomorrow or Friday? '

Whoops, I had completely forgotten that Mother had said she would have the boys for a couple of days.

'Friday would be best. Give them chance to get over the weekend.'

'Good. I'll phone you at 11 then.'

And with that, she abruptly ended the call. I didn't know where to start, so much to do. I decided to get the washing done, then pack the same clothes the boys had taken with them to Harlech, save me thinking too much about what to pack. Then I realised I probably needed to tell the boys before I packed their bags. And if I told David, he might arrange something special for just the two of us.

Jacob and Joe thought it was fantastic they were going to stay with Granny. She would take them to all sorts of places – the river, the cathedral, the little museum, and of course they would come back with new toys. David also thought it was fantastic they were going to spend quality time with Granny.

'I'm on it,' he said when I gave him the news. This was turning out to be a good week.

I filled the washing machine with the first load of boys' clothes, sorted the rest of the washing into piles ready to go in, made myself a cup of tea and counted out three chocolate biscuits, then sat down to wait Mother's call. It would be at exactly 11am. I was a bit intrigued; perhaps she just wanted to talk through arrangements for Thursday.

'Hello Mum. Are you alright?'

'I was talking to Emily Darnley, from the WI. Lovely woman, pure white hair. Very intelligent woman interested in local history. I asked her what she knew about witchcraft at the turn of the century. She told me there were tales of wise women who lived on the edge of communities, even as late as that. Of course, by then, it wasn't a crime to be a witch or practice witchcraft in itself. They had given up burning them. But if you were accused of doing witchcraft, spells or suchlike, you could be found guilty of fraud, as supernatural powers were no longer thought to exist. You could get fined or sent to prison.'

'That's interesting but why were you asking her?' I had thought this was quite personal and hadn't expected Mother to share it with anyone.

'I asked her how we could find out about it. She directed me to the Daily Gazette, the local newspaper of the time.' She paused for dramatic effect, so I played along.

'Go on Mum, tell me.'

'I've found news reports about a Mary. I'm fairly certain it's our Mary, the maid. She was fined for claiming to practice witchcraft.'

Now that was really interesting. 'Well done Mum. That's fantastic.'

'She was fined £2 and 10 shillings. That would have been a lot in those days. I'll let you have a copy of the newspaper report when I collect the boys.'

And with that she was gone. Everything we were finding out was confirming the stories that were coming to me. I had one thing left to do today. I waited till the boys were fed and watching TV (it comes in really handy as a babysitter sometimes even though I always feel guilty about it) and took myself to the downstairs bathroom. I pulled down the lid and sat on the toilet seat. Apprehensively, I looked at the floor. Eugenie and Constance were still there so that must mean there was still more to come of their story. Dorothy was still there smiling at me. 'Well Dorothy, it was really sad, what I've heard so far. Is there more to learn? What does Eugenie do next? I hope it's good news for her. She deserves it.'

As I gazed at Dorothy's pretty smile, the floor seem to flutter and move. I shook my head thinking I was dizzy, but the reason wasn't as simple as that. As I watched, another face emerged out of the pattern on the lino. A youngish woman, about 35, not old by our standards nowadays but perhaps older in comparison to the shorter life span a hundred years ago. Her hair was pulled back off her face, hidden under a cotton bonnet by the looks of it. Dark wisps of hair escaped, curling on to her face. The eyes were dark, standing out in the pale face. I felt drawn to them and returned her stare. She had a face I could trust, kindly, her head held an angle that suggested self-assurance, a confident woman.

So now we had to work out who this was. I wondered if this could be Mary. Too close in timing to Mother's findings to be a coincidence.

*****

'How could they, how could they? Where am I going to find the money to pay this fine? £2 10 shillings. What am I going to do? I'll end up in prison.' The anger in her voice faded away, turned to sadness. 'What am I going to do?'

She stared into the afternoon air, elbows on the window frame. Her body slumped, needed support to stay upright. Her shoulders shook as sobs broke free, her head resting on her hands, the frill on her cotton bonnet nodding with her cries. Daylight leaving as twilight arrived, the sobs subsided. She lifted her head, walked across the darkened room, lit a candle that did little to lift the gloom of the room. She pushed the wooden shutters into place across the glass, shutting out the night. The snaking tongues of the new lit fire sent shadows flickering across the expanse of wooden table occupying the centre of the room. A single wooden chair stood beside it; a patchwork cushion added small comfort.

'Alice, you told me I should never trust anyone, that someone was always ready to cause trouble for – well, for people like us. Why can't they just leave us alone?' The empty room listened but offered no reply.

'All I've done is help people, Alice, just like you did. I don't charge, just accept what they want to give me. You know what it's like, more often than not it's food, bit of bacon is always good, jam makes a nice treat. Mother Sybil gave me a length of warm cloth. I made me dress out of it, a good warm one for winter, with enough left over to fashion a hat. So it's not like I'm taking money off em. I'm not rich now, am I?'

She fetched water, put eggs to boil in the pot hanging down over the fire. She returned from the pantry with a mug of milk and a thick cut slice of bread, ragged round the edges. She buttered it carefully.

She took the wooden box from the shelf by the fire, counted the coins inside it.

'Me life savings. One pound, three shillings and fourpence. And I need to buy some flour. Alice, how am I going to get enough to pay that fine? Tell me that Alice. Mary the witch who cheats people. That's what they're saying about me. No such thing as magic. No such thing as witchcraft the magistrate says, but the locals are scared of me for being a witch, no matter what he says. I'll show em Alice, I'll show em.'

She sat down at the scrubbed wooden table, meagre meal in front of her. She finished her eggs, swallowed the last morsel of bread.

The warmth from the fire and the food in her belly mellowed her anger. She took down a small dark metal bowl, with a handle looping over the top. From the shelves on the wall, she selected several jars and placed them on the table, opening the jars and breathing in deep the scent of the contents.

'Parsley for strength,' she said, adding a pinch of green herb to the bowl. 'I will need strength to get through this. Knitbone and allweed for protection and prosperity. I need help with both of those. Get those who hate me under control and get in enough to pay off this fine. Vervain for inspiration and success. That should do.'

Mary moved her candle closer to the bowl, touched the wick to the dried herbs. Smoke rose in curls heading for the ceiling. She sat down, gazing at the smoke, staring at the candle and the patterns they made as the flickering light bounced off the tendrils. The tension ebbed from her shoulders; her breathing slowed. The smoke wrapped round her, caressing her still and silent form.

Her head came up, she was back in the room.

'I hope them hens keep on laying. I can try and sell more. Perhaps take them to the village store, see if she will take some as well as me usual ladies. Perhaps she'd buy some of me goat's butter. Good stuff it is.' She paused, as if gathering her thoughts.

'I'm going to have to see if I can get some work, Alice, but who will take me on. Perhaps they'll have some work at the big house. They'll remember me from when Miss Catherine was little. They'll know I'm a good worker.'

The next morning was dry and sun shone through the trees.

'That's a sign it'll be a good day. Send blessings for me Alice.'

Yet her reception at the big house was not a good one.

'You've got a nerve coming round here after what happened with Miss Catherine. The missus will never forgive you.' The housekeeper stood with her arms folded across her ample bosom.

'It wasn't my fault she ran off like that. If the missus had been more understanding, loved Catherine like a mother should, then it would never have happened.'

'Just listen to yourself, no remorse, no respect. Get yourself gone before I have you removed.'

'But I'm desperate for work. Please don't send me away. Can you give me nothing?'

The look on her face told Mary not to push any further and she started the long walk down the drive. The sound of feet running after her made her swivel round and jump to one side, fearful.

'It's alright. Don't be afraid. I just wanted to...' The young girl stopped, short of breath. 'If you need work, try Eugenie. She's dismissed some of the old staff, too loyal to Justin's memory, blamed her for his death. Accused her of witchcraft.'

'Witchcraft?' Mary was listening, interested.

'Yes, anyway she's hiring. And she may not be so quick to blame, point fingers.'

Thanking her for her kindness, Mary made her way to Eugenie's home, a long walk to the other side of the village, then across the estate. Pausing at the village green to take a drink of water at the well, she watched, through lowered lids, people staring at her, nudging each other, moving swiftly past. She hurriedly continued her journey, to rest when she reached the safety of the outskirts of the village, away from people.

Mary's progress became slower, her legs heavy, her feet sore. At last, in the distance, the square grey mass of the house came into view. Mary arrived at the servants' entrance as the sun started to dip in the sky, started its journey to the west. Her enquiry was well received.

'Wait here, I'll go and have a word with the mistress. What's the name?'

'Mary Beck.' Mary took a seat on an upturned log outside the kitchen, the sun warming her stiffened back. She heard voices in the kitchen, stood up in readiness.

'Mary, Mary, is it really you?' Eugenie herself stood in the doorway, walked towards Mary with open arms.

'Miss Eugenie, it's been a long while. ' Mary felt her eyes water at this welcome. Eugenie beckoned her indoors to the kitchen; cook brought them a pot of tea.

'I am working to improve the lot of the farm workers. There are fifteen families living on the farm which gives us nearly sixty children. Most of them are dressed in little more than rags. I seem to remember that you are a skilled seamstress. You used to make our dresses when we were still in the nursery. Would you be able to make clothes for the children?'

'That I can Miss.'

'And could you look after their health with your homely remedies? I remember well the cordials and embrocations you made to keep us well.'

Mary looked away, drew a breath then pulled her shoulders back, her head coming upright. 'Have you heard of my conviction? I treated old Farmer Kyle's cow when it sickened, its udders swollen and infected. I made a liniment with herbs I had collected during the night. Herbs are more potent before the sun has got on them, dried away their strength. The old fool didn't have the sense to know this so when someone told him that I had collected the herbs under the full moon, he claimed that I used a potion made by witchcraft. Then the cow upped and died. He told everyone I had killed the cow to spite him. He told the magistrate that I had said I could cure the cow and as everyone knew I was a witch, I meant I would cure it by magic. I never told him any such sort, but I still got a fine. The magistrate said that I was a fraud, trying to cheat him out of money.'

Eugenie reached across the table, placed her hand on top of Mary's.

'I never meant no harm Miss. I don't know why the cow died. Usually my cures do exactly that, cure. And in anyway, making medicines and such like is not witchcraft. It's what poor people who can't afford a doctor do. It's the old ways, passed from mother to daughter.'

'I know that Mary. And I also know that you are indeed a witch, but we will keep that between us. Will you work with me, to improve the lot of my workers?'

'**Mum, the Mary you found in the newspaper** – it's our Mary.' It was early, probably too early to be phoning even Mother. Her almost whispered greeting suggested she was still in bed. 'Sorry, Mum. Have I woken you?' She didn't admit it, but I was sure I had.

'Our Mary you say. Catherine's maid? Have you had another dream?'

'Yes, Mum. Well more of a vision. I could see her sat in her cottage, ranting away to Alice but Alice wasn't there. Really strange. She was furious and so upset because she couldn't afford the fine and was frightened she'd go to prison, but she did some, well, I think it must have been magic, and it looks like she found the answer to her problems. She went to work for Eugenie.'

A perfectly rational woman

The boys off to school, I took Bruno for a walk in the fields. I needed time to think as much as Bruno needed to walk. Here was I, a perfectly rational woman, hearing more and more about witchcraft, and not questioning it or laughing it off as superstition. I was glad Mary had used it to help herself out of the mess some unpleasant person had created for her. I was glad Justin could no longer hurt Eugenie and Constance. Yet there was a warning here; Catherine had used magic to get Jack to come back to her, but it backfired. She certainly had Jack, but it took the life out of him.

Bruno was full of bounce this morning and I let him off the lead so he could run off his energy. He disappeared into some bushes, sniffing at the ground, huffing at the scents he found.

'Come on Bruno. I let you off the lead for exercise not so you could hide in the bushes.'

As I walked to retrieve him, a young man appeared from behind the stand of bushes, Bruno trotting happily at his heels.

'Hello, this your dog? Lovely boy isn't he?'

'Yes, he's mine. Thanks. Come on Bruno, you scoundrel.'

Bruno was nudging his head against the tight black jeans, trying to lick the owner's hands.

'He's taken a fancy to you,' I said, a little embarrassed by Bruno's sudden affection for this complete stranger.

'Don't worry,' he said. 'I'm used to dogs. Mine's at the vets; they've removed a lump from her leg. Perhaps Bruno can smell her on me.'

'Nothing serious, I hope.'

'Just a small cyst, they think. She's a Red Setter. You'll probably see us around a lot. She needs so much exercise. I moved here a couple of weeks ago, from Wolverhampton. Great to have found this space.'

I quite liked this young man. Mid-twenties or thereabouts, chatting so easily. I told him I was there at least once a day, often twice, so would no doubt see him again soon, and I carried on my way, Bruno now interested in a flock of birds feeding low on the ground on whatever bugs they may have disturbed.

On the way out of the fields, I nodded hello to Mrs Purple Hat, who seemed to wait till I passed her before she moved away from the wooden posts marking the entrance. Was she stalking me? If so, she was harmless enough, just a bit odd. Perhaps she was lonely.

At home with a cup of tea, I decided to leave the washing up and update my book. I recorded Mary's story, being careful to record her magic spell, having to think hard to make sure I had the names of the herbs right. Did they even exist? I hadn't heard of some of them. I decided to check on the computer, see I could find any more information. Knitbone was comfrey, allweed was dill. I recorded this in my book as well.

As I was drinking my second cup of tea, I decided to record my meeting this morning with Mrs Purple Hat and also the young man. Something about the way I was meeting people seemed a little strange.

I had finished my book on witchcraft. It was all very interesting. I had learned about the eight sabbats each year to mark the changing seasons, and the rituals that witches did to celebrate them. It was more difficult to understand the magic, the spells and what they thought they would achieve. Candle magic, visualisation, using herbs and crystals, raising energy in rituals. All words on paper till I saw Mary burning herbs and drifting off somewhere inside herself. Did her actions, her spell, really bring about the answer to her problems or was it coincidence and her own ideas and actions? I thought of Fey Witch. Did she do magic?

The rest of the week was rather quiet. I had no more dreams nor visions. The boys were behaving well, enjoying the warmer weather that let them spend most of their free time in the garden. David found time to play football with them when he came home, now the nights arrived later. Mother had been quiet as well, busy with WI and her friends. I had seen the young man with his red setter in the fields when I walked Bruno. The dogs got on well, playing together, chasing, rolling over in the grass. He was staying with a friend, so he said; he'd found work locally. Most of our trek around the fields was in companionable silence. We didn't have a great deal in common, given the age difference and him living a single life while I was a full-time mom, but it was pleasant to share the walk.

Thursday rolled round. I needed a trip to Fey Witch's shop. I'd decided to make mother a birthday card rather than buy one. I knew she would appreciate the effort, even if it wasn't perfect. I always started out with an image of the beauteous thing I would produce but I had to admit that sometimes it would fall short of the ideal. I left Bruno at home so I could go straight there after dropping off the boys without feeling guilty about him waiting outside. Freedom to browse.

The shop was quiet that time of day. Mother is a mauve person, so I selected backing paper in delicate mauve with a slightly darker fleck running through it. A brighter purple paper had caught my eye; it was handmade so it felt softer and would make lovely, moulded flowers, curved over the back of spoon. White lace would add the finishing touch. And of course, I bought some other bits and pieces. The spare room was full of boxes of materials for making cards. It was a bit of an obsession. I gathered my selection and took it to the counter and was rather surprised to be met by my young man from the dog walks.

'Hello,' I said. 'Fancy meeting you here.'

'Hiya. Yeah this is where I'm working now. I'm staying with the woman who owns the shop.'

'It must be a fascinating place to work. So much interesting stuff in here.' I'd noticed the pentacle, hanging round his neck from a silver chain.

'Well, yes. Suppose you could look at it like that. I love people coming in with their animals.' He smiled. 'That bit over there is interesting.' He nodded towards the velvet lined shelves with their unusual trinkets.

I made the brave decision to take a good look while I was there on my own. There were several wands – I recognised those – fashioned from wood, one with a crystal fastened to its point which the label said was quartz. Another was wrapped with silver wire and yet another had strange straight marks burned down its length.

'Those are runes. The wands are great aren't they. Made locally so each one is unique.'

He said this as my hand was hovering over a circular black compass with a silver pentacle embedded on its face. 'Why would you need one of those?' I asked.

'How much do you know? Heard about the four quarters and the elements?' He carried on when I nodded. 'Well, when we cast a circle for a ritual, we like to have the quarters lined up with the directions, so the east quarter facing east.'

'Oh, of course. How silly of me. I'm Erica by the way. Suppose I should introduce myself properly after all this time we've been walking the dogs.'

'You're right. I'm Dale. Pleased to meet you,' he said with a chuckle. 'But not silly at all. Any questions just ask. Happy to answer what I can.'

I spent another twenty minutes admiring the many things on display, then thought of poor Bruno who would probably be crossed legged by now. I bought him a dog chew and left for home.

I really needed to sort out what we were doing for Mother's birthday next week. I had already bought her present, a silk scarf, hand printed using wooden blocks. It was very tasteful and elegant, and I was sure Mother would like it. It was also very expensive. David wouldn't mind but I would be glad to get back to work so I didn't have to worry about spending money. David is brilliant and as far as he's concerned it's a joint income, not his, but sometimes it feels a little awkward. We'd agreed that I would go back to work when Joe moved up to senior school. Knowing that helped. So that was the present sorted, the card in hand but the actual day, I wasn't so sure about. Grudgingly, I decided to give Eileen a ring, see if she had any ideas. She probably would have. She's like Mother – knows everything.

Eileen rang me back after she'd had chance to think about it. 'The White Swan,' she suggested. 'If we're lucky, the weather will be dry enough to eat in the conservatory area. It opens on to the garden. There's a play area to keep the boys occupied.'

'Sounds brilliant,' I said. So that was Mother's birthday all sorted. Just needed to finish the card. I could have started cooking dinner; I could have done the ironing; I could have done lots of things but what I really wanted to do, needed to do, was update my book. So I grabbed a cup of tea, took myself to the dining-room and settled down with my beautiful book and pen. I added my meeting with Dale and the things he had told me about the wands and the compass. Another coincidence, Dale working there of all places, living with Fey Witch.

I persuaded myself to put the book away, place it in the cloth I now wrapped round it to keep it free from dust, and to protect it – from what I didn't really know but I felt it wasn't right to leave it out in the open for anyone to see. A bit like my diary when I was a kid. I don't think I showed that to anyone apart from Jennie, my best friend. Those were my secrets and I shared them only with people who were precious to me.

I made cottage pie for dinner with cauliflower, broccoli, thick brown gravy and a handful of chips to keep the boys happy. It was ready to set on the table as soon as David walked in which was a good job as he arrived home early. I heard his key in the lock as I was turning pans down to simmer.

'Traffic was really light tonight, don't know what's different.' David kicked his shoes off in the hall, talking to me with his voice raised to carry the distance to the kitchen. 'Such a lovely night. How about we take the boys over to Swan Pool, go for a walk round the lake?'

'Sounds great. Dinner's ready. I'll call the boys.' They didn't need to be called; they must have a sensor that alerts them as soon as food is on the table. Promising an ice-cream instead of pudding, I left the washing up and we escaped to the car; Bruno leapt into the back, his face pressed up against the dog guard, so he didn't miss anything.

The sun glanced across the water, sent sparkles rippling as the breeze brushed the surface, making waves. Peacefulness drifted in the warmth, sounds distant, muffled. The boys made short work of their ice-creams, bought from the van that always lurks there on warm evenings. I made mine last, enjoying the creamy mint with chocolate. Bruno followed close at my heels till I gave him the last bit of the cone. David was ahead with the boys, quacking at ducks, wondering whether the black birds on the water were coots or moorhens. Bruno raced off to join them, scattering ducks as he pulled up in a skid. I followed them for a while, dawdling behind, then found a bench conveniently in a patch of sunlight. The path went all around the lake so David would know where I was. I sat down, looking at the boats on the water.

****

'The work is coming on well, John.'

'It is Ma'am, thanks to your generosity.'

'It's your hard work that has fixed the cottages, and brought clean water.'

'But Ma'am, without you giving me the time off the land to do the work and paying for the necessaries, none of this would be happening.'

We walked down the lane, inspecting the work. John took my arm, guiding me out of the way of a gaggle of children racing downhill chasing a hoop with a stick. Trailing slowly after them was a lad, heaving himself along on crutches, one leg dangling in mid-air. I stared at him, following his slow progress.

'Who's that John?'

'Most of the children are a picture of health, Ma'am. Your Mary has worked wonders. It's brought their mothers so much comfort.'

'But John, who is that boy? What is wrong with him?'

'That's Robert. He had an accident Ma'am. When he was little.'

My eyes filling with tears as the memory flooded back. 'He fell under the carriage didn't he? The day I came here, my wedding day.'

'It wasn't your fault, and he's happy enough. Tough little lad.'

'But he'll never be able to work on the land, will he John? Not with his leg like that. What will become of him?'

We walked on, not speaking, looking at the cottages and the gardens now used for growing food and even flowers, now that there were proper cess pits for the brick built communal toilets.

'John, I was thinking. It would be nice to organise a trip to the seaside for the youngsters.'

'Are you sure Ma'am? I mean, that would be wonderful, but it would be costly; we'd need to send someone with them.'

'If the church in the village can arrange it, then I'm sure that we can.'

'You are wonderful, Ma'am.' John's voice softened. 'You have such a good heart.'

I heard the tenderness in his voice. 'So do you John. I couldn't have done this without you.' I reached out with my hand, placed it on John's arm. Muscles earned from hard work rippled beneath the dry, tanned skin. He traced each of my fingers with his work rough fingertips, covered my hand with his.

'I'm sorry Ma'am,' said John, pulling his hand away as he remembered himself, his station.

'Don't be John.' I swallowed. 'I'm not, nor would I be if it happened again.'

*****

The cooling air sent a shiver down my back. The light was starting to fade – where were David and the boys?

'Time to go home,' said David, as the lads rushed up to me to give me the pretty weeds they had collected on their way round the lake. 'That took longer than I expected. Forgot how interesting everything can be to these youngsters.'

We headed for the car park, the boys walking slowly now, and even Bruno taking a steady pace. There weren't many cars left; the door slammed on a dark car parked across from ours. I thought the driver looked familiar, though I was too far away to be certain. I had that unsettled feeling, the hairs on my neck tingling. I was sure it was Dale.

It was so real

I woke up, sweat dripping from my body yet I was cold, my body shaking. My chest heaved; sobs wrenched from my throat. I hurt, I was in pain, my wrists hurt, pain seared between my legs.

David wrapped his arms around me, held me tight. 'Hush, hush, it's alright, it's a dream, just a dream.' He comforted me like a baby, rocking me in his arms.

'Something awful has happened to Eugenie. Terrible.'

'Are you ok? That's what's most important. What happened to Eugenie is long in the past.'

How could I answer him? Though we lived years apart, I was scared, I was sore. I felt what Eugenie went through, I knew her humiliation.

'Oh David, it was so real. It's like I was there, like I was Eugenie. I think she was raped.'

'But I thought Justin was dead?'

'It wasn't Justin. She didn't know this man.'

David cuddled me, his warmth reaching into my body, his love calming me. I slowly relaxed and must have fallen asleep.

When I woke, the sun was high enough to shine boldly through the curtains. David appeared with a cup of tea, toast and marmalade.

'I left you to sleep. You needed it after last night. That was so awful Erica.' As he passed my tea, he gasped, put the mug down and took my hand in his. 'Erica, this bruising – was it here last night?'

I stared at my wrist, rubbed it with my fingers, trying to brush away the purple stains. 'No,' I said. 'David I'm scared. How can I dream up bruises?' Tears slid silently down my face.

'Erica, I can't go to work and leave you alone, not like this. I'm going to call your mother, see if she can come and stay with you.'

My instinct was to say no, I'd be alright but then I realised that I wasn't alright.

'Thanks David, that would be great.'

'Of course I'll come over. I was coming over soon for my birthday meal, so I can come today and stop a bit if that's ok with you David.'

'That would be good, Jocelyn, if you don't mind.' David sounded genuinely grateful, no hint of the chagrin he normally showed when the subject of my mother coming to stay was brought up. He phoned work, said he would be in a bit later, took the boys to school, stayed with me till Mother arrived, carried her bags upstairs to the little guest room. 'I'll see you later love. Get some rest.'

Mother came into the bedroom, knitting in hand. 'I'm going to sit here and get on with this cardigan. Emily Darnley's daughter has had a little girl, 7lb 6oz and I promised I'd knit something for her. You get some sleep. You look exhausted. I'm right here if you need me. We can talk when you're rested.'

The rhythm of the clacking needles lulled me back to sleep. I woke, still drowsy, opening my eyes to see a swirl of white frills tipped in pink. I must have been asleep for quite some time.

'I'll go and make some tea,' said Mother, slipping out the bedroom door. 'Be right back.'

I pulled myself upright, shifting the pillow so I could lean back without banging my head against the wooden headboard. I looked at my wrist – the bruises were fading. I no longer had pain down below. I knew Eugenie survived the attack, would get over the physical pain but would she ever recover? I tried to keep calm but still the tears were very close to the surface; I struggled to hold them back.

'Let them out Erica. A good cry will make you feel better, get rid of the tension. And drink your tea. I've brought up some biscuits. Something sweet will help. You're still in shock.' Mother had also placed a box of tissues by the bed. I now cried in all seriousness. Mother was so thoughtful.

My tears subsided from full on wracking, shoulder heaving sobs to the sniffly sort, then stopped. I felt worn out but calm. Mother was right, I felt better, the tension lifted. After a shower, the warm water washing away the remaining knots, I dressed and headed downstairs.

'Erica,' said Mother, 'what are you going to do about all this? It's getting too much for you. And the bruising? I'm worried.'

'I don't know Mum. I don't want it to stop. I need to know what happens to Eugenie. In anyway, I don't know if I can stop it.' I had no answer.

'I think we should go and speak to that woman at the witchy shop. She's the only one I can think of who may be able to help, or even understand. I've a feeling that if you go to your doctor, he will either prescribe you medication for anxiety or make a referral to mental health services.'

I chuckled. I loved that my mother was telling me that the rest of the world may think I was delusional. On a more serious note, perhaps I was.

'OK Mum. Sounds like a plan.' We set off to see Fey Witch.

The shop was empty, the morning rush after dropping the kids off at school had come and gone, and the post school rush was yet to come. I was pleased to see that Dale wasn't there, presumably his day off.

'Fey, I need some advice.'

'How are you doing with the people coming to you? it can be unsettling,' said Fey, putting the kettle on and producing three mugs.

'It is. It looks like I am going to find out my family history. I've learned a lot already that I had no idea about. My family used to be into witchcraft.' I looked at Fey as she made the tea, trying to see her reaction. She showed no sign of surprise at all, not a flicker of her eyelashes even.

Fey pulled up a couple of stools, brushing bits of hay and cat litter off the faded tops. 'It's not that surprising really,' she said, as if answering my unspoken question. 'People in the past were more in tune with the natural world, closer to it in their day-to-day existence. Nature could bring bounty or famine. You learned respect. You learned how to work with natural forces.'

'Hmm, well. The thing is, I don't know why I'm seeing all these things now. Some of it is really upsetting.'

'Tell me everything that happened last night.' I didn't have much option but to do what Fey asked.

'I dreamed of Eugenie, who I think is my great-great-aunt or something like that. She is my great-grandmother's sister. She had been hurt, raped. I felt everything she was feeling, the fear, the humiliation but more than that, I woke up with bruises on my wrists, where she had been held down.'

Fey listened, thoughtful. 'Now that is unusual. A physical manifestation. The connection between you must be very strong. But I can't see why she should want you to feel the hurt. What was the reason she was raped? Was it a revenge attack? A punishment?'

'I don't know. I just knew that she had.'

We all drank our tea, deep in thought. Fey stood up suddenly.

'It might be the spirit of the attacker coming through.' She moved to the witchy section of her shop, ruffled through boxes.

'This is a hag stone, a stone with a natural hole in it. Make this into an amulet that you can wear. It will protect you from anything evil, from whatever spirit it is that wants to hurt you.'

Fey explained how to personalise it, make it mean something to me, how to bathe it in the smoke of burning herbs to cleanse it, surround it with candles while I focused on it and what I needed from it. I chose dark blue waxed cord to hang it from and on sudden impulse chose a small silver pentacle. If it was important to my ancestors, that made it important to me.

I needed herbs to burn. Fey recommended rosemary and yarrow to protect against negative energies, pennyroyal to protect my energy from other's energies, and sage to purify and cleanse. She added small round charcoal discs to burn the herbs on. I chose four matching candles, stubby white ones that would burn for a long time. 'Anoint them with this oil before you begin,' said Fey, handing me a small brown bottle of cinnamon essential oil.

'How much do I owe you?' I asked Fey.

'Nothing. Take it as a gift. I couldn't possibly charge for advice on this.'

'Thank you so much,' I said as Fey wrapped my purchases and put them in a small brown paper carrier bag. Mother had remained quiet through most of this but now she nudged me. 'Erica.'

I turned to see what she wanted and saw the man dressed all in black who had unnerved me when I had met him in the shop before. He was standing there, straight backed, his head tilted to one side, taking note of everything that was going in the bag. He moved his shaded gaze to me as he realised I had seen him. A smile crept over his mouth, one that I couldn't decipher. I shuddered, wanting to run from the shop but I refrained as I didn't want to upset Fey by rushing off. I moved in between him and the counter so he couldn't watch as Fey finished packing the bag.

'Thanks,' I said again.

'Let me know how you get on. If you have any more trouble, come back to me. Remember, you can tell me everything.' Fey smiled, a wide-open smile that I had not seen before. She normally presented as somewhat aloof, even scary but no longer. I felt that she was a definitely a friend, someone I could call on. I picked up my bag, and Mother and I left the shop, brushing past the disturbing mysterious man in black.

We stopped for lunch at Greggs, sitting outside the busy shop in their tiny seating area, a couple of tables scarcely fenced off from the main footpath. Tandoori chicken baguette for me and tuna and cucumber sandwich for Mother later, we selected a cake each for when we got home.

'Fey was very concerned by what happened to you. The way she insisted that you could tell her anything. And the way she gave you that strange stone and things. She's a good friend to you.'

We finished our coffee, gathered our bags.

'I think we need to do this thing with the stone today,' Mother said. 'I can't bear the thought of anything worse happening to you.'

I had wanted to do this when I was on my own, but Mother was right of course. It needed to be done before I had any more dreams.

We had time before the boys came home. I threaded the strange holey stone on the blue thread, secured the pentacle with a knot. I looked on Yahoo to see how to make those slidey knots that you can use to adjust the length of the necklace. I took a fine point permanent marker from my stash of craft debris. On the back of the holey stone I outlined a heart for my love for my family, no matter how far removed, and drew a tree with many branches, room for those of my family I had yet to meet.

Mother found a small plate that didn't match the rest of the set. 'You can use this to put the charcoal on'. She also found small dishes that would keep the candles safe while they were alight. I took the cinnamon oil and anointed the candles – such an archaic word – smearing oil onto the waxy surfaces, concentrating as I did so, focusing on why I was doing this, not letting myself get distracted.

Mother had set up a coffee table in the dining room, locked Bruno out to prevent his waggy tail causing accidents. I set the candles in a square. I lined up the corners of the squares with the directions of the compass. I knew which was east as that was where the sun rose to wake me up in the morning, no matter how much I wanted to stay asleep.

I ignited the charcoal, following the instructions on the foil packet, waited for sparks to bristle across its surface. Trying not to burn my fingers, I placed it on the plate in the middle of the candles. The candle flames sputtered as I lit them, wobbled, then rose straight up, fingers of light pointing to the sun. I added a pinch of the dried herbs to the now hot charcoal, remembering what Fey Witch had said – sage to purify this space, yarrow and rosemary to deflect negative energy and pennyroyal to protect my energies. I wrapped my hands round the amulet, held it to my heart, kissed it, then placed it right by the charcoal where the smoke was drifting, falling before it rose to the ceiling.

'I'll leave you alone now,' said Mother.

'no, stay Mum. Please. We are both in this,' and she sat on a dining chair behind me. I let myself drift with the smoke, let my eyes travel with the candlelight, telling my hag stone what I was doing and why, my need for protection while I found out what my ancestors wanted me to know.

The herbs burned away, and I eased myself back into the room. I reached for my amulet, put it round my neck, slipped it under my blouse so only I knew it was there. I was calmer, relaxed. Mother was asleep, her head resting on her arms on the dining table.

'Mum,' I said, rubbing her shoulder gently, 'I'll go and fetch the boys from school.' I left her still comfortable with her head on the table, closed the door firmly to make sure Bruno did no damage, and set off for school, feeling lighter than I had for a while.

Mother cooked dinner while I brought my book up to date. I had a lot to share with those pages; things that I couldn't really share with Mother or David, like just how scared I had been, and how I felt that I couldn't go on living. My logical brain told me that it was Eugenie's thoughts, but it was difficult to separate them from my own. I knew, just as Eugenie did, that I couldn't take my own life – my children didn't deserve that. Eugenie resolved to live despite the shame so that she would be there for Constance. I recorded the process of making my amulet for protection, how I now trusted Fey Witch and the discomfort I felt when that strange man in black was around, that odd smile that hovered on his lips.

Dinner was up to Mother's usual standards, though how she achieved it with the contents of my freezer, I'll never know. After taking Bruno for a walk – when we ran into Mrs Purple Hat again – David put on a film that we could all enjoy. The boys went to bed without any argument given that they weren't tired. Mother had promised their favourite fairy cakes with peanut butter and orange icing for supper. Mother and I told David about our trip to the shop and showed him the amulet. We agreed that I would carry on for now, letting dreams, visions, whatever, come to me as they would, but we also agreed that if I came to any harm again, I would ask Fey Witch how to get out of it.

*****

After three months, Lucy was certain. Eugenie was with child and although Lucy did not know who the father was, she was certain that it had not been an error of judgment, a liaison out of loneliness. Eugenie had been withdrawn, tears too ready to fall when she thought no one was looking. Lucy remembered the night Eugenie had come back with cuts on her face, and wore long sleeves even though it was a hot day. A fall on the way home was the explanation she had given, but Lucy also knew that her undergarments had been torn. Lucy had mended them.

Lucy heard shouting in the yard outside the estate manager's office.

'Lucy, Lucy, come quick.' John had Eugenie in his arms, carrying her through the door. 'She collapsed, just fell to the floor while we were talking about which fields to plant up this year.'

'Bring her this way, quickly.' Lucy took them to the bedroom, fetched water to cool Eugenie's face. Eugenie had come round but was disorientated, her breathing fast and shallow. She lay back on the pillows and appeared to sleep.

'What's wrong with her Lucy? Should I fetch Mary, send for a doctor?'

'It's alright John. She hasn't been eating properly, and it's so important at a time like this.'

'What do you mean, at a time like this?' Lucy didn't reply. 'Come on Lucy, if Eugenie is ill, I need to know.'

'Oh well, you will know soon enough. Eugenie is pregnant.'

'What? Who? I didn't think there was anyone else.'

'There isn't, John. This was not her choice.'

I disturbed in my sleep, woke enough to roll over, cuddle closer to David, then drifted straight back to sleep.

I was at a church, outside, waiting with just a handful of simply clad people who cheered as Eugenie and John walked proudly onto the steps outside, followed by Constance in the prettiest of dresses. John held Eugenie's hand as they walked away from the church under a flurry of flower petals.

Mother's birthday

'So Mum, it looks like she became pregnant from the rape. That would have been something to be ashamed of back then, rather than pitied. I thought John was sweet on her. Looks like he did the honourable thing and married her, to save her reputation, although I bet people still talked about her, marrying one of the farm labourers. I think it was lovely; she had someone to love her at last.'

We were getting ready for Mother's birthday meal. The boys were clean and shiny, wearing shirts and ties, looking so grown up. I knew Mother would appreciate the effort, but I doubted if the boys would, not for long in anyway. We had agreed to go out Saturday, so we had no rush waiting for David to get home from work, and no problem with the boys staying up late on a school night. I planned to give Mother her present on Sunday, her birthday, but she was faffing around, looking distressed.

'What's the matter Mum?

'I don't feel right, I packed in a hurry and I forgot the wrap I intended to wear with this dress.' Her dress was pale blue with darker blue flowers. She looked lovely, so I told her so.

'That's very kind dear but I would feel better with something round my neck.'

I fetched her present. 'Here Mum, open this today.'

Her face lit up when she carefully undid the wrapping paper. 'Thank you so much, Erica. It's perfect.' She curled the scarf round her neck, arranged the folds till it draped just so. I wore the proverbial little black dress, my go-to for those posher occasions. The White Swan was quite upmarket, somewhere you feel you have to make an effort, especially as Eileen was going. I know you're supposed to love your sister, and yes, I do, but I always felt not up to her standard, probably because she and her husband both worked in top jobs in the city and both being career minded had decided not to have children. So their home could have been featured in a magazine, and their frequent holidays were in places reviewed in quality broadsheets. I thought sometimes Mother's critical eye was more so because of the contrast between me and Eileen and had been since we were children. Eileen was keen at school, got far better grades than I did, and worked her way through university into a great job. I worked in admin till I got married and the children came along. Not in the same league, not at all.

Eileen and James were seated, having secured the ideal table in the conservatory, close to the entrance to the garden where the boys could play, yet sheltered from the breeze and bathed in the late afternoon sun. James and David headed to the bar while I laid down the law to the boys about how to behave in the play area, and Eileen gave Mother her birthday gift. Mother opened the gift box to reveal two champagne flutes, perfect in their simplicity, Baccarat no less. The other box, wooden and packed with straw, contained a bottle of Dom Perignon which would taste superb in those glasses. Mother was ecstatic. She appreciated the finer things in life though I couldn't help but feel that two glasses was a bit insensitive now that Dad was no longer there to share.

'Are you going away this year, David?' James had just finished telling us about their latest holiday to Cyprus.

'Yes, of course, everyone needs a holiday don't they?' David laughed as if he had made a joke.

'Where?'

'Oh, we haven't decided yet. Thought we would see what last minute deals are on offer.' The truth was closer to 'we're going camping in Wales as we can't afford to go anywhere else this year.'

'That's so hit and miss David. Surely you would be better off booking in advance, so you don't end up with a complete disaster.' Of course Eileen would say that.

'There's a lovely little place we stayed at last year in Greece. I'll text you the details.' James was trying to be helpful, I supposed.

'Yes, Erica,' said Eileen. 'You really should try it – or aren't you able to go somewhere warm like that this year?'

Mother thoughtfully tried to steer the conversation in a different direction.

'We really must tell you, Eileen, what we have found out about our family history.' She started to explain about Catherine and Eugenie.

'And you honestly believe these dreams are true!' The tone in Eileen's voice said it all. She thought I was being ridiculous.

'Don't tell me. This has all come from that face on your bathroom floor, hasn't it?' The evening went downhill from there. We finished our desserts in silence. By the time coffee arrived, we had managed to make polite inane conversation about how good the weather was for this time of year, and how well the boys were doing at school.

'I love your scarf Mum,' said Eileen.

'Thank you. Erica and David gave it to me. Absolutely perfect, isn't it?' Anger flashed briefly in Eileen's grey eyes.

James insisted on paying the bill, and we parted company.

'I'm sorry Mum' I said, as we got into the car. 'We were here for your birthday. It wasn't fair to ruin your evening.'

'It wasn't your fault Erica. I should never have told Eileen. Not here. It must have frightened her.'

I hadn't thought of it like that.

'At least the food was excellent.'

'Almost as good as yours,' David said to Mother, which brought a huge smile to her face.

*****

'The twins are an awful handful,' said Lucy. 'They still talk in that strange language between themselves, when they don't want people to know what they're talking about. Their poor nanny is run ragged. Listen. '

In the distance, Nanny could be heard calling. 'Fredrick, Douglas. Come here this instant,' exasperation clear in her voice.

'They're boys, Lucy. They are bound to be more trouble than Constance. Girls tend to be quieter, not running round all over the place.' Mary spoke softly, without much conviction.

A flash of red hair sped past the kitchen window, closely followed by another. Nanny's flustered larger frame moved more slowly, as if giving up the chase. A smile lifted the corners of Mary's mouth.

'They are horrible to Connie,' said Lucy, not letting levity change the course of the conversation. 'I've seen them pinch her when they think no one is looking, even broke her favourite doll. Said they'd knocked it on the floor accidentally, but you could tell they were lying.'

'The problem Lucy, is that we don't know anything about their father.'

'But John's a wonderful man.'

'Not John. Their real father. The bastard who raped her.'

'Yer right there. They say blood will out. Mary, is there anything you and I can do to find out who it is? Anything in Alice's book?'

Mary and Lucy walked deep into the woods, pushing branches out of the way, brambles snagging on their skirts. Mary carried a large bag over her shoulder. The waxing gibbous moon that rose in the afternoon was now large and bright, not yet full but shining enough to light their way. Small animals rustled in the undergrowth, disturbed by their passing. A fox barked in the distance. The way became easier, opened out to a clearing amongst the trees. Both women walked around the space the way of the clock, mumbling under their breath, creating their safe place, open to the skies, bathed in moonlight.

Mary stood in the centre, moved away twigs and dead leaves, made a place to light a fire. She produced kindling from her bag, placed the twigs and a fallen branch over the kindling. The kindling took and as the flames took hold, tendrils of smoke drifted to the moon.

Both women gazed at the flames, mesmerised, immersing themselves in the stories they told.

'Truth sought out in moonlight,
Reveal yourself in daylight.'

They repeated these words over and over, till they no longer had meaning as individual words but entered their hearts, their minds and lingered there.

The fire dipped low. 'I think we are done,' said Mary, pulling herself to her feet. Lucy followed suit, rubbing her hands in her eyes, struggling to get back to the solid world. They walked widdershins around the circle they had paced out earlier, retracing their steps, and with one final look at the moon that shone bright above them, they made their way to the edge of the silent woods, then went their own ways.

*****

Mother turned her card over, inspected the structure, how the lace was attached. 'You really ought to think about selling these cards you make.'

'Thanks for the vote of confidence,' I said, 'but I'm not sure that anyone would buy them.'

'They are beautiful; I would buy one, and the money might help a little.'

'Do you really think so?' My mind was racing ahead. I had enough time to make cards, and I loved doing it. But would anyone like them enough to buy them? And where would I find people to sell them to?

'I know a shop that sells handcrafted cards. Make me some samples and I'll go and speak to them. See if they would be interested.'

Mother was going home later that day and she wanted to set her plan in motion before she left. We went to Fey Witch's shop to purchase supplies. She had generously said that she would pay for whatever I needed to craft the samples.

'Hello Dale,' I said as we entered the shop.

He nodded a response as he was dealing with a customer. Of course, it took me ages to select the items I needed. Each card would need to be different and also spectacular. I could hear Dale still talking to his customer. At last I had chosen my purchases and moved to the counter. The customer finally left. I realised it was the man in black with the upright bearing that said he expected to be obeyed. Weird how he wore dark glasses all the time, and that leather hat with the brim that covered his face, no matter what the weather was doing.

'Sorry about that,' said Dale.' He just wouldn't leave. At least not till he saw you coming to the counter. Glad you did,' he said with a smile.

'Who is he Dale?' asked Mother. 'He seems an unusual character.'

'I'm not sure, but he knows his stuff. Asks me all sorts of questions about the witchy things we sell here, and often gets me to order things in for him, herbs and suchlike that we don't normally stock. It's a learning curve for me so it's not all bad.'

As we left the shop, heading towards Gregg's for our farewell cake, Mother nudged me and flickered her eyes over my shoulder. I turned in time to see a long black coat swing out as if its owner had hurried round the brick corner of the chippy.

'He was watching us Erica. I'm not sure I feel comfortable about that man.' I had to admit, neither did I.

I helped Mother load her bags into the boot of her car, apologised once again for the awkward atmosphere that had spoiled her birthday meal (she assured me it hadn't) and promised that I would make five cards ready for the next time she came over.

William

'William has been drinking. Not fit for work again.'

'We need to do something about him John. He can't keep getting away with it,' said Thomas, his face rumpled in a frown. 'I know he's been through a lot, but we can't carry him. He shapes up for work or he's out.'

'But his family, the lad, Tom. What will happen to them if we tell him to leave? They'll have to give up their cottage.'

'Have a word with him, John. Perhaps see if Mary can help. Do something for him, or we'll be left with no choice.'

John walked away deep in thought. William wasn't the sort of man you could talk to like that. He had a temper on him, and the men had learned the hard way to steer clear of him when he was in drink. John took the path off the estate towards Mary's cottage. It would take him a while to get there, good half hour walk, but he hoped that's where she would be. He hadn't seen her in the Row that morning nor by the house when he went to see Thomas.

He saw curls of smoke through the trees and smiled, relieved she was at home.

'Good morning Mary,' he called as he entered the clearing to her cottage, his voice raised so as not to startle her. Mary came to her door, opening it wide as she recognised John's voice.

'Hello John. What can I do for you?'

'What makes you think I want anything?' joked John.

'Well, you've never called a-visiting before.' Mary chuckled to herself and invited him in with a gesture, moving the kettle back on the stove to heat up again.

'You're right Mary. I am after something. I could do with some advice about one of the workers. Been at the farm from a lad, brought up on the estate, took over from his dad when his dad died young. Looked after his mum till she followed his dad to her grave.'

'So what's the problem that you need to speak to me about him?'

'He's started drinking, heavy like. Gets a temper on him when he's had a few. And he's started having days when he can't work for the drink.'

John took the mug of tea Mary handed him.

'If he don't stop the drink, he'll have to go. And he has a wife and kid. They'll have nowhere to go. He was a good man, Mary, a good worker, till the drink took him.'

Mary watched John as he drank his tea, could see the tenderness in his heart. 'What started him drinking John? Was it slow or did it come on quick?'

'He's always enjoyed a drink, like all the lads do, but for him it started to be a need inside him that he can't do without. Been like this for a few of years now. Nothing happened to him sudden.'

'Anything in his past?'

'Well, there was that bad business with his son, little Robert.'

'The lad who can't walk properly, the damaged legs? Tell me what happened, John. I always thought he was born like it.'

'No, he was a lively lad, into everything. Curious, no fear. That's what got the better of him. The day Eugenie came here, the wedding day. Little Bobby was so excited; he wanted to get as close as he could, so he could get a good look at the pretty lady in the lovely dress. But he fell. Slipped under the carriage wheels.' John told Mary how Justin was mad about the delay, refused to wait while they pulled the lad from under the carriage, forced the driver to carry on, the heavy carriage rolling over his legs, crippling little Robert for life.

'No wonder he drinks. He must be filled with hate but with Justin dead there's no one to focus his hate on. So it'll be eating into him.'

'But he didn't start drinking heavily till some years after that. Robert is ten now.'

'I suspect it's still at the root of the problem. Leave me to think on this John. I'll see if there's anything I can do.'

Mary waited till john had had time to be well away from her cottage. She took old Alice's book from its hiding place and pored over the pages of spidery writing till she found the section she wanted. Then she went to the cupboard with the dark wood doors, opening them to reveal shelves of dried herbs, carefully stored and labelled.

John called on William a few days later, armed with the herbs Mary had given him, the instructions for taking them repeated till Mary was sure he had got it right.

'Hello Nellie, William. Bill, I need to talk to you. On your own, like.' Nellie stood firm, not moving till William told her to get out. She pulled Robert to her, taking him out into the road outside. There was nowhere else to go in this small cottage which would give John and William privacy.

'Your drinking Bill. It's getting out of hand.'

'Who do you think you are Mr High-and-Mighty John, or should that be Sir John now?' Anger flared in Bill's eyes. 'Telling me what to do.'

'I'm not here to argue William. And I'm not here to tell you what to do. But I am here to tell you what will happen if you don't stop your drinking. But I don't need to tell you, do I Bill? You already know. You're not a stupid man.'

William didn't say anything, lowered his head.

'I'm also here to bring you stuff from Mary, herbs that will help you curb the drinking.' John raised his bag, pushing it towards William. 'She's a good woman Bill. She knows what she's doing.'

Bill still didn't speak.

'Let us help you Bill. I may have married Eugenie, but I lived here just like you. I know how hard the life can be and I also know how much harder life will be if you have to leave the Row. Think of your missus, and Robert.'

Bill looked up at John. 'I know you're right John. I will try. I don't know what will become of Bobby.'

John called Nellie back in.

'You need to take charge of these herbs, Nellie, make sure he takes them right. Milk thistle seeds - take one teaspoon a day. It helps with the liver. Dandelion root. It's dried. Make it into an infusion with boiling water and give him a cup to drink every day. And valerian root. You don't need a lot, only a pinch. Steep it in boiling water for at least ten minutes, strain it and let him drink it half an hour before bed. It will help him sleep. And make sure he eats apples. Mary said they will help the bad stuff from his system.'

'Do you think this will work John?' The bluster had fallen away, replaced with fear.

'Only if you want it to Bill. The herbs will help but you need to do this for yourself. Mary said the first few days will be hard. You'll shake and feel real bad. Take the week off work Bill. I'll see to it that you still get paid.'

'Acting the big man, making out we should be grateful. It's er fault this all happened. Er and that bastard that crippled our Bobby.

'Enough woman.' Nellie held her tongue as William raised his hand to her.

'You're wrong Nellie,' John said. 'Justin yes, but Eugenie? She's done you no harm. I hope this goes well for Bill, for both of you.'

Bobby had heard everything from his post at the doorway. He stepped back to let John leave, watched him till he was out of sight.

Albert

'Erica, there's a man across the road staring at our house.'

'What do you mean David?'

'Exactly what I said. He's been there for a while now. Just standing there.'

I went to the window, followed David's lead, peering through the nets, making a note that they needed washing.

I jumped back, away from the window.

'Are you alright?'

'I know him David. He's the man from the shop.'

'Not that witch place again? Erica, you've got to stay away from there. All these oddballs.'

'What are we going to do?'

'I'm going to have a word with him. Ask him if he wants something.'

'Be careful David.'

I watched as David walked down the path, spoke to the man in black. I could feel my heart beating, pounding in my chest. I didn't know this man, other than I didn't feel right when he was nearby, and I certainly didn't know how he would respond to David's brave approach. They seemed to be talking fine and then most oddly, the man in black showed David something which glinted in his hand. David nodded his head and took it from him. They shook hands and the man in black went on his way.

I flew to the door as David came in.

'What did he say?'

David held out his hand. In it lay a pen, glossy red, decorated with shiny gemstones. My pen!

'What? How?' I could scarcely speak, the relief, the surprise, the total lack of comprehension.

'He said he found it on the floor by the shop just after you'd walked away with another woman. I presume that was your mother. Very nice of him to bring it round for you.'

'It was, but David, how did he know where I lived?'

'I really don't know; I never asked. He wanted to come in and speak to you, but I said you were busy with the boys. Somehow, I didn't think you would want to speak to him.'

****

He strode down the lane towards the Row with his shoulders back, his head tilted upwards looking across the fields into the wide-open distance, where the sun was dropping from the sky to the ground. He stopped, breathing deeply as if trying to pull the essence of the land into his lungs. The bulging rucksack on his back scarcely weighed down his broad shoulders. The khaki uniform marked him as soldier. As he neared the Row, he slowed down, looking around him, taking time to savour the familiarity and note the changes.

He heard the children coming long before he saw them and stepped to one side as they rushed past, the lad at the front whipping the hoop with his stick.

'Hey up,' shouted one of the older lads. 'That's our Albert, that is.' The lads stopped in their frantic run, bumping into one another, turning round to look. Albert had already made good headway past them as they started trotting along to catch him up. The lads raised a cheer, alerting those at home on the Row, who came out to see what was happening.

'Albert lad. Thank God you've come back.'

'Good to see you lad.'

Well-wishers followed him to his dad's cottage, a self-contained building set aside from the rest of the street. Albert lifted his hand to knock the door as the door swung open. Thomas, with tears in his eyes, wrapped his arms round his son, clapping him on the back.

'Come inside son. Come inside.' Thomas closed the door on their reunion.

The onlookers realised there was nothing else to see and made their way back to their cottages, chatting as they stood on doorsteps, agreeing how wonderful it was that Albert was back safe and sound. Only one person remained by Albert's home, leaning on a fence as the fading light covered him in gloom. He spoke as if to himself, his words barely sounding in the dusk.

'Thomas's son runs off to war, comes back a bloody hero. My lad will never have that chance. He will always be a cripple, no use to anybody.' He stayed there till the dark masked his movements completely and he slipped quietly away, back to where Nellie was waiting for him.

'Bill, please say you haven't?'

'No Nellie. Give me credit. I've not touched a drop.' Nellie went to hug him, but he shrugged her away.

*****

I collected the spray bottles, cloths and the mop and gave myself the next half hour to clean the small bathroom. It wouldn't take that long but it was a bit of a squeeze. I started by getting rid of the cobweb I'd noticed hanging from the ceiling which is what had provoked the cleaning spree. I removed the dead leaves from the window ledge. This poor plant – an African violet possibly - had survived longer than most but looked like it was on its way out. I polished the taps. Even the mirror sparkled. All that was left to do was the floor.

'Good morning Dorothy. Are you ok today?'

I pushed the mop over her face, which felt a bit rude.

'And you Connie and Eugenie?' I stopped and took a closer look. There were still faces in the same spot on the floor, or should I say face. Now there was only one face. Eugenie was no longer there, but from the head of shiny curls, I thought this must be Connie but grown up.

'Hello Constance. You've grown into a lovely looking young lady. I hope your mum is alright.' I felt quite sad; I wanted to know Eugenie's story, how it ended. Now she wouldn't tell me. I hoped Constance would finish the tale.

****

Albert rested as instructed by his mother and father, eating well 'to fatten him up' as his mother kept repeating, offering him yet something else tempting to eat. After two days, he could stand it no longer.

'Dad, I need to do something. I can't just laze about. Tell me what you need doing.'

Thomas was about to argue with him, tell him to take his time, then saw the anger bubbling close to the surface, the battle Albert was having to keep it under control.

'OK lad, there's plenty of work to be doing round here.'

They walked to the stables. Albert had always worked with the farm horses, loved their gentle nature.

'It's quiet, Dad,' he said, his head cocked to one side, listening for the welcoming noises he remembered from the stables. 'Are we ploughing?'

'There's not many horses left on the estate, not anymore. They took most of them away.' Thomas stopped, not wanting to stir up memories for Albert.

'The bloody war effort. Dad, the horses over there suffered something terrible.' Albert fell silent, rubbing his eye with the back of his hand.

One lonely horse whinnied as they entered the stable. Albert ran a practiced eye over the horse, patting her neck, tracing the muscles in her withers. He frowned at patches of mud clinging to the white hair down the legs, at the tangles in the tail. He started to separate the clumps with his fingers.

'I'll be alright Dad. You can leave me here. I'll give this one a good grooming. A treat for her, and me.'

Albert had lied, to his dad and to himself. He wasn't alright. He heard again the terrified whinnying of horses living in hell, amid the sound of the shellfire, the thick mud sucking them down into an almost certain death. He saw once again the pitiful thrashing of horses trying to escape the mud, then worn out with trying, sink into long sought peace to their death. Horses who had fallen into holes blasted by shells, breaking legs, screamed in pain. The fortunate were put out of their misery by a bullet through their brain.

His hand trembled as he picked up the curry comb, gently removing dirt from the mare's dark brown coat. As he switched brushes, gradually moving to a softer brush to smooth the brown to chestnut gloss, the tremble had gone, swayed away as he leaned in close, breathing in the scent of the horse, feeling the horse relax under his deft movements. Albert spoke quietly throughout, telling this horse of the horrors he had seen, knowing he would never be able to tell a soul without tearing himself asunder with grief. He stood at the horse's head, gently stroking the soft hair, cleaning away the dust from the fields. Albert looked into the large dark eyes and knew that this horse had heard and understood every word. Albert broke into sobs he couldn't contain. A broken man.

Thomas stepped quietly into the stables, trying to catch sight of Albert, to see how he was doing there on his own, without him realising that Thomas was watching. Thomas saw the tears flow, kept to the shadows.

'It'll do him good to get it out of his system,' thought Thomas, waiting, ready to step in when needed. The trembling stopped, Albert sniffed, blew his nose.

'Here lad, I've brought you some dinner.' Father and son sat down on a bale of hay and shared cheese and apples.

'You had it rough over there, eh son? You were just a child when you went. You should have been having fun, looking for a sweetheart, and instead...' Thomas fell silent, not knowing how to continue. How to tell his son it was alright to be upset, to not have to be strong, at least for a while.

Albert kept his eyes on the floor.

'It was the horses that hurt the most Dad. We chose to be there, most of us. We had something to fight for, our country, our pride, the people back at home. But the horses – they had no choice, whisked away from the life here and sent into what was hell for them. As soon as they died, they were replaced, just like bullets or shells, a wheel on a truck. The brass didn't see them as anything more than a tool, to use till it's broke then replace it.'

He faltered, his voice slipping away in memories. Thomas waited.

'They didn't ever have enough food, they weren't looked after proper, no one had time to groom them, they were in gas attacks, mustard gas.' Again Albert halted, his words trembling to a stop. Thomas sat still, quiet.

'The gas, Dad, it comes at you like a ghost, moves across the mud like a phantom reaching for you. They sound gongs, to tell you there's gas looking for you. All you could do was put on your gas mask and pray.' Albert paused, muttering beneath his breath.

'The horses didn't stand a chance Dad. Not even a mask to protect them. Do you know what it does to you Dad? You breathe in, you have to, and you breathe in gas that blisters your throat, your lungs. You choke, you suffocate. The horses died. Even if it doesn't kill you from breathing it in, it gets on your clothes, raises blisters on your skin. You have to strip off your uniform, get it away from your skin. The horses were soldiers, serving just like us, but they had no uniform. Their suffering, Dad, it was terrible. All I hear is their screams. In my dreams in the dark of the night, in my daydreams in broad day light. How can I stop thinking Dad? When will this leave me?'

Rumours

I woke with tears streaming down my face. Poor, poor Albert. He volunteered for love of his country, yet the war hurt the things he loved most: his love for the beautiful horses like those he had worked with on the farm, learned their gentle ways, betrayed.

My phone rang, brought me quickly back to the real world. It was Mother.

'My red pen? Are you sure? The one with gemstones?'

I listened to Mother as she described the pen that she had found in her bag. She was adamant it was mine.

'It can't be, Mum.' I stared at the pen on my bedside table, picked it up for a closer look. 'I have my pen in my hand. Definitely.' I could tell that Mother was getting distressed. She told me that it had to be my pen that she had in her possession, that she would never had bought such a pen, nor would anyone have gifted it to her.

I had a sinking feeling as I explained to Mother that the man from the shop had returned it to me.

'Yes, Mum. The strange one. He brought it to the house.' I also had to tell her that I had no idea how he knew where we lived.

'I'm coming to see you Erica. I want to show you the pen I have here.' She fell silent, then… 'I think we need to talk about these strange people that are following you. Something just isn't right Erica. I'm worried.'

Mother insisted she was coming over the next day so of course, I got out the vacuum, polish and duster and started cleaning.

Bruno, relegated to the garden, sat in the closest patch of sun to the back door he could find, not impressed.

I heard a key in the lock as David let himself in, made his way to the kitchen.

'Your mother coming to visit?'

'How did you know?'

He chuckled, a sheepish look on his face.

'The 'fresh linen' air spray, the sparkling windows and the tempting aroma of roast beef gave me a clue. But the bottle of chianti on the dining table was the clincher.'

We both laughed as David opened the peace offering, poured us a glass.

'She's worried about that man who brought my pen back to me. He couldn't have found it. I haven't lost it. Mother has it.'

It was a good job that we had already had a glass of wine. David's skin changed shade to match the crisp white kitchen units. Without speaking, he poured another glass.

'We'll talk about this tomorrow, when your mother's here. For tonight, we'll just enjoy that meal you're cooking and pretend we're back before all of this – whatever it is – started.'

I didn't sleep well that night. The wine hadn't helped like it usually did, and it wasn't strange dreams that disturbed me. It was worry. Mother was right. I had been ignoring the strange things happening around me because I really wanted to find out more about these people who had dropped into my world, with such interesting stories. So I kept telling myself that everything was alright. The dreams weren't so bad and Fey Witch's involvement hadn't seemed a problem at first. I had felt she was being helpful. But. Big but. I had to admit, Mother had cause for concern. And David had already raised his concerns over the impact it was having on my health. I decided to ask Annie if she would take the boys for the evening so we could talk without being disturbed.

Annie was remarkably good about my request, given that I had been ignoring her so much just lately. We knew each other so well, it would have been difficult to not tell her what had been going on. We walked from school to her colourful, child friendly home where we stopped for a coffee while the boys ran riot. Annie's two boys were the same age as Jacob and Joe, in the same classes, so they headed off to explore the toys with no hesitation.

'How are you Erica? You look tired. Are things ok with you?' Annie always came straight to the point, no pussy footing round things. It made her a strong friend, even if a little disconcerting. No hiding your troubles with bland niceties.

'There's certainly been a lot going on since last time I saw you,' I said and gave her a potted version of my dreams.

'And this all started with that face on your bathroom floor?' At least Annie hadn't laughed at me, or suggested I should see my doctor. 'How fascinating.'

I glanced at my watch. 'I should be getting back now, get dinner ready for when David comes home so we have plenty of time to talk.'

'The boys can stay overnight Erica. They can borrow clean clothes off my lads.'

Jacob and Joe thought this was a fantastic idea and waved me off without a second thought.

'Thanks Annie. I can't say thank you enough.'

'Say thank you by keep talking to me. Don't shut me out. I'm always here for you Erica. Remember that.'

We hugged, then I rushed home, feeling much better for having shared this nonsense with someone who wasn't in the centre of it, someone who had an independent perspective.

'But David, we know Erica's not just making it up. We've checked the facts. A lot of it is there in black and white.' Mother was more animated than I had seen her for a long time.

'But there's a lot of it we have no way of knowing! It could all just be overactive imagination.' David wasn't used to Mother being so directly assertive with him. Usually Mother got her own way by persuasion rather than table thumping. 'She is exhausted Jocelyn. She's on edge all the time. Either that or rushing off to be on her own so she can daydream these fantasies. She doesn't interact with the children in the same way, always too tired. They're missing out.' David sighed. 'I'm missing out.'

'Excuse me. I am here you know. I can hear what you're saying.'

'Then say something Erica. We're here to discuss what's happening to you and you've said practically nothing all evening. Although, I must say, dinner was very enjoyable.' From Mother that was high praise.

'Look David, I want to show you something.' Mother produced the red pen from her bag. David rushed up stairs to the bedroom, ran back at risk of breaking his neck falling downstairs, holding a red pen in his outstretched hand. They were identical.

'What the hell is going on?' David's brow pulled down into a frown. There was no denying the concerns this raised. We talked about the scary man in black, the way the woman in the purple hat always seemed to be conveniently just about to enter the fields whenever I walked Bruno. I remembered how I had met Dale as a dogwalker, then found he worked at Fey Witch's shop, and even saw him when we went out for the evening to Swan Pool.

'I don't like it Erica. It's too much of a coincidence – all these goings-on after you've asked Fey Witch to have a look at the face in the bathroom floor. I want to have a word with her. See what she has to say about it.'

'No Mum. You can't do that.'

'Well what else do you suggest?'

David had been quiet for a while. 'I think for now I will take over walking Bruno, see what happens. If they are still there, then it's just coincidence. If they stop being there, then it would seem like they are stalking you.'

I started to protest.

'No Erica,' said David. 'We can't take the risk, not with the boys.'

I had to accept that, put the way David said it.

'Also Erica, I want you to stop it. These dreams. All of it. It's no good for you. for any of us.'

'David, I can't just stop. It's not like I ask for these dreams to come. It's something that's happening to me, not that I've asked for.' I felt tears stinging into my eyes. 'And I don't want to. I need to find out what the dreams are with me for. To find out more about our family.'

David walked out of the room, exasperation showing in his brisk walk, his tense shoulders.

'Erica, you have to be reasonable. You don't want to end up arguing with David about this.'

'It's my life Mum, me who's living with this. I would have thought that you would be as intrigued as I am, a bit more supportive.'

'Erica,' she snapped, 'that is uncalled for. I am here because I am concerned for you. And for David and the children.'

I couldn't trust myself to remain civil. 'I'm going to bed,' I said, thinking how relieved I was that Annie had kept the boys overnight. I realised later that I hadn't even said goodnight.

*****

Rumours spread in small communities. Everyone was sworn to secrecy. No one would admit to talking out of turn. Yet whispers now circulated about Eugenie, John, the twins. William. He didn't turn to drink when little Robert was injured. He was angry but William had always been an angry man. The people living on the Row had waited, nervously, excitedly, to see what William would do, how he would make Justin pay for his callousness. Then Justin died and no matter how they looked at it, they couldn't make it William's fault. Rumours moved on to Eugenie.

Then William's drinking rapidly got out of hand, no longer a few pots with the lads when the work was done, but a way of life. It took hold of him, possessed him. What had started it, no one knew. And they were too wary of William to talk to him. He kept his reasons to himself, backed up with his fists.

The women were the first to make the connection. Eugenie and John's marriage had come out of nowhere and there was lots of talk about that. Then the twins turned up so soon after the wedding. Born early, it was said. Twins often are.

'But those babbies aren't tiny. Not for twins. They're a good size. They weren't born early.'

And so the whispers continued.

'Our John is a good man. He would never have got her in the family way.'

'But he married her quick. No one saw it coming.'

And then someone, it might have been June at the cottage next to William's, said that it was about then that William started drinking heavy. So they worked back the dates – on washing day, as they hung the clothes to blow in the breeze. June was thinking, you could see it on her face.

'Do you remember when Miss Eugenie had a fall, so they said? Her face was bruised all down the one side. I saw her when I went on an errand to the big house. We didn't see her much on the Row for a while. That was before the wedding.'

And so they came to a conclusion. Their collective mind knew that William had raped Eugenie, was the father of the twins, that John had stepped up and done the right thing out of the goodness of his heart. That William had taken out his anger against Justin on Miss Eugenie.

'I don't think they know who it was. They can't, can they? Or John would never have helped William the way he has. He's done so much to get William off the drink.'

This was a puzzle which left them with much to think about.

Friends

When I finally woke up on Saturday morning, David was already out of bed. I could hear the clattering of dishes from the kitchen. I needed coffee, so I pulled on a dressing gown and made my way downstairs. I wasn't looking forward to meeting David or Mother, not looking forward to the atmosphere. I suspected I needed to apologise but then why should I? They needed to apologise to me as well. The evening simply hadn't gone well.

I heard the kettle on the boil before I made it to the kitchen. Mother had two mugs waiting. The kitchen had been cleaned of last night's debris. I paused at the door to the kitchen, not sure what to say. Mother made coffee, then turned round with a mug in each hand.

'I'm sorry.' We both spoke at the same time. Mother put the coffee down on the table, put her arms out and hugged me. I hugged her back.

'David has gone to fetch the boys from Annie's, and he's taken Bruno with him. Said he will take the boys with him into the fields to get the bounce out of them and Bruno.'

'Mum, does he really mean to stop me walking the dog?'

'Just till we know what's going on Erica. We only want to keep you safe. Who are these people who seem to be watching you?'

'But they are people who know Fey Witch, and I trust her. She has been so helpful all the way through this.'

'Then shall we go and talk to her?'

I had to admit defeat. Resigned, I agreed to go with Mother to speak to Fey but what to say, I had no idea.

'Fey, I want to ask you something, but I don't really know where to start.' Mother was standing close by, in ear shot, but looking at card blanks.

Fey looked at me for what seemed like an eternity. 'You're troubled,' she said. 'Are they getting too strong for you?'

'Who?' I asked, surprised.

'Those who speak to you. Are the dreams coming more often? More powerful?'

'They come even when I'm awake.' I said this quietly, almost to myself.

'Are you grounding yourself properly, as I showed you? These things can drain your energy.'

I hadn't been grounding myself at all.

'You will find that things will be easier if you do.' Fey assessed correctly that I hadn't. 'And if you need to talk, there is always someone here for you. Edith has been taking the time to be around for you whenever she can.'

'Edith?'

'You know her.' Fey smiled. 'The little lady with the overweight dog, and that unmissable purple hat.'

'And Dale?'

'Yes, Dale too. I asked him to stay here for a while. I thought with him being younger you might find it easier to talk to him, ask him questions. Discovering you are a witch can be quite traumatic if you've had no inkling of it before.'

'I wouldn't say that I'm a witch.'

'Well, you have affinity for things that others don't.'

I couldn't argue with that. 'It's really thoughtful of you to enlist the help of Dale and Edith to keep an eye on me.'

Mother looked over at this stage, which made it clear that she had been listening all the way through.

'How about the other man? The one in black who followed us home?'

Fey frowned. 'He's not connected to me. Not at all. Be careful. Don't trust him.'

Mother paid for the card blanks and more crafting supplies, thanking Fey for her help, and we headed to Greggs for cake and coffee.

'I feel much better now that we've spoken to Fey. Very good of her going to all this effort.'

I nodded, not speaking as I manoeuvred a large creamy, jam doughnut to my mouth.

'Really Erica, you are making such a mess with that.'

'I licked the excess cream oozing from the side of the doughnut. 'I know, but it tastes heavenly.'

Mother changed the subject. 'How are you getting on with the card making venture?'

'I haven't really done much.'

'I didn't think so. You've had so much going on with all these dreams and things. But I feel that it will do you good to have an interest, even more so than making money.' She went to hand me the bag of goodies she had bought from the witchy shop, then changed her mind. 'Never mind,' she said, 'you can look when you've had chance to wash your hands. Have you got a pen? I want to write the details on the back of this receipt. You will need to keep full records for when your business has got off the ground.'

I licked my fingers and delved into my bag, handing Mother my pen. She stared dubiously at the glittery red object as if it were an abomination. I said nothing but felt firmly told-off. Perhaps I deserved it, after all, it was probably sticky as well.

David and the boys were back from their walk when we arrived home. The boys rushed over to tell me all about their stay at Annie's while Mother spoke to David. I caught snippets of their conversation.

'Yes, David. I'm certain these people are fine. Fey is really thoughtful to have people looking out for Erica. I'm certainly not convinced that Erica is a witch.'

David interrupted with 'well, I wouldn't rule it out completely.'

'David, really. Be serious.' But I could tell she was also amused. 'Anyhow, this Fey witch may be over the top, but her heart seems in the right place. It's that man in black I'm concerned about. Even Fey said not to trust him.'

The boys had had a wonderful time and now their favourite breakfast food was pancakes with maple syrup and bacon. I would have to make sure they realised this would be a treat, not a daily breakfast.

Mother made lunch for the boys, including David, and we left them watching the football match on TV while we went to look at the card blanks and papers that she had bought earlier. We put colour schemes together, and I sketched out some designs. I showed Mother the one card that I had actually managed to complete, a birthday card for 'the one I love'. I had gone to town with lace and glitter, a deep red heart nestled amongst the frippery.

'It's beautiful Erica. Perfect.' High praise indeed. 'When do you think you will have finished the samples?' Always the little knock – good but….

David poked his head round the door. 'I'm going out for a bit, meeting Les down the pub to commiserate on the match. We lost big time.'

'Off you go then David,' said Mother. 'Have a good time. I'll look after the boys for a bit Erica, and you can get on with making these cards while you have a chance.'

And with that, I was alone.

****

Albert stared at the contraption in front of him. A mound of metal, large wheels at the back, smaller at the front.

'It's alright son,' said Thomas. 'We can't get enough horses for the ploughing. Talked it over with John, and we decided to try one of these new-fangled tractors. It's come from America. They use them on the big farms over there.'

Albert didn't respond, continued to stare.

'It's a Fordson, lad. Will work as good as horses, probably better, definitely cheaper, and doesn't need grooming.'

'Alright Thomas?'

'Yes John. Come to see us try this beast?'

The team who had brought the tractor from the dealership stepped up to the tractor. 'In warm weather like today, it'll start easy enough. But if it's cold, it takes a bit more effort.' The driver cranked over the engine. It fired into life first time, loud, harsh, demanding, the noise breaking through the quiet of the farm, scaring birds who scattered like petals blowing in the wind. A lonely horse in the stables whinnied its fear.

Albert threw himself to the ground, crawling on his belly to take cover behind bales of hay. He screamed at the shells flying overhead, adding his shouts to the sounds of the men dying around him, their bodies torn and bloodied by the impact of the shells. He covered his ears with his hands, sobbed.

'Cut if off.' John shouted to make himself heard over the noise of the machine.

Tom ran to his lad, arms around him. 'It's alright lad. You're safe. The war's over.'

The Fordson

Mother and I parted company amicably but on the whole it hadn't been a good visit. I felt like a naughty child again, with my failings highlighted and my chores laid out for me as punishment. I knew I was being childish. Mother hadn't intended it like that at all. She was worried for me, cared about me enough to worry. Yet that was the way I felt, like I had done from childhood. Eileen had always been the successful one, the well-behaved one, the one Mother was proud of. The one who Mother updated her friends with her wonderful job, her wonderful husband, their wonderful house.

David and I skirted round each other, extra polite, avoiding the things we wanted to say. At last the children were safely in bed, the kitchen cleaned, a cup of tea made, the TV on low in the background. We had run out of excuses. It was time to talk.

'I know what you're saying David, but I have no choice in this. I can't stop. I don't invite the dreams, they invite themselves in. And if I'm honest, I don't want to stop. David, this is my family. I'm sure of it. And if so, there must be a reason for all this.'

'Slow down, Erica. It's alright. Your mother and I had a talk about this. I can see how important it is to you, and thinking about it, I know you have to see it through. But I am worried about you. Some things need to change.'

'David, I can't…'

'Woah, let me finish.' He smiled that lovely smile of his, looking straight in my eyes, his dark brown eyes shining. 'You need some help round here. I haven't been pulling my weight. You take care of everything for the house and look after the boys. It doesn't leave time for you, to do anything for yourself.'

'But you work full time David.'

'So do you, we just work differently. So I'm going to take over the dog walking, and I'll take the boys with me. I can spend more time with them, take them to the playground. It'll give you an hour to work on your card making enterprise. I saw that wonderful one you made. So professional.'

'Thank you David. Are you sure? It's a lot to take on.'

He leaned over, cupped my face in his hands, kissed me. 'I'm sure,' he said. 'I love you.'

'Though there is one thing. Is there any way we can check out the history more? To find out if this is really your family. I know your mother said some of it is about people she knows, but can we pin anything down?'

'I'm not sure David. I wouldn't know how to start. Mother's friend led us to the newspaper report about Mary. I'll ask Mother if she has any ideas on how to dig up more.'

We went to bed, slept wrapped in each other's arms. I had no dreams that night, I slept peacefully, knowing that David loved me.

We woke up early, before the alarm went off. I felt the benefit of a good night's sleep. I almost felt bouncy, instead of my usual dragging steps. I had time to make us a special breakfast – pancakes with bacon and maple syrup, although I pointed out to the boys, including David, and to me, that this was a one-off occasion. I could get too used to this, and my waistline would suffer, especially if I was handing over Bruno's walks to David for a while.

'I'll drop the boys at school today, save you going out.'

'Thanks David,' and I gave kisses all round in a haze of coats, bags and lunch boxes. Bruno looked at me with dark doggy eyes making me feel guilty, but he would soon get used to his new routine. 'Later Bruno,' I said ruffling his fur.

I decided to start on the card making, so I had something to show I was making good use of the extra time I now had. I started on a design with a bouquet of handmade paper flowers, lots of tiny blue and pink flowers mixed in deep green foliage. I needed to cut what seemed like hundreds of circles of paper, clipping the edges of each one to make petals. The job was easy, repetitive, but would take a long time.

****

The Fordson wouldn't start, the cold weather making it difficult, hard work. Albert cranked the engine again, and again.

Men stood around him, watching. Men who hadn't been to war, didn't understand the terrors that wouldn't leave. There was whispering, a few chuckles, as they watched Albert trying to master this tractor, get it going.

'Here lad, let a real man do the job.' William pushed forward from the crowd, approached Albert.

'What do you mean, a real man?' Albert stood up, his lanky frame paling against William's bulk.

'Let me see,' said William. 'Someone who won't run crying for his mommy, frightened of the noise.'

'That's enough William.'

'Let him alone.' Worried murmurs spread from the gathered men.

Albert pulled himself upright, shoulders back to attention, showing how broad he was, the potential in his build.

'What? You think you're a real man. A coward who stays at home on the farm when we were dying out there for our country.'

'I had more sense than to go over there. Why die for this country? It's owned by people who don't give a shit about people like us.'

'Who gives a damn about shit like you? Such a big man. Were you being brave when you raped Miss Eugenie? Was that you fighting for your pride, hurting a woman who couldn't fight back?'

William tensed, growled, fists clenched. 'You shut yer dirty mouth.'

'Deny it William. Tell people you didn't.' Albert was no longer the young lad he'd been since he came back from war but the soldier he had been when at war, strong, fear pushed away where it could do no harm.

The muttering in the crowd grew louder as more people came over to see what was going on.

'Is it true William?'

'Tell us man.'

Unable to deny it, William felt trapped, losing face. He turned to face the crowd. 'Taught that bitch a lesson didn't I? My babby crushed under her fancy carriage, her and that Justin. She deserved it. I was owed a reckoning.'

The murmuring crowd hushed, and parted. John strode into the clearing they created.

'That right William? You did that to Eugenie? Foisted your brats on her?' His voice was low, steady, but William felt the menace in it, tried to run. Albert was behind him, pushed him back towards John, the crowd forming a circle round them.

The first blow connected with his jaw, the force staggering him backwards. The second blasted the air from his body as his ribs broke. William dropped to the floor. Nothing and nobody would protect him from the hail of blows that battered his life from existence.

Exhausted, John allowed himself to be led from the devastation.

*****

'It was me that did it. We were fighting. William started it. I should have stopped but well, the war and all that, you know.' Albert stood tall in front of the local Bobby.

The assembled crowd nodded in agreement. William had started it, goading Albert. They all told the same story. That William knew of Albert's nerves, how Albert couldn't help himself when the terrors crept in, didn't know when to stop.

William had picked a fight, picked the wrong fight. Albert had acted in self-defence. It was a fair fight and William lost, look at the size of William to Albert. And after all, Albert was a soldier; the war made him a hero.

*****

John sat, head in his hands, in Thomas's cottage, set back from the others on the Row.

'I can't do it. I won't do it. Not let Albert take the blame.'

'You can, and you will. Miss Eugenie can't take any more sadness in her life. She doesn't deserve it, and certainly not at the hands of that William again.'

'But Albert...' Thomas cut him short.

'Albert will be fine. William started it, and it was a fair fight. Everyone says so. And no-one is going to question that. We all know that William was a low-life, and that Albert is a hero. William had it coming. He deserved it.'

Thomas came closer, laid his hand on John's shoulder. 'Eugenie needs you. We all need you John. This place is running better than it's ever run before, with you in charge. The workers' lives have changed for the good. You're safe here.'

*****

'I've spoken to most of the men who were there, and they all say the same thing. Looks like William set up his own downfall. But there was something puzzling me. What's this about William and Miss Eugenie?'

'What do you mean? What was said?'

'It was just old Bob – muttered how bad it was for something like that to have happened here on the estate. A disgrace, he called it.'

'Not sure what that is about, but you know what Bob's like. Not all there nowadays, gets a bit confused.'

'Then we won't say no more about it John. Don't want nasty rumours like that spreading about, do we?'

'No, we don't. Thank you Sergeant.'

'We should tell the twins John.'

'Tell them what Eugenie?   That their real father was a vile, violent man. And on top of that, tell them he's dead. No Eugenie, we will not tell them a thing other than the truth they believe.   That I am their father.'

'They have a right to know their father's dead.'

'And you have a right not to suffer any further.   What that man did to you was evil.   It has left you sick to your heart, you have not recovered, not fully.   Raking this up would set people talking about you, about us. We would have no peace.'

'I suppose you're right as usual. And they like to go and help Albert with the horses. They wouldn't think the same of him, would they?'

Laura?

I could get used to this time to myself. David was taking the boys to school most mornings and taking them over the fields with Bruno most evenings. The boys were loving spending more time with Daddy, and David was certainly in a better mood. I think part of that stemmed from the day he realised his jeans were no longer tight on him, when he had to fasten his belt to the next notch.

As soon as David and the boys had left in the morning, I was working on the cards. Cleaning and shopping was relegated to afternoons. The design took up a lot of time. At first I was thinking that I would never be able to sell them for enough to make it worth my while doing it in terms of the time it took. I was explaining this to Mother when she called to check I was actually doing them.

'I'm not checking on you Erica. I'm interested in how you are finding it and what styles you are making. You're so creative.' I felt a bit sheepish when she said that, so I chuckled and told her that I knew that, of course. She pointed out that the design would take a while but once I had the basic designs worked out it would get easier. 'You will have a range of similar designs I suppose, perhaps in different colours. Say you have five main designs but offer them in different colourways or with different sentiments, then you have a large number of different cards catering to different tastes.'

As usual, Mother was right. I had to start thinking in terms of this being a business, not just making a card for Mum. I soon had five designs worked out and had made two of each in different colours. I had gone for the classy end of the market, so muted and delicate colours; the kind that I would keep, not wanting to throw them away. I called Mother to see if she wanted to come over to see them. Naturally, she was keen to do so, and I was to expect her on Monday.

As the boys got ready to leave for school with David, I thought I had better forewarn them that they wouldn't be able to go dog walking with Daddy that night, not if they wanted to spend time with Granny before bed. They put up a fight, which surprised me. Usually they can't wait to see Mother.

'We want to go, Mom. Please let us.' Jacob looked at me with pleading eyes.

Little Joe hadn't learned these tactics yet. He pouted, and almost shouted at me. 'But I want to see Laura.'

'Who's Laura?' I hadn't heard this name before.

'The lady with the dog.' His face showed he thought I was stupid for not knowing. Jacob scowled at Joe. I fixed my gaze on Jacob.

'Who is Laura, Jacob?'

He looked at the floor. 'She walks with Daddy when we take Bruno out, and we play with her dog.'

I didn't quite know how to respond to that but I felt a bit like the Inquisition, so I changed my line of questioning.

'Oh,' I said with a lighter touch to my voice. 'What sort of dog is he?'

'I think he's a Collie dog. He's black and white and runs ever so fast. We chase him, then he chases us back.'

I thought it a bit odd that David hadn't mentioned this Laura at all, and neither had the boys but perhaps I was just being paranoid with everything that was going on.

Mother duly arrived. The boys stayed in, remembering probably that there was likely to be presents for them in her bag. David took Bruno for his walk. Mother spent time with the boys, revealing the contents of her bag. A gleaming red racing car for Joe and a new book for Jacob.

'Where are you David?' I said to myself. It was getting late and the boys needed feeding soon before they got cranky. The pasta bake was drying out in the oven. Much longer and it would be inedible. I cooked some chips to go with it. David still hadn't returned so I plated up a meal for him. He would have to microwave it when he got home.

The boys tucked up in bed, Mother asked if she could have a look at the cards. We got engrossed in the designs, making plans, lists of things to do. Mother was delighted with the finished cards.

'I'm taking these to the shop as soon as I get home. I'm sure they will love them.'

Mother insisted that once we had worked out the pricing on the cards we should work out a wider range – wedding stationery – invitations and place cards. And get some business cards printed. I heard the music blare on the TV, which reminded me I wanted to watch Charmed, my favourite, and I knew Mother liked it too. Which also made me realise that David wasn't home yet. There was no way that he could still be walking Bruno. That dog may like long walks but there comes a stage when he just sits down and refuses to go any further.

The demon defeated and the world safe again for now, I heard David in the hall, just returned from his three-hour walk. Bruno headed straight to the kitchen and I could hear him lapping at his water bowl.

'That was a long walk.'

'We weren't walking all that time – that dog is getting lazy. Started walking slower and slower. Actually, I stopped at the pub on the way back. Barry rang me, wanted to know if I was up for the big match next month. He's got a spare ticket, so I met him for a pint and a chat.'

'How come he's got a spare ticket? I thought they were like gold dust.'

'They are. But Brucie can't go. Big family wedding and his wife has put her foot down.'

'Good for her.' I laughed; David laughed too, and he took himself off to warm up his dinner.

****

'Lucy, Mary, what are we going to do about Mummy. She seldom leaves her room and when she does her eyes are ringed with red as if she has been crying. It's not just me that's worried. I can see how hurt John is. He does his best, but he is so busy with the farm and the rest of it that he doesn't have time to sit with her.'

'I think the boys get her down sometimes. I know five-year-old boys can be a handful but these two won't take instruction from no-one. And the way they still use that strange talking of their own is not right. I'm starting to wonder if there's something wrong with them.' Lucy and Mary exchanged glances in a silent language of their own. They were both aware of the circumstances of the boys' conception, Eugenie's secret that only they and John knew for certain. The rumours had been squashed following William's death, though people queried why John had kept on Williams' wife in the cottage on the Row, and set Robert as an apprentice type setter, giving him a trade he could do despite his damaged legs.

They fell silent, giving thought to the problem.

'I think,' said Mary 'that it would help if she had something to take her mind away from the boys and the farm, a new interest, perhaps meet new people.'

'That's a good idea,' said Lucy. 'There's nothing new to say to people on the estate, not often, we all know each other's business.'

'Leave it with us to think about, Miss Constance. We'll see if we can come up with some ideas.'

Connie left the kitchen, returned to the parlour and the book she should have been reading.

'I don't know how Miss Eugenie can stand to look at those boys, knowing what was done to her by their father. No one can blame her for not loving them the way she does Connie.'

'She does her best but now John avoids them it's all too much for her. But I'm not surprised at John after, well, with what happened with William.' Mary and Lucy fell into deep thought.

'I'll have a look in Alice's book,' said Mary. 'See if anything springs to mind.'

Mary walked home taking the path through the woods, the leaves turning to hues of autumn, dropping softly as she walked, skittering through the branches till they reached the sheltered ground. 'I wonder if Eugenie has seen Catherine since she left home. They were really close as children.'

Alice's book covered a large part of the table, the lamp spreading light on its musty pages. Mary rubbed her eyes, squinting at the lettering. 'I'm getting old Alice. My eyes aren't what they used to be.' She used her finger, moving it along to help her focus on the text. Her finger paused in its travel. Mary read the passage again. 'A spell to heal families, thanks Alice.'

Mary made herself a cup of tea, cut a slice of the cake she had made that morning, a simple sponge, light and fluffy from the fresh eggs her hens had laid. Despite the late hour, she gathered the items she would need for the spell -two long candles and paper to roll round them. Then she took a small knife from her shelf, the white wooden handle marked with signs of the crescent moon.

Sitting at the table, Mary took the knife in her hand and cut the wax of one candle in half, yet not severing the wick. She pulled the ends of the candle away from each other so that the wick was visible in between them. Picking up the knife again, she made marks along the side of both the broken ends of the candle, brushing away the tiny curls of wax that lifted as she dragged her knife. Catherine was named at one end, Eugenie at the other. Mary laid them on the paper. She placed the other candle in a holder, in front of her, then lit it, the flame flaring, bouncing as it flickered into stillness. Mary gazed through the flame, stilling her mind, putting all day-to-day concerns away from her. Only one thing mattered – the work in front of her. When her mind was clear, Mary said the words of Alice's spell.

> 'What parted you happened long ago
> You're still the people you used to know
> Lose the pain, let it go
> Together there will be no more woe.'

Mary took the lighted candle, letting wax drip over the wick showing between the two halves of the candle. 'This wick is the tie that will always be there between family. Your relationship has stretched but it's not broken. Be healed, be as one.'

Mary wrapped the repaired candle in the paper, pulled it tight to keep its shape till it was cold. Then she placed the now whole candle in the holder, lit it from the healing candle, and left it to burn in the night till it was gone. She woke early in the morning, full of the energy that she always felt after practicing magic. 'We'll just have to wait and see what it brings, eh Alice.'

****

'Mummy's received a letter.' Constance was excited, bouncing from foot to foot. 'It's not a business letter. She opened it, looked at who it was from, then put the envelope to one side.'

'That was quick.' Lucy spoke quietly to Mary so that Constance couldn't hear. Mary's face opened in a wide smile.

'That is exciting Miss Constance but don't rush your mother nor pry into her business. Give her time to read it and see how her heart feels.'

Constance lingered by her mother's room most of the day, hoping her mother would come out, arms open and share the contents of the letter. She was disappointed, heading to the dining room when dinner was ready. Frederick and Douglas were already there, chatting to each other in their strange, muttered language. They fell silent as Constance came into the room. Constance seated herself across the table from them without speaking.

Eugenie and John walked hand in hand to the dining table. Constance was instantly on the alert; it was unusual for both of them to be present at dinner. She waited, almost patiently.

'We have some news for you,' said John. 'We will be welcoming a newcomer to our home.'

'My sister Catherine has two children, girls a bit older than you Constance. The oldest, Edna, is not keeping well. Doctors think that a change of air would be good for her, away from the smoke of the city. She will be staying with us, at least for the summer. Hopefully, her health will improve.' It was the most Constance had heard her mother speak for a long while.

'I expect you all to make Edna welcome.' John turned his gaze to the twins who were muttering to each other. 'That includes you two. It will be daunting for her, moving away from the city and leaving her parents and sister behind, so it is up to us all to see what we can do to make it easier for her. Understood?'

Constance smiled, almost clapping her hands in delight. Someone to play with, well not exactly play with given their ages but to talk to. The twins didn't respond; at least they ceased their muttering and fell silent.

'When will she be coming Mother?'

'In two weeks' time.'

The man in black

Edna arrived on the train from Birmingham. We met her at the station, John and me. She had travelled on her own, the guard entrusted to put her off at the right stop.

I cast my eyes over the people waiting on the platform, looking for a frightened young girl. The only younger person was a straight-backed woman, her head held high, her eyes casting about her, a travel bag clutched in her hands.

'Edna?' I spoke politely, carefully, not wishing to offend this confident person who surely couldn't be my niece.

'Aunt Eugenie?' The voice was low pitched, quiet but clear.

'I am so glad to see you Edna. This is my husband John. That is, your Uncle John.' The carriage home gave Edna chance to survey the scenery. She stared from the window, asking questions.

'Aunt Eugenie, what is that black and white animal?'

'That is a cow. We have lots of them on the farm.'

'I didn't know they were that big. That's where we get milk from isn't it?'

'That's right. You will also see sheep, pigs and hens.'

'I know what hens are. I see them hanging up in the market. And sometimes you see whole pigs ready to be cut up for sale.'

As they approached the house, Edna fell silent. John pulled up the carriage, walked round to open the door to help Eugenie step down. Edna didn't move.

'Time to get out Edna,' said John, offering his hand.

'Is this where I'm going to live? It's bigger than our street!'

Constance came running out of the house, stopping abruptly in front of Edna.

'Hello,' she said. 'I'm Constance.'

'Constance, why don't you take Edna and show her where to put her things, and let her freshen up after her journey, then come down for some refreshment.'

'Yes Mummy. Your room is next to mine, Edna,' and the girls walked into the house. 'Come and meet Sweetheart, my puppy. He's adorable.'

****

The dreams, visions, whatever they were, were coming thick and fast, almost continuous.

'Mum, I'm struggling. If I'm not actively doing something that I need to think hard about, I drift off. I don't know whether it would be best to just stay in bed for a couple of days and get it all over with.'

Mother was worried by that suggestion. 'What if you can't get out of your dream world? What if you just, well, get trapped there?' This was something I hadn't thought about.

'Do you really think that could happen?'

Mother didn't know. She thought we ought to visit Fey Witch, ask the question.

'When shall I come over?'

I gave this some thought, then remembered that it was this weekend that David was going to the big match with Barry.

'I'll be over Saturday then, let David get off first. I presume they'll be going for a drink before the match.'

Mother thinks she has the measure of David. Perhaps she does.

Saturday arrived. David was excited; I was really glad he was going. He had been so supportive lately, taken on a lot for me. It would be good for him to get away, let his hair down, well what was left of it.

'That's a huge bag!'

'Just bits and pieces. I'm not wearing my shirt down there, not on the train. You never know who else is going to be travelling.'

They had decided to get the train, rather than cope with the congestion by the ground, and they could have a drink without worrying, without the car. I have to admit, I did worry about them getting into trouble. You got some unpleasant people at football matches, especially with the alcohol.

'Have a great time David. Love you.' This was a bit soppy for me, but I really did appreciate what he was doing for me.

'Er, yeah, thanks.' And off he went.

I'd scarcely had time for a cup of tea when mother arrived. She rushed us straight out.

'Let's get this done,' she said. The boys were happy enough to walk to the shops.

'Can we have chocolate?' said Joe. 'Pleeease Mom.'

'Of course,' said Mother 'and you can choose a cake to have after lunch.'

OK then, I would just step back and let Mother take charge for a while.

Mother stopped at the newsagent and let the boys choose a comic. A clever strategy, I thought. That would keep them occupied while we talked to Fey Witch. While I was waiting for the boys to look at every single comic on the shelves before making their choices, I looked at the display of cards by the window, comparing prices and quality with my hand made versions. A man dressed completely in black, hat crammed on his head, walked past the glass. My heart skipped a beat.

'Mum.' She must have heard the urgency in my voice as she came straight to the window. 'It's him, I'm sure it is. The man who had my pen.'

She opened the shop door, the digital beep sounding above her as she looked out.

'Probably just coincidence. He hasn't stopped. He's walked round the corner at the top.'

We gathered the boys and their comics and left the shop. I checked up and down the street.

'He probably lives locally Erica. These may be the shops he uses daily, just like us.'

'Perhaps,' I said, but that didn't make me feel any better.

The little bell tinkled as we entered the witchy shop. It was quite busy today, people doing their Saturday shopping for their pets to last them for the week. I began to think that we wouldn't be able to speak to Fey Witch today. She would be too busy. I waved at

Dale who was at his corner of the shop, talking to three teenage girls who appeared to be very impressed with the unusual things on the shelves, and with Dale himself who was being very obliging with his explanations of the items. He waved back, excused himself from his entourage, and came over to us.

'Did you want to speak to Fey?'

'Yes, we did but it looks like she is too busy.' Mother is always direct.

Dale waited for a chance to speak to Fey. She looked up, then beckoned us over, pointing to the door to the back room. Dale took over from her, talking to customers, wrapping their purchases.

As I stepped into the back room, I heard the bell on the door tinkle. A shiver ran down my spine. I pushed the door to behind me.

Fey listened to what we had to say and sat in silence, as if giving our question some thought.

'I am pleased at how well you are doing,' she said 'allowing these thoughts through. I don't see that it can do any harm, increasing the frequency of the dreams. These are not really spirits that you are seeing but simply memories of the past.'

'But the faces on the bathroom floor?'

'Yes, I believe those are spirits making contact, but they aren't the people you are seeing are they? They aren't forcing themselves to your attention; they are simply enabling you to see the past. What have they told you so far? Have they shown you the magic in your ancestors?'

It made sense the way she explained it.

'Keep yourself grounded. It will help you cope better with all this. I feel you will find that there is something important you need to learn from these dreams, so take heed of what they are telling you and be prepared to put in work to help them. And remember, I am always here for you. It will help to share what you are seeing with me. I can help you keep it in perspective. And others like me, my friends, you can speak to us at any time.'

'Time to go boys.' Mother's voice roused the boys from their comics, and they got up from the floor where they had been sitting, legs crossed, noses so close to the pictures, I'm surprised they could see anything.

'Thanks Fey,' I said as I opened the door to the main shop. The bell over the external door was still tinkling as if someone had just left the shop, slamming the door behind them. I chilled when I saw a retreating figure dressed all in black, leather hat pulled down over his ears, hurrying from the shop, dodging cars, heading towards the corner.

Sweetheart

Edna soon became a favourite with everyone. She had an old head on her shoulders but a sunny and outgoing nature. She was entranced with the animals around the farm, especially the towering horses, and was in raptures when she saw her first piglets. Though hating the thought of having to eat them when they grew, she was realistic enough to know that it had to be done. The house soon echoed to the sound of happy young girls talking and laughing. Connie was loving her new friend who also made time for Eugenie, restoring smiles where for so long there had been sadness. The twins however kept their distance, never speaking to Edna, nor speaking in her presence, not even in their own muttered language.

Edna was very interested in Mary's work, and insisted on helping with visiting the sick on the farm, and soon was helping to make herbal potions and tisanes.

'Mum looks after the sick using the same sort of remedies.'

'Your mom was always good with healing. She started learning from me as a young girl. I'm glad to see she carried on.'

'It helps us get by.' Edna confided to Mary what a struggle they had putting food on the table, with Dad out of work so often. Mary had a word with cook who provided Edna with specially made bone broth to 'build her up'. With good food inside her, and fresh country air without the fumes from the factories, Edna's health improved, her breathing easier and overall she was not so frail. Eugenie wrote weekly to Catherine to share the good news of Edna's improving health. Catherine responded seldom. The cost of a stamp could not be spared weekly.

****

'David, breakfast is ready.' The boys were up and dressed, shovelling their breakfast into their mouths so they didn't miss a mouthful. Pancakes again.

'Boys, we need to go. We're late.'

'Wait a minute. They're just finishing their breakfast.'

'Perhaps you should get it ready earlier then. I'm fed up with this rush every day, just because you're late getting the boys sorted. It's not much to ask, seeing as I'm taking them.'

'I said now.' David shouted this at the boys who scurried to grab their bags, racing out of the house. My eyes stung as they filled with tears. That accusation may have been true, but its delivery was a bit harsh. And there was no need to shout at the boys. David's pancake lay untouched on the plate.

*****

'It was lovely Mum to see so much fun in that house, in fact in any of my dreams. They have held so little joy, mainly misery and terrible things happening. Connie had a puppy that went everywhere with them. Sweetheart she called it. Do you remember how much she loved that dog she had, till Justin killed it in front of her?

'It's good to see you happy, you know. You've been quite withdrawn lately.'

'I think I'm learning how to separate it out. I've been doing as Fey Witch advised, and practising that grounding every day. It helps.'

'Shopping trip today I think. Lunch in town and a bit of mother/daughter time. Plenty of time if we leave now, and still be back in time to pick up the boys from school. What do you think?'

'That sounds good to me'. I rushed to put on smarter clothes, settling for a skirt and jacket with a cotton blouse underneath. I was about to leave the bedroom when I stopped and added a smudge of lipstick.

I would have been quite happy with a new jumper, but Mother insisted on treating me to an entire outfit. I wasn't sure when exactly I would wear it but Mother insisted she would have the boys so David and I could go out for the night. We decided to do Chinese for lunch, one of these all you can eat buffets. I always feel conspicuous going back up for more but today I didn't have that problem, I was enjoying the food that much. The sweet and sour sauce looked more like it should have been on a pudding, bright red and shiny. Of course, I dropped some on my white cotton blouse.

'Go and wash it off quickly, before it stains.' I rushed to the ladies and started dabbing at it with wet tissue, succeeding only in spreading the stain further.

A toilet flushed and a cubicle door opened. A woman stood next to me to wash her hands.

'You look like you have a problem there.'

I thought that was a bit of a cheek, then I realised it was Sue, Brucie's wife. I didn't know her that well, but we had enjoyed several glasses of wine in the pub with our menfolk to celebrate birthdays.

'Hello Sue. I haven't see you for ages.'

'Must be nearly a year now. Last time was for Brucie's 50th.'

'That's right, at the Hen and Chickens.'

'How are the boys?'

Of course I said they were doing fine but I was running out of conversation. Then I remembered something.

'How was the wedding?'

'Wedding?' Sue looked puzzled.

'You know, the one where you said Brucie couldn't go to the football. I was really impressed with you for standing your ground and making him go to the wedding.'

Sue didn't reply for a while, checking her lipstick, puckering up her lips.

'I'm not sure what wedding you're on about,' she said. 'And I wouldn't dare tell Brucie to not go to a match. He's not missed a match since he was a youngster.' She paused, glanced at me briefly, then looked away again. 'Anyway, got to go, he's waiting for me, just paying the bill.' And with that she was off.

I stood there, bemused, staring at myself in the mirror noticing every grey hair, every wrinkle, the badly applied lipstick. Why had David lied? And even if he had made a mistake about Brucie going to the wedding, if Brucie had gone to the match, where did David get the ticket from?

I went back to Mother who was enjoying a glass of dark red wine. I couldn't bring myself to tell her. I wasn't sure I would be able to speak without crying.

'You don't look well Erica. Eaten too much sweet and sour?' She said it kindly, with laughter in her voice, but my eyes filled with tears.

'Come on darling. Let's get you home.'

We picked up the boys on the way back.

'Jacob, are you going to walk Bruno with Daddy tonight?'

'Yes, if that's ok with Granny.'

'That's fine love. Of course you can go.'

'And you Joe? Do you want to go or are you tired out after a long day at school?'

'I want to go. I want to see Dill.'

'Who's Dill?' asked Mother.

'Laura's dog,' said Joe, clapping his hands.

****

It was that dark I could scarcely make out what was happening. The big house was in front of me, few windows lit up. It must have been late. Lights were showing in the servants' rooms and in the master bedroom. Everywhere else was in darkness. I heard a door open, muffled as if someone was taking care to be quiet. A small dark figure crept out of the door, stopped as if checking for something, then beckoned, and a second figure emerged, weighted down by a large bag.

From their size, I could only think it could be the twins. What were they up to at this time of night, sneaking out in the dark? The bag was moving, and I heard one of the twins hiss at the bag, then he lashed out at the hessian. I felt uneasy; they were up to no good, I was sure of it. What could I do but watch?

The twins left the grounds, carrying the bag between them. They took the path towards the Row. The clouds lifted letting moonlight shine through, a full moon escaping from its dark cloak of clouds. A cat screamed into the night. They turned off before setting foot on the gravel road by the cottages. My heart started to race as I realised where they were going – to the new well that Eugenie and John had provided. The moving bag! My heart sank.

'No, please no. Not poor Sweetheart.'

The terrible scene played out in front of me like a horror movie. Fredrick undid the rope securing the neck of the bag, pulled the little puppy out by the scruff of its neck. At first Sweetheart tried to lick Fredrick's hand, excited. Fredrick cuffed it while still holding tight to its neck. They walked right up to the well. The wall was high to prevent people falling in. Douglas climbed on to the wall, sat with his legs dangling over the side. He stretched his arms out to Fredrick to take poor little Sweetheart from him.

I'd heard Mary and Lucy discuss how unpleasant the twins were; I'd seen them being nasty to Constance. This was on another level. Constance didn't deserve this. It wasn't fair: to have her first dog killed by her insufferable father and then this dear little puppy that she loved so much drowned by the twins. It just couldn't happen. My heart beat fast, my body tingled. Blood pulsed through my veins, my anger grew larger till my body could no longer contain it. I heard screaming; it was a while before I realised it was me.

Hands held on to my shoulders, shaking me, calling me back to the present. I didn't want to return, not yet. I wanted to watch the outcome, to see the end of this story.

Sweetheart cocked his head, as if listening, then drew out a last burst of energy. He struggled as if possessed. He escaped Douglas's grasp, jumped at his chest, amazing strength for a little dog. Douglas lost his balance, the unexpected impact knocking him backwards, and as Sweetheart jumped to the ground, Douglas fell into the well. His dying scream will remain engraved on my brain, as will the sight of a little dog making his joyful escape back to Constance.

I snapped back to the present, David and Mother fussing over me.

'Erica, what is the matter?' Mother spoke calmly, firmly, as she had done when I was a child, demanding an answer.

'I killed him Mum. I killed Douglas.'

There was no wedding

'Erica, it's just a dream. It's alright.'

'It's not alright Mum and yes, it was a dream, but I was so angry. I couldn't let it happen, and then.' I stopped talking. How could I explain it to Mother when I couldn't explain it to myself.

David arrived with a cup of tea, and a bottle of brandy, dusty from where it had lain in the cupboard since Christmas. He gestured and Mother told him to top up the cup. David wrapped a blanket round my shoulders. The warmth of the tea, the brandy, and the forced return to the present day – I started to shake off the horror. Mother sat with me while David attended to the boys. I realised I must have drifted off on the settee while watching TV.

'When you're ready, Erica, no rush.' Mother sat on the armchair close by.

'The boys are in bed,' said David. 'I told them you were asleep so they can claim two kisses in the morning to make up for not getting one tonight.' My eyes moistened as I saw how far these dreams were affecting my family.

I owed Mother and David an explanation for tonight. 'The twins were going to kill Connie's puppy. They are so spiteful. I saw them with Sweetheart tied up in a bag. Douglas climbed up the edge of the well. I couldn't let it happen to poor Connie, not again. I was so angry.' I paused; I wasn't sure how to describe what happened next.

'I felt a tingling throughout my body. That anger, the fear, my love for Connie, it came alive. I saw the air shimmer around me as it left my body and headed straight for Sweetheart. The poor little thing had given in, was lying there exhausted. Then this stream left me, connected to Sweetheart. I could see it. He revived, started to struggle, jumped up at Douglas – a huge push for a little dog. Douglas toppled backwards. All I could hear was his scream as he fell.'

'How is that even possible?'

'I don't know David. I wouldn't have believed it myself a few hours ago.'

'Well, he deserved it. Spiteful little brat.' Mother always had a different outlook.

'Perhaps he did Mum, but it shouldn't have been at my hands.'

'Erica, I know what you think happened, but logically, how can you be responsible for a death that happened years before you were born?'

She was right of course but it seemed to me that increasingly often, logic didn't come into it. Something older and unknown was overriding the comfortable order that had been my life.

****

They found Fredrick lying on the grass next to the well. He was unable to speak, wouldn't tell them what had happened.

Lucy had raised the alarm when the boys didn't come down for breakfast, not long after Connie came looking for Sweetheart and found him outside, traces of blood on his coat. Thomas and John organised a search. They found the sack covered with dog hair and smears of blood – on the inside.

'It's a bad business John,' said Thomas as they watched the men recover Douglas's body. 'Bad blood in that family; first William, now this.'

'That's as may be Tom, but it's my family now.'

****

'I will be late back from work tonight. There's an important meeting scheduled for five and we are invited to go for dinner afterwards. I can't really get out of it. More of a demand than an invitation.' David was rushing to get out.

'Oh, OK,' I said. 'Hope they take you somewhere nice.' What else could I say? Seemed a bit strange that he hadn't mentioned it before.

'I'll take Bruno out for a walk then. I'll wait for the boys to come home from school. Perhaps we will meet up with Laura. The boys love seeing Dill.'

The door slammed as David left the house.

Mother took the boys to school, called at the bakery on the way back. Cake and coffee appeared on the coffee table within minutes of her being back in the house.

'OK Erica. What's going on?'

'What do you mean Mum? There's all sorts of stuff going on, and you know all about it. I tell you everything.'

'Yes, about the dreams you do. But what's up with you and David?'

'Nothing! What makes you think there is?'

'The late nights, your questioning the boys about Laura and Dill, his sudden interest in football again.'

She was spot on of course. I couldn't deny it. And I didn't want to. It would be a relief to share my suspicions.

'Mum, I'm sure he's having an affair with Laura.' I didn't cry. I'd spilled too many tears last night.

'That weekend he was away at the football? With Brucie's ticket? 'When Brucie's wife put her foot down and made him go to the wedding?' She didn't. There was no wedding. Brucie went to the football.'

'So where was David? Do you think he was with Laura?'

'Yes Mum. I'm sure he was.'

'Have you said anything to him? Asked him what's going on?'

'I'm scared to Mum. He's had to put up with so much from me with all this stuff about the dreams. Perhaps it's nothing. Perhaps I'm being oversensitive. Should I trust him?'

'Well, it's your decision. But if I was in your situation, I would want to know.'

****

Edna was loved by everyone she came into contact with at the farm, apart perhaps from Fredrick, but especially Mary who found her a quick and willing student, helping look after the children on the farm, collecting herbs, mixing medicines, showing mothers what normal health looked like and when to seek help. Mary had taught Catherine how powerful magic can be, and realising that Edna was aware that her mother had special skills, Mary saw fit to share the foundations of her own powers so that Edna could grow and develop her own.

Eugenie and John were outside enjoying a walk in the sunshine.

'Look John. The girls will be here soon.' They watched Edna and Connie race across the field in a very unladylike fashion. 'Her health is so much improved John. I feel it's time for her to return to her family.'

John placed his arm round her shoulder, to still the shudder that would turn to tears.

'You are right, my love. But we will stay in touch and we will see her again.'

That night, Eugenie sat down with Edna, discussed her health, and her future.

'It's time to go home isn't it? I will be glad to see my mother and father again, and Lily, but I will really miss you all.'

Eugenie wrote to Catherine and received a letter by return.

'John, I can't believe this. Catherine is going to come and fetch Edna, so that she can meet us all and see for herself the wonderful place that has cured her daughter.'

'That's what she said? It will be good for you to see her again. It's a long time to be away from your sister.'

Connie was bereft, her happiness ripped away from her.

'But you knew that I would be going home, Connie. I am healed now, thanks to you and this wonderful place you live, the kindness of the people here. I have to return to my parents. They need me. And I have a little sister who I miss.'

Connie became calmer, but could see no further than Edna leaving.

'Connie, I will always see you not just as a cousin, but as my other little sister.'

'And you will be the big sister I never had.'

'Connie, will you do something for me? Can you be a big sister to Fredrick? He must be so lonely now that, well, you know, Douglas.'

'That is a hard task Edna. He hates me. He won't even talk to me.'

'He won't talk to anyone. I think it is grief and also perhaps guilt. They were both in that plan to hurt Sweetheart, yet it was Douglas who died.'

'I promise I will try Edna, but I won't promise that it will work.'

The train pulled into the station, puffing smoke into clear air. Eugenie watched expectantly, looking for Catherine. Eugenie felt a child again, seeing the straight back, the hair pulled back from her face, the plain, patched skirt, but seeing only the sister she remembered. They approached each other, not knowing what to say. Catherine reached out with her hand; Eugenie grasped it in both of hers.

'Edna is waiting at home. I thought it might be too emotional a meeting to take place in public.'

'Thank you for your thoughtfulness,' said Catherine, declining John's help to step into the carriage.

They travelled country lanes in silence, Catherine remembering the once familiar landscape.

****

Catherine stopped overnight, spending most of the time in the drawing room with Eugenie. As she told Edna, they would have plenty of time to talk when they returned home.

'Catherine, I regret not having tried to make contact with you. What happened to you was awful, I don't think I will ever forgive our parents for the way they treated you. I have no contact with them. But I felt so guilty for taking Justin from you. I am ashamed to confess that I shamelessly threw myself at him, even though he was courting you.' Eugenie waited anxiously for a reply.

Catherine laughed, a stuttered sound as if she wasn't used to hearing it. 'I didn't love Justin. I hated him. It was our father who wanted the relationship to prosper. I had hoped that he would prefer you, ask you to marry him. There is no need to ask for forgiveness.'

Eugenie threw her arms round Catherine who stiffened then relaxed into the hug.

'Eugenie, I love my Jack. I did the right thing back then and have never regretted it. Life has been harsh for the girls though. It wasn't their choice to be poor and for that I am sorry.'

'I regretted marrying Justin. You were right about him. Terrible man. But without him in my life, I would not have my beautiful Constance, nor John.'

The sisters talked late into the night. One subject was close to Eugenie's heart and she refused to back down, no matter how many objections Catherine put in the way. Eugenie would provide for Edna to train to be a nurse, rather than her having to take work as soon as she could to help support the family.

'It makes sense Catherine. It will give her a chance to work her way out of poverty. You said the only thing you regretted was the way your children suffered from your decision. Let me put this right at least for Edna. I am after all her aunt.'

One other thing they agreed on. They would keep in touch, and when the time came, Catherine would move back to the country, to live with Eugenie and John at Lansdowne Farm. Eugenie had suggested that Catherine move there now.

'It's good of you to offer but I don't think it would work for Jack. New things are difficult for him. He knows where he is in his own home, he can walk out in the streets and know his way back.'

The sun shone brightly as Catherine and Edna set back to the bustling city, a last burst of country clean air before they returned to the perpetual smoke haze. Connie clung to Edna till John unclasped her hands and hugged her tightly, allowing Edna to climb on the train that disappeared in the distance.

Operation David

'Good news Erica. Monica loves your cards. She wants to place an order for twenty.' Mother was so excited she was practically yelling down the phone. Most un-motherlike.

'I had better get cracking then, hadn't I.' The conversation was short; Mother was meeting with Emily Darnley as they were planning to spend the day doing some research to see if they could find out more about what I was seeing in my dreams, find out if any of it was true. I had been a bit wary at first sharing so much with an outsider, but Emily had helped Mother discover the newspaper report about Mary so perhaps it would work.

I set out my craft stuff on the dining room table, but my heart wasn't in it, not today. What was going on with David? We have always rubbed along, up and down like any couple, but things had been going so well; although these dreams were stressful in some ways, it had brought us closer. We were even saying mushy stuff like 'I love you'. Then Laura appears on the scene. Laura and Dill. I needed to see this woman. Find out if I was right about her and David. I sat with my head in my hands for a while. Then I made a decision. I needed to fight for David. Catherine fought for Jack. If you love someone, you don't just let them go.

I worked on the cards for the next two hours, sticky dots and paper trimmings littering the table. While my hands worked, so did my mind. A plan of action was forming – Operation David. Good food rather than quick cook meals, time to talk when he got in from work, ask Annie to have the boys for the evening so we could go out somewhere nice. I could wear that new outfit Mother bought me. I needed to get out of the habit of wearing baggy comfy clothes all day every day.

With this plan fresh in mind, I set off for the local shops, Bruno in tow; I thought steak would be in order followed by apple pie and custard, David's favourite.

'Wait there Bruno. I won't be long.' Taking Bruno into the butchers was just too tempting for him – dog drool all over the floor is not a good look for a shop. I hitched his lead to the post outside. A poster in the window said there was a band on at the Old Cock. The butcher cut steak for me, chatting away while he did so. He's a lovely chap, known him for years. I emerged with my parcel stowed in my bag to find that Bruno wasn't there, his collar lying empty on the floor, the lead still attached to the post.

I looked round frantically. Where was he? I heard shouting up the street, saw Bruno's black and tan coat disappearing round the corner. I started to run towards him, but the slight hill soon slowed me down. A man, dressed all in black, walked in my direction, Bruno following him closely to heel, which he would never do for me.

'What are you doing with my dog?' As soon as the words left my mouth, I realised that sounded a bit harsh.

'He slipped his collar. I am merely returning him.'

'He's never done that before.' I was suspicious. After all this was the strange man in black, my stalker.

'I think he wanted to play with that dog up there.' I saw a lean black and white collie trotting behind a young blonde woman, her short swirly skirt swishing as she walked.

'So that's Laura,' I thought, the shapely legs and long blonde hair bouncing on her shoulders making me cross.

'How did you know it was my dog?' I demanded.

'I've seen you around,' he said, commanding Bruno to sit at my side. Bruno responded immediately and stayed there as the man in black strode away. I realised I had forgotten to thank him.

Annie agreed to have the boys. It crossed my mind that I should really offer to have her boys to mine one night.

The steak was sizzling nicely in the pan; I had been careful not to pierce the outside skin once it had been sealed, so I knew it would be juicy inside. The warm smell of baking apple pie spread throughout the house. A bottle of white wine was chilling in the fridge. I had thought of putting a vase of flowers on the dining table but that felt a little over the top.

David turned the key in the lock, and I flicked on the already hot kettle, to have a coffee ready for him by the time he made his way to the kitchen, like he usually did. I waited, with a smile on my face, for him to walk through the door, which became forced with the waiting. I decided to go and find out where he was - perched on the arm of the settee, his mobile phone in hand. His phone disappeared into his pocket as soon as he heard me.

'Hello, David. How was your day?'

'Fine.'

'Busy? Or has it got more manageable now that big contract has been sorted?'

'Yes. Er, no. Thanks,' he added as I passed him his coffee.

'Dinner's ready. I'll dish up, shall I?'

'Give me a minute.' David went upstairs.

I arranged food on the plates, attempting to make it look as tempting as it smelled: button mushrooms next to the juicy steak, fresh fried hand cut chips, finished with grilled tomato and a handful of green salad.

The steak stopped sizzling, the fat pooling white as it cooled.

'David,' I called, 'dinner's on the table.'

There was no reply.

'It's going cold David.'

'I'll be down in a minute.' It wasn't what he said, but how he said it – angry, as if I was an interruption.

I sat at the dining table, staring at my steak. This wasn't going the way I had planned. I picked up my knife and fork and started eating. David joined me some ten minutes later. He poured us a glass of wine, and prodded his steak. He ate the steak, toyed with the salad, left the chips which were now cold.

'Sorry Erica,' he said. 'I had something to sort out.'

'No problem. Apple pie and custard?'

'Yes please. Thanks.'

'You haven't tried it yet.' I tried a joke to lighten the mood.

'Not just for the apple pie, for this.' He waved his hand over the plates, the glasses. 'For everything.' He paused as if he wanted to say something but wasn't sure. 'I've said I'll meet Mike for a pint or two.'

'But I thought we could go out tonight. The boys are at Annie's. There's a band on at the ..'

'I said, I'm meeting Mike.' He interrupted before I could finish my sentence. 'You shouldn't have sprung it on me like this.'

'I'm sorry,' I said. I turned away to hide the tears smarting my eyes. David left the table without touching the apple pie. I reached over, and ate his as well.

****

The little church was quiet, almost empty. Eugenie, John and Constance sat in the front pew. Fredrick watched Charlotte as she walked down the aisle to where he waited for her. She had no family to celebrate this special day with her. Two people sharing their loneliness. Their responses to the vicar failed to break the oppressive silence of the church. No one attempted to join in the hymns, the vicar boldly singing solo in his age-gruff tones.

John shook Fredrick's hand as they stood on the steps of the church. 'She's a lovely girl. You take good care of her.'

'What else did you think I would do?' Fredrick looked to where Charlotte was wrapped in Constance's arms, Eugenie smiling fondly at both of them.

'Don't take offence lad, nothing was meant by it, save to wish you well. Are you coming back to the house? Eugenie has laid on food.'

'I'll not be back to that house again.'

'Maybe not, but you're happy enough to live in the house that your mother has provided for you. You are an ungrateful wretch Fredrick Wright. Not what I had hoped to see in a son of mine.'

'Your son? My name is Fredrick Underhill. And you killed my father.'

John staggered, turned, strode away. Today wasn't the time for it.

'And remember Charlotte, if ever you need anything, we're here for you.' Eugenie and Constance waved them off in the carriage that was to take them towards the village, to their new home. Fredrick refused to look at them, keeping his face turned away.

Eugenie looked at John, his taut face, the tension in his stance.

'Now John, we know he's a troubled young man and with what happened to him, I'm not surprised.'

'Eugenie, you are blind to him and his faults. Yes, it was a terrible thing with Douglas, but he was part of that. It wasn't your fault, yet he treats you like the enemy. He is happy enough to take from you - the house you've given them, the allowance so he doesn't have to find a job to support his new wife. I pity that young woman.'

'He's still my son John. What am I supposed to do? I can't just turn him out, turn my back on him. Not like my parents did with me.'

'No, I suppose you can't. You are too good a woman for that.' John planted a kiss on the top of Eugenie's head, holding her close to him so she couldn't see his face. The warmth of his hug spread through her as a chill breeze scattered confetti.

Britain at war

The drawing room was full of people, uneasy because of where they were, uneasy because of what they were waiting to hear. All eyes were drawn to the wireless, the large, polished box with its efficient dials sited proudly on the sideboard, tuned to BBC radio. The clock sounded 11am. Hush fell. Then the announcement. Germany had failed to respond by the deadline. Britain was now officially at war.

A ripple of anger and disbelief moved through those listening. John was talking to the men.

'You're in essential work for the country. We need to keep producing food. I doubt if you will be conscripted.'

Eugenie watched as Charlotte wiped her eyes on a white lace edged handkerchief. They were both thinking the same. Fredrick wasn't in essential work. He wasn't in any work. At his age, he would be conscripted, sent away to fight for a peoples across the sea, that weren't his own. And given his age, just twenty-two, one of the younger ones, he would be called up soon.

****

David let himself in quietly, or so he thought, the jangling keys, the kicked off shoes, the creaky board on the stairs alerting me that he was on his way upstairs. I wasn't asleep. My head was too full of thoughts. Now I'd seen Laura, I was almost certain that there was something more to it than just walking the dog. His increased nights' out for a drink with the lads, that weekend of the wedding when his story didn't match up with Brucie's wife's version – where exactly had he been if not with his mates at the footie? – and his attitude towards me tonight. To me it all added up when I thought of her long legs showing under her flirty skirt.

His breath stank of alcohol, made me feel queasy when he rolled over to face me.

'Did you have a good night?' I said. I didn't want to be that wife who stays angry, throws accusations without any evidence.

'Not bad.'

'Where did you go?'

'The Old Cock.'

'Bet you had a good night then.'

'Nah, bit boring. Too quiet.'

'Oh, I thought there was a band playing there tonight.'

I rolled over away from him. He cuddled up to me, his arm draped over mine. I smelled a perfume I recognised. Youth Dew. I loved that perfume, heady, long-lasting, the one that David always gave me on our anniversary, but I also knew that it wasn't my perfume that I was smelling. Mine had run out months ago.

****

'How could you?' Charlotte's face, raging red with anger, crumpled into despair, colour draining to white.

John stood next to the chair she had dropped to, her head in her hands.

'All you needed to do was to say he worked here on the farm.'

'I couldn't lie to the tribunal, Charlotte. People knew he didn't work here. And it wouldn't be right, not for the other lads who are going away to war, not for the lads who would enlist at the drop of a hat but have to remain on the farm.'

'But I need him,' Charlotte said, turning to Eugenie.

'You're expecting aren't you?' said Eugenie.

Connie was by the door listening. She came in, put her arm round Charlotte, took her to the kitchen to get a cup of tea.

'John, is there nothing we can do?'

'No, Eugenie. He shouldn't have tried to scrimshank his way out of his patriotic duty. Bloody coward, just like his dad.'

****

'Mum, I've finished the cards. They're all ready to go to Monica.'

'Wonderful. I can come over today to pick them up. I'll stay overnight if that's alright with you.'

'That would be fantastic Mum.' My voice trembled as I fought back tears.

'Don't cry Erica. I'll be over soon. We can talk about it, whatever it is. Always better face to face,' and with that she was gone, no doubt to get her bags packed. Even though I didn't know if I could tell Mother about David and this affair, it would be good to have her here, someone to talk to apart from the boys.

****

Eugenie listened to the radio, tears streaming down her face. The first bombs had landed on Birmingham.

'You don't know for certain that it's Birmingham Eugenie. It just said a Midland town.'

'But John, you know it's going to be Birmingham. Hitler's after the factories. And there's the British Small Arms where they make the sten guns.' Eugenie stopped. This was war, so different from the Great war. It wasn't all happening over there; it was here.

'John, I'm so scared for Catherine and Edna.' John wrapped his arms round her; no words he could say would allay her fears.

'I feel so useless Eugenie. I should be doing something to help.'

'There's nothing you could do. You're too old to fight and in anyway you're needed here, to keep the farm producing as best we can.'

****

Charlotte looked nine months gone by the time she was six months into the pregnancy. Lucy and Mary watched her carefully. Her worry for Fredrick was taking its toll, and her eyes darkened with exhaustion and crying.

'Mary, do you think she could be carrying twins?'

'It's possible, there's twins in the family.'

Mary and Lucy would be present at the birth. Charlotte had refused to go anywhere near the hospital, wanting the comfort of her own home. When the time came, it wasn't twins but one large, sturdy bouncing baby girl. Frances was the name Charlotte eventually gave her, taking time to recover from the difficult birth. 9lb 10 ozs was more than a healthy size for a first baby.

'It's the baby blues Lucy. Not surprising given the worry, what with no news of Fredrick for months now, and let's face it, that birth didn't go easy.'

'We'd better keep a close eye on her, Mary. Make sure she's coping with little Frances.'

They had no need to worry about Frances. As soon as she saw her, Constance fell in love with the chubby baby with the fuzz of red hair and soon learned how to see to a baby's needs. She was at Charlotte's home every day, playing with Frances, feeding her, changing her, keeping the house clean, chivvying Charlotte along, doing her best to keep Charlotte's spirits up.

Constance was there the day the telegram boy arrived at the door, his uniform smart, his belt buckle gleaming. His bike was leaning against the hedge.

'Telegram for Mrs Wright.' He waited for her to come to the door, waiting as required to see if there would be a reply. Charlotte's face rained tears, unable to deal with the telegram. Constance took it from her hand, read the dreaded words 'we regret to inform you…'

'He's missing in action.' Constance put her arms out to support Charlotte as she slid to the floor.

'No reply'

'Sorry for your news,' said the telegram boy, getting on his bike, and riding away.

****

I was no longer crying by the time Mother arrived. I'd told myself I was being silly, imagining things. David wasn't like that, and he was entitled to some fun with his friends. I was being unreasonable.

'These cards are wonderful. You are so talented.' Mother didn't ask why I had been crying, not at first. I thought I had got away with it, then…

'What had upset you this morning Erica? It's no good pretending that it was nothing. I could hear the pain in your voice.'

I welled up again, then had to tell her.

'It's just me being silly. David would never do that.'

'Erica, I know you are under a great deal of stress at the moment, and you are feeling vulnerable. But that doesn't mean that you are wrong. Unwilling as I am to say it, I think you may well be right. You at least have sufficient reason to challenge him.'

She was right. I couldn't pretend any more.

'A change of scenery would do you good. You scarcely leave this house apart from school and the shops.' Practical as ever, Mother had a plan. I agreed to go back with Mother, to stay at hers for the weekend with the boys.

'You can come and meet Monica at the shop, talk to her about your ideas and find out first-hand what she thinks of your designs.'

I phoned David while he was at work, something I didn't usually do, but felt it only fair to give him some warning that I wasn't going to be there by the time he came home. We planned to leave straight after school. I took Bruno for a walk over the fields, waving to Mrs Purple Hat as she popped up from nowhere. Bruno raced off as soon as I loosed the lead, sniffing under bushes, chasing back to me then off again. The sun was warm on my skin, and my spirits lifted as I gazed around at the trees, noticing the changes in the skyline and the colours. I stopped, rooted myself on a patch of daisy sprinkled grass, and practiced the grounding technique that Fey had taught me.

'Home time, Bruno.' He came reluctantly but trotted behind me obediently. And of course, there was Dale.

'You're out of work early!'

'She let me off for the afternoon; it was far too quiet in there for both of us.'

'Lucky you.'

'We've had some new card stuff come in today. I think you'll love it, just your style. Will you be in tomorrow?'

'That's a shame. No, I won't, I'm away for the weekend. Hide some away for me.'

The weekend was a success. Monica loved my designs and she had plans to broaden my services to include bespoke wedding stationery. All quite ambitious but very exciting. We took the boys on the cruise boat down the river, and to the fairground, just the right size for two young boys, then ate fish and chips as daylight faded and twinkly lights came on. Mother cooked a wonderful Sunday lunch. She invited Emily from WI who brought with her a sheaf of papers full of details confirming that my visions appeared to be accurate. Names and dates of birth, the blitz in Birmingham, conscription ages and protected occupations. So now I knew that I wasn't just making it up; this was my history, my family. Now I needed to know why it was so important for me to know all this. And why did Dorothy want me to know it now?

We arrived back home Sunday evening, the boys going straight to bed, worn out by Mother playing enthusiastically her role as grandmother. I was feeling much more generous towards David, willing to believe that he was still the man I trusted and who was only grumpy because I was pushing him into it.

I took my overnight bag to the bedroom, to put my dirty clothes in the laundry basket. As I opened the door, stepped into the bedroom, I breathed in the scent of Youth Dew. The perfume I no longer had.

Perfume

David came to the bed, leaned over my huddled body, brushing damp hair from my face.

'What's the matter?'

'Who is it David?'

'What do you mean?' His surprise seemed genuine.

'The perfume David. Is it Laura's?'

'Youth Dew? It's your favourite isn't it? Have I got that right?' He took a package from the bedside table.

I opened the elegant paper bag, took out the cardboard packaging and read the name of the perfume emblazoned in gold. Youth Dew.

'I sprayed some earlier, to see if I could remember if I'd got the right one.'

'Oh my lord, David I'm so sorry.'

'You just don't trust me do you Erica.' He walked away, shaking his head. I cried some more. I don't know where David slept that night, but it wasn't in our bed.

Morning arrived, sunny and bright. David was up before me, I could hear him in the bathroom. I quickly dressed and headed to the kitchen to make coffee. We were polite to each other, but the atmosphere was cold, stilted. It's difficult to make conversation when you are ashamed of your behaviour. There wasn't time to talk about it; sometimes life gets in the way of the important things. At least, we were talking; it could have been a frozen silence. David left for work; I took the boys to school, Monday morning reluctant.

I decided to update my Book of Shadows. I slipped the key from the chain round my neck, felt it warm in my hand. I ran my hand over the soft chiselled leather, enjoying the smoothness and the satisfying patterns under my fingers. I opened the book wide and started to turn the pages to where I had last finished writing. As I passed the pages through my fingers, I came to a page that was crumpled, folded down. I paused. I hadn't done this. I was so careful with this book; it meant so much to me. I smoothed the page to make it straight, trying to press the creases flat. The paper tingled under my skin. It was telling me, warning me. Someone else had definitely handled my book. I leaned forward, pressed my nose to the paper, breathing in deeply. Youth Dew. I knew it. Laura. But why would Laura go through my Book of Shadows. Why had she been here?

I was angry. I felt violated. David had made me believe that it was all in my head. That he was innocent, and I was a possessive, jealous wife. But to let her touch my book, to damage it, to read my innermost thoughts – that I could not forgive.

I apologised to my book for not protecting it. I don't know how she had opened it. The lock didn't seem damaged. I carefully updated it with my recent visions, with the details that Emily had found for us. It took me a long time. By the time I was finished, I knew that I was going to have it out with David.

****

'I know this is a terrible thing to say** but I truly feel that it would have been better for Charlotte if he had died in the fighting. Then she could have dealt with the grief and time would let her mend. But this not knowing, the constantly waiting to hear something, hoping he will come home, it's not good for her.'

'It's not good for you neither Eugenie but I know what you mean.' John fought for something positive to say, to take her mind off Charlotte's troubles. 'I hear Edna is putting her nursing training to good use, helping with those injured in the blitz.' As he said it, he realised it wasn't the best thing he could have said. Eugenie looked away, to hide her tears.

'Look love, I didn't mean it like that. I just meant that it was a good thing you did, setting her up with training.'

'I know John but I'm fearful for Edna, Catherine, all of them. There's no one there for them.'

John listened, feeling useless.

****

'How could you?'

'Could I what?'

'Don't act all innocent David. I'm not stupid, and your little ploy to hide the fact that you'd had her here in our home, in our bedroom, didn't work. The perfume? I know you had a woman here.'

David shifted uneasily, not raising his eyes to me, not able to look me in the face.

'It's Laura, isn't it? Despicable, David, using the boys as cover so you can meet with your fancy woman.

'And it's not the first time you've spent the weekend with her is it? Did you really think I wouldn't find out about the weekend when you said you were at the football. Some mate you are, expecting your mates to lie for you.' I was on a roll now, letting out all that I knew with all the venom I could muster. David stood there like a little boy in front of the headmaster's desk. He didn't speak.

'And you even let her paw through my Book of Shadows.'

That stung him into speech. 'And that's it isn't it? That's the worst thing for you. Shows us where your priorities lie. Forget about me and how lonely I've been, how cut out of your life I've been. All you care about is these visions and your newfound witchy stuff. That's it, I'm out of here.'

'David, wait,' but he didn't hear me over the slamming of the door. I heard the car start up and pull away with roaring engine, and then the quiet. What had I done?

****

'I've enrolled with the home guard.'

'Why John, just tell me why?'

'I have to do something Eugenie. I can't stay here, hiding on the farm, when our people, our own family, are suffering in the city. I'm going to be staying with Catherine, so there will be someone there for her, to help with poor old Jack.'

Eugenie knew there was no fighting his decision. John was an honourable man – he showed that when he married her – and she knew how he felt that he wasn't doing 'his bit' for the war effort.

'You're a good man John Wright. I am so proud of you, and so lucky to have you.'

****

'He's left me Mum. I was right in my suspicions he was having an affair. I called him out on it. He didn't try to deny it, just stormed out, said he was leaving.' I paused as I took a deep breath, wiped my eyes. 'What am I going to tell the boys?'

****

News from the war came thick and fast. Albert had lost his life, a hero to the last, single-handedly taking out a machine gun placement that was holding down his platoon, saving the lives of nine soldiers who were trapped under fire.

Fredrick was no longer missing in action. He returned home to Charlotte, his right leg amputated above the knee, where he had been blown under the tracks of a British tank by an explosion which also damaged his hearing and peppered his face with scars. He fell in love with Frances; having missed out on the cute baby she had been, he made up for it with the active toddler, giving her the affection that his wife wasn't able to give.

Constance was no longer needed to keep an eye on baby Frances. No longer needed and no longer wanted. She stepped into John's role as farm manager, learning what she needed to know from her mother and the old hands who knew how the farm should run.

****

Mother moved in for the first week after David moved out, to help with the simple logistics of getting the children to school and back, walking the dog, shopping and everything else a household entails, which was hectic enough with two adults but much worse with one, especially when my heart wasn't in it, and all I wanted to do was sink into my duvet and cry.

Jacob asked fewer questions than Joe. I suspected that some of his friends had dealt with a daddy moving out, so he knew it happened, even if that didn't make it any easier for him. Joe simply didn't understand where Daddy was and asked continually 'Where's

Daddy? Why isn't he here?' He cried himself to sleep at night. I cried with him.

David phoned to arrange to pick up some stuff and to ask if he could take the boys out on Sunday for the afternoon. Of course, I said yes. I wasn't going to let the boys suffer any more than I could help it.

Mother left on Saturday. She didn't want to see David; she doubted that she could be civil to him. She took twenty cards with her, and some flyers advertising my wedding range. Keeping my hands busy kept the tears at bay.

After the boys left with David, I took Bruno for a walk. The weather was warm and sticky, breaking into patters of rain that threatened to pour but faded in the sunlight reaching through the clouds. I needed space, the house walls closing in on me. David and I had remained polite and sounded friendly in front of the boys. At some stage, we would have to meet alone to discuss the future.

I walked Bruno towards the stand of trees at the far side of the fields. I didn't usually venture that far, keeping to the more open dog walking routes. It was dark amidst the pine trees, their branches shielding from both the light and the rain, the floor covered with prickles that deadened all noise, like walking in a cave. The birdsong sounded distant. I enjoyed the solitude even though it was a little eerie, scary almost.

Someone coughed. I stopped, looked round. A man dressed in black walked slowly towards me. My heart beat faster. What was he doing here? I couldn't avoid him, the path between the trees narrowed. He walked towards me, slowed down but did not stop.

'I didn't mean to startle you.' His voice was low, quiet. 'Laura is not who she seems. David does not know this. Don't let them isolate you. You will need friends.' And he carried on walking as if he hadn't spoken.

I also didn't stop, sped up to get out of the trees. Relieved, I spotted Mrs Purple Hat at the edge of the darkness. I waved to her, happy for a friendly face, but carried on walking so I didn't have to speak to her. I didn't feel ready for chit chat with anyone at that moment.

I went over his words again, and again. This was a strange message, and also the way he delivered it, as if he didn't want anyone to know he had spoken to me. A shiver trickled down my spine.

Bombs fell on Nechells

In March 1941, bombs fell on Nechells. Houses shattered to the ground, leaving skeleton fingers pointing to the sky. Catherine and Jack's home lay in pieces on the ground, the ageing shoddy building collapsing, unable to withstand the battering.

John was on duty that night, helping those trapped to climb from the wreckage, taking the wounded to receive medical care. He worked throughout the night, directing people who were left wandering with nowhere to go, reuniting people with missing loved ones, comforting those who couldn't comprehend what had happened. Catherine had joined him, comforting those who had lost loved ones, tending to injuries as best she could. Angels moved amongst them, people would say later.

As the new day dawned, pale rays rising from the east, pushing through smoke and dust, John heard crying in a tottering building. It was a child, not very old by the sound of it. John pushed the door, but it was jammed by fallen masonry. He pushed his head through the blown-out window, lifted his weight onto the ledge strewn with shards of glass.

'No John. It's too risky.'

'It's a child, Catherine. Listen to the cry.' John ignored her warning and heaved his body through the window. Catherine watched in despair as she waited for him to return. In minutes, she saw him at the window with a small child in his arms, so covered in dust that it was impossible to say if it was a boy or a girl. Catherine ran to the window, grabbed the baby from his arms, heard a rumble.

'John, John, look out.' Too late; the wall collapsed to fill the empty space where the window had been, bricks bouncing off the surrounding walls. Catherine saw John fall to the floor, hidden under bricks and rubble. She scrambled over the remains of the wall, grabbing broken bricks in her bare hands, searching for John. She heard a groan, a sigh of breath pushed out of his body. She uncovered his face. Wiped the dirt from his nose, his mouth. Saw the blood seeping from his ear, from the back of his head, staining his hair, the rubble.

'Don't leave us John. We need you. Eugenie needs you.' Yet she knew it hopeless. Too much blood. The laboured breathing.

'I'll stay with you John, till help comes.' His breath came in jagged gasps, further and further apart. Catherine leaned over him, placed a gentle kiss on his forehead.

Too late, she felt the rumble as what was left of the bomb struck walls gave up their battle to stay upright. She died next to John, crushed under the rubble. Clouds of dust settled over them like a shroud.

The child wailed its loneliness from the paving where she had laid it.

****

'Mum, I know what happened to Eugenie and Catherine.'

'Don't tell me over the phone. I'm coming over this afternoon. I have an order for you for wedding invitations and place cards.'

I knew that Mother was using any excuse to come over, to 'keep my spirits up' and I really appreciated her support.

'I love you Mum.' I'm sure I heard a sniffle in her voice as she said goodbye. I decided to make an effort and baked a cake, a

Madeira, and was most impressed with myself when it actually had that special crack in the top. I'd never managed that before.

We sat at the kitchen table with a cup of tea and a slice of cake, the rest of the cake close by in case we needed seconds. Bruno sat hopefully under the table.

'John and Catherine lost their lives in the blitz, rescuing a baby from a bombed-out house. He was so brave. They both were.'

'What happened to Jack?'

'He went to live on the farm with Eugenie.'

'How wonderful.'

'It really was. Jack had forgotten a lot, but he remembered how to groom a horse, so he spent his days with the horses. Constance took over running the farm, letting Eugenie take it easy.'

'How sad that Catherine and Eugenie had so little time together. Finding each other after all the time they had spent apart. Making plans for the future. And then this.'

****

Frances grew up strong and independent, wise beyond her years. She early learned to cook and clean, to do the chores that were necessary to keep a household running. She helped Fredrick, pushing his wheelchair on the days when he was too tired, in too much pain to move it himself. She fussed around Charlotte, encouraging her to eat, to bathe, to get out of bed. The baby blues turned into something more sinister over the years, that tore the joy from Charlotte's heart, that left her wishing to leave this life.

Help came from an unexpected quarter. William's wife Nellie had never remarried after his death. A good Christian soul, she reached out in forgiveness to William; after all, she reasoned, his transgression against Eugenie had also been a transgression against her, denying their marriage vows. The vicar told her every Sunday that we should forgive those who trespass against us. Nellie prayed for William, for she knew with great certainty that Justin and Eugenie were the cause of everything that had befallen her family.

'Our poor little Robert,' she told the vicar, 'it was what happened to him that was at the bottom of it all. That brute Justin urging the coach onwards after the poor mite had fell under the wheels. William couldn't forgive that evilness, all done just to impress that stuck-up Eugenie. He worried what would become of Robert, for his future, not able to run around with the other lads, nor work on the land like his dad.'

The vicar firmly believed that one shouldn't speak ill of the dead, so he never interrupted to point out that William had a temper on him before any of this had happened, that he was known for it.

'And then Justin died without anything being done about the way he'd treated our little Bobby, everyone too scared of him, feared they would lose their job and then their home, not that those cottages could be called proper homes back then.'

The vicar pulled his coat further on to his shoulders, straightened his Bible and his notes for the sermon he had just delivered. Nellie didn't notice his preparations to leave, so intent was she on explaining to the vicar what she had decided to do.

'Of course, what he did to Eugenie was wrong. There's no denying that but he was beside himself with grief. He kept it all inside till it festered and just exploded. You could tell how remorseful he was. That's when he started drinking heavy. All down to that Justin again. And look what happened next. That John thinking himself a big man after he married Eugenie, threatened to get rid of him, throw us out of the cottage. And William, bless him, turned himself around, stopped the drinking. He didn't even touch a drop when that Albert come swaggering home the hero. Our poor little Bobby will never have the chance to be a hero. William had to live with that. That Justin again.'

The vicar stood up. 'I can see you've given this a lot of thought Nellie.'

'You're right there Vicar, I have. You see I reckon that it was John that killed my William, not Albert like the police said. And John and Eugenie kept quiet about the real father of the twins, so I never got to see them, not up close and if you think about it, they were my children, sort of. And now poor Fredrick is a wreck of a man, with his leg and all that, what with having to go to war when he should have been at home on the farm. He needs help, and that poor young girl Frances with so much on her hands, well she's like my granddaughter. I'm going to see them. Offer my help.'

'That's kind of you Nellie. A true Christian gesture.'

'I'm so glad you see it like that Vicar. Someone has got to put right the harm that family has caused. Justin may be dead, but Eugenie has a lot to answer for.'

The vicar placed his Bible on the table, kept his hand on the simple cover.

'Nellie, what you are planning on doing is a noble thing, but you said you were doing this in the spirit of forgiveness. You need to put aside your anger against Eugenie. She has suffered a great deal.'

'Forgive me Vicar for questioning your words, but how can you support her? Everyone knows she is a witch, has used magic to get what she wants.' Nellie crossed herself, and walked away, leaving the vicar in troubled peace.

'Erica, Erica, come here.'

I tracked her voice to the downstairs bathroom. 'Are you ok Mum?'

'There's another face Erica. Look.'

And there was indeed another face in the bathroom floor. A young woman with a broad, round face, her auburn hair falling in curls around her shoulders. Her mouth was drawn tight in a line, her brows pinched together.

'Who are you?' I asked. 'You look harassed, as if life is too much for you.'

'She does, Erica, as if she's carrying the weight of the world on her shoulders.'

The only person I could think of was Frances. In my visions, I had only seen her as a young child. I knew she'd had little time to be that young child, having to support her depressed mother and her disabled father. Perhaps this was the grown-up version of Frances, still looking after everyone else.

'She will reveal herself to you, Erica, but you mustn't let it wear you down, you have enough to deal with.'

We went to the witchy shop to look at the new craft supplies they had in stock and I spent a good hour choosing items to make samples to show the client. Dale watched closely, showing us the new range of papers. He also showed us the new leather-bound books they had in stock.

'Don't you think these are wonderful?' A deep red book with a crescent moon picked out in gold on the cover caught my eye.

'You must be ready for a new book,' he said. 'Your old one must be nearly full, with all the stuff that's happened. What else do you put in it?'

I must have frowned as his attitude changed a little.

'Sorry, I'm only asking as I'm interested in what people put in their Book of Shadows. You don't get to see many as they are such private things. Have you ever seen another one? An old one?'

'No, I haven't. I'm making this up as I go along.' I wasn't lying, not really. I hadn't seen another book in the flesh, so to speak. Only in my dreams.

I smiled at him, paid for my purchases and left the shop, feeling ill-at-ease.

'What was that about Erica?'

'I'm not sure Mum. How does he know about my Book of Shadows? Fey sold it to me before Dale started at the shop. And how does he know I have lots to write about? They must have been talking about me.'

'Perhaps Fey did tell him. She would have to explain why she'd asked them to be around for you.'

'Perhaps you're right. I'm seeing trouble in everything nowadays. But it's odd that he asked if I had seen an old one. Almost as if he knew.'

We shopped for dinner, shepherd's pie, chips for the boys, broccoli and carrots for the grown-ups, picked up the boys and headed home. I carried the shopping straight into the kitchen to get the minced meat in the fridge before it spoiled.

'Mom, Mom, come here.' The urgency in Jacob's voice made me run to the living room. I stopped short at the devastation in front of me. The lamp and the coffee table were overturned on the floor. Every drawer in the dresser was pulled out, contents falling over the edges, the cupboard doors were open with boxes and CDs spewing onto the floor. My collection of miniature white vases lay shattered on the carpet, fragments of china like fallen petals.

Mother took charge of the situation. 'Everyone out of the room. Come to the kitchen. Don't touch anything.'

'Erica, you need to phone the police. Tell them you've had a break-in, then go upstairs see if they've done anything up there.'

Jacob and Joe sat at the kitchen table with a biscuit and a glass of orange squash.

'Mommy,' said Joe. 'Where's Bruno?'

'Bruno, Bruno.' We listened for a response. He was in the garden, a rope passed through his collar and round the magnolia tree. He was quite comfortable out there, not distressed. And now I could see how they had got in. The glass in the dining room window had been smashed and the window opened.

The police arrived while I was upstairs. It was the same as in the living room. Every drawer and cupboard had been opened, even the drawers under the bed.

'So nothing has been taken?'

'Not that I can see Officer.'

'Yet apart from the window and the vases, nothing has been damaged?'

'It's all just as you can see.'

'It seems an odd one this. If it was kids breaking in out of boredom, I would have expected to see more damage, graffiti, that sort of thing. If it was professionals, well, why didn't they take the computer or the TV? Your jewellery?'

As he said this, I knew he was right. This didn't seem a typical break-in.

'And the other thing that troubles me is your dog. You said he was happy enough tied up in the garden. He's a big dog. I suspect he must have known the person or persons who broke in. Most people would be wary of tackling a dog that size.'

Mother arranged for the window to be boarded up and insisted on calling David to let him know. He came straight round, said he would stay the night. Angry as I was with him, I was glad to have him around.

I fell asleep as soon as I settled my head on my pillows, but the sleep was troubled. Voices bounced round my head, a constant distressing drone that rattled my nerves, dragged me down.

'Justin thought he was so much better than everyone else, his workers that kept his farm going, made him the money so he could live his posh life. Never mind spending anything on the cottages.'

'Justin crippled our Bobby, ruined his life.'

'William never got over it.'

'And that Albert took the blame for William's death. But everyone knew that John did it, murdered him in cold blood. And he got away with it.'

'Where's the justice? Leaving those little boys to be brought up by the man who murdered their father.'

'And then Douglas died. The dog just lurched at him like it was possessed. That must have been Eugenie. It's a witch, she is.'

'And that horse reared up and kicked Justin. That wasn't normal, neither.'

'Fredrick was crippled in the war. John made him go, out of spite I reckon, wouldn't say he worked on the farm.'

'I was left here on my own, carrying a babby. I couldn't cope, Frances. It's John and Eugenie's fault I'm no use to anyone.'

'She only ever loved Constance. Didn't care for me nor Douglas, her own flesh and blood.'

'Wasn't our fault what our real dad did. Wasn't fair the way they treated us.'

'And she came from nothing. All airs and graces. Yet she ended up with the farm and the estate. After she killed Justin with her witchcraft.'

'That Mary taught her all she knows. Old Alice left her the cottage and all her secrets with it.'

The hostile voices kept on and on, weaving into my brain. Poor Frances, how did you deal with this?

****

Frances dealt with it by leaving home. She packed her bag and found haven in Notting Hill. London was shaking off World War II and transforming itself into a place full of freedom, of hope and promise, of excitement, assisted by LSD and marijuana. The Beatles sang of love, bright colours wove optimism into life – everything the opposite of life at home.

Nellie kept to her word and supported Charlotte and Fredrick, finding usefulness in looking after them. Robert never returned to the farm. He was ashamed of his father.

Floppy hat and hippy beads

At first, I was more worried about the effect on the boys, rather than for myself. I was glad David was about more for the boys' sake. The boys found his presence re-assuring, playing football and walking Bruno were familiar activities, although the slightest noise in the house sent them running to me, to check everything was alright. Yet it pulled my nerves tighter, having to be pleasant to him when I wanted to scratch his eyes out, abandoning me for another woman, such a cliché it made me feel sick.

Then the niggles got into my head. First Laura goes through my Book of Shadows, Dale was asking questions about it and if I had seen another one, then someone breaks into my home looking for something and to top it all, it seems to be someone whom I know, or at least Bruno knows. And then there was that strange warning from the man in black. Why would anyone want to steal my dreams? Did they think they revealed some terrible secret, like a great uncle was a bank robber and he would leave me a clue as to where he buried the money? Even as I played out the scenario in my head, it sounded ridiculous. I was letting my mind run riot. Stay in touch with reality, I told myself. My visions were enough fantasy for now.

****

Frances returned to her childhood home, belly swollen with child, which she disguised with a loose kaftan that flowed down to her Birkenstocks, her long, tousled hair topped with a floppy hat, beads jingling round her neck.

'There's no mention of the father,' said Nellie.

'It's this hippy free-love thing. All very well when you're singing songs about it but another thing altogether when you're left bringing up a child on your own.' Charlotte remembered how hard it was looking after Frances when Fredrick was away at war.

Both women shook their heads and waited for Frances to tell them her plans, not wanting to scare her away. By the look of her, she was close to her due time. Frances spoke to Mary and Lucy, asked them to be present at the birth.

'Do you not want to go to the hospital? They have much better facilities there.'

'No, definitely not. I don't want no doctors interfering.'

'It's these new age values,' said Lucy to Mary. 'They believe in natural childbirth.'

'It's not really a new value is it? It's the way it was always done.'

When the time came, Mary and Lucy had their hands full, not one but two babies.

You have a boy and a girl, Frances. Both healthy little things and I do believe,' said Mary, 'they are going to have red hair like yours.'

'I'm going to call the girl Georgie and the boy Harrison. After the one in the Beatles. He writes such wonderful songs.'

* * * * * *

David stopped coming round so often. Things had settled down – well, at least the boys were no longer jumpy whenever I left the room. The police had finished their enquiries and said it was unlikely they would be able to find who had broken in, but they would let me know if they found out anything.

I resumed walking Bruno and found I was glad of company; Mrs Purple Hat met me most days. Enid made a good walking companion, chatty but also well informed about witchcraft and she was happy to share this knowledge with me. I learned a great deal over the next few weeks, and it was good to have someone to share stuff with about the boys, now that David wasn't there to listen.

The client was happy with my designs and my cards were selling well, so I got myself into a routine. David had the children from Friday night to Sunday every other weekend, as well as taking them out two evenings a week. We hadn't really talked about the future. I was hopeful that we could get over this and did my best to be friendly and welcoming whenever I saw him.

I re-found my interest in baking, trying out new recipes on the boys – and Mother when she came to visit.

I made a Victoria sponge, filling it with raspberry coulis and Chantilly cream. I placed a slice in front of the boys when they came home from school, to fill that gap between home-time and dinner.

Joe took a couple of bites, then put it back on the plate and pushed it away.

'What's the matter Joe? Didn't you feel like cake today?'

'I don't like it. Laura puts strawberry jam in hers.'

Well that told me. Not only was she still seeing my husband, but she made better cakes.

Jacob ate all of his, then finished Joe's abandoned slice as well. I don't think he was being greedy. I think he was trying to save my feelings. I hated David at that precise moment, for putting his family through this.

****

'**You can't really be thinking of doing this.** Call yourself a mother?' Nellie was fuming. Charlotte was sobbing, tears staining the front of her blouse, making dark patterns.

'I'm leaving because I can't cope with this anymore. You do nothing but complain and moan about life. Mom wishes she were dead. Dad has given up on life, just sits there in his chair, with a bottle of Davenports in his hand. Fat lot of cheer it brings him. What life is this for me?'

'But the babbies, Frances. You can't take them travelling across India. They'll die of disease.'

'That's why I'm not taking them Nellie. I can't take them with me, but I need to go. If I stay here, I'll end up like Mom. No good to them, to anyone. Better to give them up for adoption, so they stand a chance of a better life.'

'You will not put them up for adoption.' Fredrick disturbed from his reverie, his voice clearer, more forceful than it had been for months.

Frances walked out of the room, away from the angry voices, her voice lifted in song. *Here comes the sun, and I say it's all right.* George Harrison confirmed that she was doing the right thing.

****

Nellie called at the big house, asked to speak to Constance. She sat on a comfortable upholstered chair and looked around the room at the decoration, the dark wood furniture with its fine carving, the paintings on the wall. By the time Constance arrived, she was on edge, bitter about the difference in lifestyle.

'Hello Nellie. It's William's wife isn't it? How can I help you?'

'Let's not beat about the bush. I know you don't want me here, don't want to be polite to me but this concerns both of us. Young Frances is leaving us, going off to India to find herself or some such nonsense.'

'What about the twins?'

'Exactly. That's why I'm here. She doesn't want them. She's leaving them here while she goes swanning off. You know what Charlotte and Fredrick are like, their circumstances. They can't manage to look after them. I'm fit enough but I have to admit that I wouldn't be able to look after two little uns, and them two as well. I need you to do something for us.'

Constance waited for Nellie to explain what she wanted.

'Will you take the little lad? You've got a lot of space here, and a cook and hired help. You wouldn't notice him really, and it would be a great life for him on the farm. And after all, he's your family too. I'll keep the girl. I can't let them both go.'

'I'll have to talk it over with Mother.'

'Well don't take too long thinking about it. Frances is setting off soon.'

******

Harrison stood in line with his fellow students for the obligatory photo, mortarboards hovering in the air above them like crows ready to swoop. Constance opened wide her arms as he walked towards her, a smile broad across his face, rushing in to return her hug.

'I am very proud of you.'

'I owe it all to you,' he said. 'You've been so good to me all these years. Thank you so much.'

'No need to thank me, I've loved every minute you've been with us. We all have.'

'Wait while I get changed and I'll come home with you.'

You'll do no such thing, Harrison. I'll be fine. Go and celebrate with your friends.'

****

'Come on Nan, sit up and let's try to eat something.' She put her arm round Nellie's thin shoulders and sat her up, pushing pillows behind her to keep her upright. She lifted a spoon of soup to Nellie's mouth, but it was a waste of time.

'No love. I don't want anything.' Georgie didn't catch the words but knew what she meant. Nellie was dying. The anger had gone out of her; she no longer spoke of Eugenie and Justin, nor blamed them for the troubles in their life. Nellie prayed often, muttering prayers that no one could hear apart from her maker. She seemed at peace.

Assault

'Erica, can you come over?'

'Mum, are you alright?' Mum sounded shaky, not at all herself.

'Someone was in my house, Erica. The police are here.'

'Are you ok?'

'He was still inside when I got home. He pushed me as he ran out the door. I fell.' Mum broke into tears. 'I'm not hurt,' she said, 'just shaken.'

'I'm coming Mum.' I called David, asked him to get the boys from school. Then I phoned Annie. I had no need to ask, she straight away offered to drive me to Mother's. She's such a good friend.

The police had not long left when we got there. This wasn't just a break-in like at my house. This was an assault. Mother had said she wasn't hurt, but there was a bruise creeping across her face, where she had hit the wall as he pushed her. Nothing had been taken but the place was a mess. The door on her lovely Welsh dresser lay on the floor, ripped off as the photo albums had been pulled out, thrown across the floor. The drawers had been pulled out, emptied of their contents. Every room was the same devastation.

'Mum, I think you should come back to mine.' I had my arguments prepared. I didn't need them.

'Are you sure Erica? That would be lovely. I don't think I could be here on my own.'

My mother scared, defeated. I'd never known her like this before.

'Thanks Annie for your help. You've been a godsend, but you get off now. I don't want you to be late picking up your boys.'

'Are you sure? I can stay, drive you back.'

'It's ok, Annie,' said Mother. 'I'll be alright to drive.'

I saw Annie to the door, walked her to her car, gave her a hug. As I watched her drive away, I felt a shiver run across my shoulders. My safe world was crumbling. I turned to walk the flower edged path back to the house. A flicker of movement caught my eye. I swivelled round in time to see a figure across the road walking quickly away – a man dressed all in black.

****

Constance had disappeared from the bathroom floor.

I recorded this in my Book of Shadows. I gave it some thought. At first I felt cheated almost. I wanted to hear the rest of her story, and I'd thought that through Constance, I would have been shown the rest of Eugenie's story. Mother came to sit with me while I worked.

'But you do know what happened to Eugenie, mostly. She lost John but she still had Constance. She'd found Catherine again, and although they didn't have much time together at least they made peace before she died. And poor Jack lived the last of his life looking after horses, what little he had left. It sounds like her old age was peaceful after the upheaval of her earlier life.'

'I suppose you're right. I hadn't thought of it like that. And we know that Constance took over the running of the farm. There was no sign of a special someone in her life though, no children of her own.'

'But what about young Harrison? She loved him, took good care of him if he graduated from university.'

'What does it all mean Mum? Dorothy is still there and Frances. At least that's who I think it is. What is it I'm supposed to learn? I wonder where it's going now.'

Mother went to her little room upstairs. 'I feel tired. I'm going to lie down for a while.'

'You go ahead Mum. You've had a shock. It will take you a while to get over it. Rest will help.'

I watched her go, her shoulders drooped. I hadn't really thought of Mother as old, not till now. She was always so capable and full of more energy that I could ever muster. Who was doing this to us? And why? The two break-ins were linked. Of that I was certain. That man in black was at the root of it. He must be. He was always there, watching. Was he looking for something? Or just trying to scare us?

My anger boiled in my chest. I felt my body tingle, pulsate. My head was full of light, my senses stretched beyond my body, reaching out into the air around me.

'Leave us alone. Whoever you are, trying to hurt us. Stay away from my home, stay away from my mother.'

My anger left me, moving like streams of light. What had I done?

I felt lightheaded, but calm. The tingles stopped, I relaxed into my chair. I picked up my pen, recorded what had just happened. Is that what they call magic?

Then I sat back in my chair and felt slightly ridiculous. 'You're getting carried away with all these dreams,' I told myself firmly. 'You're not magical. You're just plain old Erica.'

****

Mum stayed for a few days and didn't seem to want to go back home. While I didn't mind her being with me at all, I was worried that she would lose confidence and find it difficult to get used to being on her own again. It had taken some time for her to become independent when Dad died. It had taken her a long time to take charge of the house, to realise she was capable and strong enough to do it by herself.

'Mum, shall we go to your house, water the plants. It would be a shame if they died for want of water. You put so much effort into them. We can come back here after we've done that.'

That worked. We dropped the boys at school and set off. Mum put the key in the lock, pausing to take a deep breath before turning it and pushing the door open. The house was exactly as we left it, the debris of her life scattered across the carpet. Her eyes glistened with tears.

'Come on Mum, it'll be fine. We can get this sorted.' First of all, I put the kettle on, checked the date on the milk. Mum was picking up photos when I carried the tea into the living room. We spent a while examining the pictures, remembering the happy times on holiday with Dad, at parties with all the family. There was a picture of Dad, and Mum in the shortest of miniskirts, a kaleidoscope of colours.

'Look at you Mum! And Dad with his hair past his shoulders. How old were you there?'

That was back in the 60s. Tony and I must have still been in our twenties. The world was a new place. The possibilities were endless, everything bright colours and loving.'

'Same sort of age as Frances, then. Still, it seems a bit extreme to abandon your children and set off like that.'

'Given what she faced at home, the lure of a happy life must have been compelling.'

We gathered the rest of the photos and put them back in the dresser. It took ages, far longer than I expected as we took time looking at them. I didn't rush Mother as I could see her mood lifting at the memories. We had time in anyway. It was David's night to have the boys.

The plants were drooping a little, so I filled the sink with water, gathered all the pots and let them soak up the water before letting them drain. The living room was almost back to rights. Mother was putting some paperwork back in a drawer.

'Erica, come here.'

'What's up Mum?'

'My address book – look.' Jagged edges showed that some pages had been torn out.

'Who's addresses would those be?'

Mum flipped through the pages.

'Eleanor Bennet – an old friend from school. We still exchange Christmas cards.' She stopped. 'They've got Eileen's address.' Some more frantic turning of pages. 'And Patricia's.'

'Mum, we should tell the police.'

'What good are they going to do? No, we need to tell Patricia and Eileen. Warn them.'

Mum made the phone call to Patricia while I phoned Eileen. Eileen outright dismissed what I was saying.

'Don't be so dramatic Erica. Why would anyone be targeting our family?' Then she became a little more amenable. 'In any event, James and I have a state-of-the-art alarm system. We need it what with the things we have in our home. Every door and window is alarmed and there are cameras outside covering the doors and the drive. I don't think we have anything to worry about.'

'I'm glad to hear that,' I said, a little miffed by her attitude.

'Perhaps you should consider improving the security at your home. James would be happy to give you advice on a decent system, given that David isn't there to help you.' It took all I had not to slam the phone down on her.

'How did you get on with Patricia?' I hoped Mother's call had gone better than mine.

'Patricia listened to what I had to say. She was very concerned about me, and you, but she didn't see why anyone should try to break into her house, not related to me and you in anyway. She did however promise to make sure her doors and windows are kept locked and no valuables are left in sight.'

It's just nonsense

David's car pulled up outside, the door flew open and Jacob and Joe jumped out. I was watching through the window, waiting for them to come home. I couldn't get used to the boys not being around, much as I loved the quiet time to myself. Problem was, nowadays I had too much time to myself.

I was about to open the front door when I noticed Joe at the passenger side door, his arm reached in, jumping up and down excitedly. Two long legs emerged from the front seat, a short floaty skirt swirling around them.

'Dear God,' said Mother, watching from behind me. 'Is that woman coming to the house?'

'I don't know Mum, but I think I'm going to head them off at the door.' And as I opened the door, to guard it, Laura stood up, brushed her skirt down, smoothed her clingy top and took Joe's little hand. Her heels made her so much taller than him that his arm was raised up to her. They walked from the car but as Laura put her foot on the path, her foot twisted, and she fell to the ground. I watched as David ran to her, tried to help her up, but she sat straight back down, holding her ankle. She seemed to be in pain.

David tried again, and half carried her back to the car. Laura would not be coming into my home today. High heels are so impractical, especially with children around.

The boys waved to David, rushed up to me. 'Can we play in the garden?'

'Just for half an hour, then it will be time for supper and bed.'

Mother looked at me with a wry smile on her face. 'Well done Erica.'

'What?' I said, puzzled.

'Your spell worked. Didn't you ask for those that intended you harm to stay away from your home?'

'Oh,' I said. 'I did.'

That night, after the boys were snuggled up in bed and story read, after Mother had gone to bed exhausted, I went to my Book of Shadows, read what I had written. When I did whatever it was that I did, I had meant whoever had broken into my house and Mother's – that sort of harm. I hadn't been thinking of Laura stealing my husband away. Perhaps I needed to be more specific. And in anyway, I hadn't intended anyone to be hurt.

'It's just nonsense,' I said to myself. 'Pure coincidence,' yet I felt quite proud of myself. I'd said to leave my home alone and she hadn't made it in. Perhaps I am powerful after all. I chuckled. A bit of entertaining nonsense. I raised my hand and made as if to cast something from my hand outwards. 'Take that,' I said. 'and that', moving my hand round the room, pointing my fingers at the photos and vases on the window ledge.

The rose exploded, petals falling onto the ledge, surrounding the base of the vase, toppling onto the carpet.

I jumped up from my chair and fled to the door, my heart beating fast. I looked back, laughing at myself.

'Just a rose dying from lack of water.'

I could see the vase was dry, no water reflecting light through the glass. 'Get yourself to bed Erica before you spook yourself.' I shut the dining room door, walked steadily down the hall, then fled upstairs to my solitary bedroom, closed the door firmly behind me.

****

I eventually drifted into sleep. I think. It may have been a waking vision. I was looking at a familiar face; not a face I knew straight away but one that jogged my memory.

'When you've finished the deliveries, could you go to Grandma's, check they are ok.'

'OK Mum, no problem at all.'

'And Dorothy, give Granddad Jack a kiss for me.'

'Yes Mom, see you later,' she said, as she perched a hat down on her head at a jaunty angle.

The woman pulled on her blue dress, adding a white apron emblazoned with a cross on the front, marking her as a member of the Red Cross, a belt cinching it tight. She slipped her feet into sturdy black shoes, smoothing her stockings into place. A cap atop her head, her uniform was complete.

With a start, I realised that this was Edna, a fully qualified nurse, proud in her uniform, the younger woman the Dorothy of my bathroom floor. I watched fascinated. Edna walked through the city streets, her back straight, head up, walking as proud as Catherine had when she was younger.

She walked down Elvetham Road, turned onto Bath Row, approached a large building. The sign outside pronounced it the Midland Nerve Hospital. I followed her as she made her way down the ward lined with beds at either side, greeting patients lying prone in their neat beds, blankets folded with 100% accuracy at the corners. The work of the busy hospital continued relentless.

'I hope there's no air raid warnings today. These men can't cope with it, not after all they've been through.'

'Yet they are safer here, nurse, than still overseas fighting. If an air raid comes, we will deal with it professionally and without any drama. Remember your training.'

Edna was moving down the ward, straightening blankets, checking notes, smiling and talking to keep up spirits, to keep patients calm. Shellshock added to what would have been otherwise minor injuries.

A wail started, sirens impossible to ignore. Nurses sprang into action, moving patients to the safe place below the hospital. Minimum panic, a well-rehearsed drill. Edna went back up to the emptying ward to check that everyone had been removed to safety, just in time to hear the whine of a bomb falling, a direct impact on St Thomas's church opposite.

'Dorothy,' she cried. Then stood quietly, breathing deeply, concentrating on the flames. I heard her muttering, speaking not to herself but not to anyone in the room. Her arms stretched out, her hands beckoning. I couldn't make out what she was doing. It was like she was gathering something in, and shaping it into a ball. Then with an almighty surge of energy, she threw the non-existent ball away from her.

Edna faded from my sight; instead, I saw Dorothy, huddled with Jack and Catherine in the cramped, dark Anderson shelter. The darkness faded as they were bathed in white light, surrounded in a bubble, protected, safe.

The vision faded.

****

I ran downstairs to the bathroom.

'What are you trying to tell me Dorothy? How did she do that? Was she a powerful witch? Did she learn it from Catherine?'

Dorothy didn't answer me, not in words, but I'm sure her smile was broader than it had been before.

****

'Mum, the things I'm seeing, we can prove it. It will be written up in a book somewhere, or on the internet. Shall we go to the library? They have computers there, as well as books, and the staff can help us if we get stuck.'

We tiptoed into the library, found an empty desk with a computer, and started work.

'Erica, look at this. There was a St Thomas's church on Bath Row. It was bombed in 1940. What was left, they made into a Peace Garden – it's still there.'

'And look Mum.' I pointed to sentences further down the screen. 'The Midland Nerve Hospital was on Bath Row. And opposite and just down the road was Davenports Brewery. That's who delivered Fredrick's beer.'

The article on the blitz made sad reading, so many injured, so many buildings damaged. People made homeless, including a direct hit on Nechells, where Catherine and Jack lived.

'Mum, do you see what this means? I'm not just imagining things, or listening to a story. This is real. It's the history of our family.'

'It certainly looks that way. You can't have known all this before you started having visions. Most of this I didn't even know.'

'And you know what else it means? If the history is true, then it looks like witchcraft is part of our family.'

'I really don't know what to think Erica. It seems so strange.'

'I've seen some good outcomes and some terrible ones. We need to give this some thought Mum. It's quite scary.'

While we were at the library, we took out some books on witchcraft. I know I'd read some before, but it was half-hearted, just holiday reading. Now we were going to do some proper research into the subject. We also stopped at the newsagents to buy a notebook and new pens. I ran my hand over the paper and surreptitiously sniffed the pages. The notebook was perfect.

The good times

David came to collect the boys.

'No Laura today?' I asked.

'No. Not today. Actually, it's a bit odd. Laura said she doesn't want to come here at all. I said that you were fine with her coming here, there'd be no unpleasantness.'

I gave this some thought – not a great deal – but it was reassuring to think that he still thought me a reasonable person, even given his deplorable behaviour. My acting skills were improving.

'But she's adamant she won't come to the house.'

'Oh dear,' I said, 'perhaps it's just the circumstances that make her feel awkward about it.' I confess I did wonder if it had anything to do with my spell.

'David, are we really over? After all the good times we've had together?' The boys were still in the garden playing football and hadn't realised David had arrived.

'Yes Erica, I think we are.' He had the courtesy to look uncomfortable, guilty even. 'I feel bad for leaving you on your own with the boys, but I can't help the way I feel about Laura.' He stopped as if he was searching for words. 'You and I, well, we were getting on fine but once I saw Laura, I knew she was the one. She means everything to me.'

'It's a mid-life crisis David. An infatuation. Why can't you see that?' I turned away so he didn't see my tears, walked to the back door to call the boys.

'Daddy's here.' The boys raced in, running straight for him, forcing him to lift his head and place a smile on his face. There was a rush of bags, shoes, coats, a whirlwind that banged the door, and they were gone.

The peace didn't last long. Mum arrived shortly afterwards. She was often here on the weekends when David had the boys.

'What's up Erica? You don't seem yourself today.'

'I'm fine Mum. Just tired.'

'Did you say anything to David today?' She just always knew.

'He said it's over Mum. That means divorce. We might have to move, I can't afford to keep up this place on my own.'

Mum sat quietly for a moment. For once, she didn't have an answer.

'It's going to be hard Erica, but you are strong, you will get through this, and I'm here for you every step of the way.' She came close, wrapped her arms round me, held me close while I cried.

'Let's get out of here, go somewhere nice for lunch, do some shopping.' Retail therapy and food was always Mother's response and it almost always worked. We had lunch in a bistro café, that served meals you didn't expect to like but were delicious, accompanied by a glass of white wine, followed by a sinful dessert, topped by luxurious coffee selected from the widest range I'd ever seen.

We drew Saturday afternoon shopping to a close, returned to Mum's car with an armful each of bags.

'Let's stop at Fey's shop before we go back to yours.'

'I don't really need anything. I have all the stuff for the next order.'

'I was thinking more of doing some research. We can have a word with Dale, or even Fey herself if she's there.'

The bell over the door tinkled, announcing our arrival.

'Hi Erica. Alright?' Dale was enthusiastic as ever.

'Hi Dale.' Mum and I walked over to the witchy counter where he was working, looked at the ornate chalices, decorated with carved figures and a pentacle on the front.

'Dale, what sorts of witchcraft are there? Are all witches the same?'

'Not the same, no. A lot of people nowadays are Wiccan. That's fairly new, started in the late 40s, early 50s. Gerald Gardner it was who wrote a book about it, but he reckons he was just telling the world of what already existed. Some people though follow the old ways. As you probably know, witchcraft is a very old tradition.'

'I always thought it had died out following the witch hunts, you know hundreds of years ago.'

'It just went underground. Witches didn't really shout about it, kept it to themselves. Still the same nowadays, lots of us about but you wouldn't really know that. Unless you join a coven, get together with other witches, but that's not that easy. It's hard to even find us. We tend to be secretive. People still don't trust us.'

Fey came out from the back room.

'Hello,' she said, 'How's your Book of Shadows coming along?'

'I'm still working on it, writing up anything interesting.'

'And is this the first time you've ever seen such a book? Many families have some sort of book passed down through the generations. Some might call it the family Bible. A big book perhaps with all the family history written down.'

I glanced at Mother who returned the look.

'No, I haven't. I'd not heard of anything like it till you put the idea in my mind.'

Mother nodded her head in agreement. 'Not heard of anything like that in our family. Obviously, we're not from witchy stock.'

Fey looked me straight in the eye. 'Oh, I don't think that's right. You're a natural at this.' She smiled and headed back to her private room.

'That felt a bit uncomfortable,' said Mother, as we stood admiring the cake shop window, or rather its tempting displays.

'Perhaps she's heard about the break-ins, is trying to work out what they are looking for. Mum, it couldn't be anything to do with it, could it?'

'I wouldn't have thought so.' We concentrated on choosing a cake for supper, despite it being our second of the day. My waistline temporarily wasn't a priority.

****

'If you're going to pick up the boys, you might at least tell me. Save me the bloody journey.' David's voice was harsh, angry, scarcely lessened by the distance.

'What are you on about David? Pick the boys up from where?'

'Don't play games. Football, this morning. It's not your weekend to have them.'

My heart stopped.

'David. I don't have the boys. They're supposed to be with you. Are you telling me you haven't got them?' I could feel my stomach tying itself in knots.

'You mean you didn't pick them up? What the…' His voice faltered. 'Erica, I went to collect them from football practice, but they had already been picked up. I thought you and your Mum had collected them.'

'It wasn't me. So who's got them David?'

Mother was now at my side, taking charge. I passed the phone to her.

'David, call the coach, ask him who picked them up. Were you late getting there? Perhaps they went with a friend's mom.'

'Of course. That makes sense. And yes, you're right. I was a bit late.' I could almost see his shoulders sink from the tone in his voice. Mother had the phone between us.

'Go and put the kettle on Erica.' I realised Mother was suggesting action to delay the onset of panic.

We sat at the kitchen table, our hands busy with hot tea, waiting for David to call us back.

'Coach said that the boys were picked up by a woman in a car. He said the boys knew her, ran up to her when she got out the car. Who could it be?'

'David.' Mother interrupted him in mid flow. 'We will start phoning round, see who has picked them up.'

'Erica,' said Mother, 'it's probably just one of the other moms has picked them up, rather than leave them waiting for David. Get your phone book and start ringing.'

I worked my way through the phone round list that me and the other moms had set up for emergencies and to share information like snow days. I'd started with Annie, for moral support and because I thought she would know who else's sons went to football.

'Oh my God, Erica, how awful for you. I haven't left the house this morning. The boys have gone with their dad to see his parents. I'm on my way. I can make phone calls. Make tea.' She arrived within minutes, and sat next to me, jotting down names to try.

Thirty minutes later, between us, we had phoned everyone we could think of. No good news. No one had them.

'David, I've phoned everyone I can think of. No one has got them.' I was standing by the window, watching in desperation, waiting for a car to pull up, for this to all be a huge mistake, for the boys to come waltzing down the path. I picked up the photo frame on the sideboard, the photo from when we were on holiday, David, Jacob, Joe and me – before Laura, before it was all over, a lifetime ago.

Crisps and a cat and fizzy pop

The boys walked down the front path one hour after they had gone missing.

I ran to open the door, grabbed them both up in my arms, fell to my knees and hugged them, tears dripping down my face.

'Come on Erica, let's get them inside.' Mother always knew what to do. She asked them gently if they were alright. They had no idea where they had been, nor who had taken them.

'I thought it was Aunty Annie. She looked just like her. She said Daddy was late and she would take us home.' Jacob was telling their story. Joe stayed on my lap.

'I'm sorry Mommy. I really thought it was Aunty Annie.'

'Where did she take you? Can you remember?'

'It was a house with a garden.' Not helpful, I thought, that could be anywhere.

'She gave us crisps and fizzy pop.'

'And sweets,' added Joe.

'We played with her cat, and then she brought us home.'

'Mommy, I'm hungry,' added Joe.

Mother was in the kitchen, making food.

'Erica,' she called to me. 'Can you come here please?'

I gave both boys a hug and left them with more TV while I went to see what she wanted.

'I've phoned David to let him know the boys are here, safe and sound. But you need to see this,' she said, handing me a letter.

NOW YOU CAN SEE HOW EASY IT IS FOR US TO TAKE YOUR BOYS. WHERE IS THE BOOK? IF YOU WANT YOUR BOYS TO STAY SAFE, DELIVER THE BOOK TO ME. YOU HAVE ONE WEEK. DO NOT TELL THE POLICE.

'It was in Jacob's bag.'

'Mum, what is this all about? It's like something out of a movie. What book?'

The letter was made up of bits of print, different sizes and styles, cut up and pasted on to A4 paper.

'The only book I can think of Erica, is the book that we keep being asked about.'

'What? My Book of Shadows?'

'Well, someone had a look through it didn't they? But no, if that was it they would have taken it when they broke into your house. I was thinking of the old one, the family Bible that Fey asked about.'

'Oh my God, you mean the one from my dreams.'

******

I hugged the boys before I tucked them up in bed. I read them a story, and another. Jacob had reached his arms up to me, wrapped them round my neck.

'I'm sorry Mommy.'

I held him tight, told him everything was ok. I sat with them till they fell asleep. I checked their windows were locked, checked again before I left their room. Then I came back, with a pillow and the duvet, cleared abandoned cars and Lego bricks out of the way, lay down on the floor. I couldn't bring myself to leave them on their own.

****

David arrived early, on his way to work.

'Erica, I'm sorry about yesterday. I feel so guilty. I shouldn't have been late. I didn't think I was that late, ten minutes maximum.'

'Why were you late David?' asked Mother.

He coughed a little, cleared his throat. 'Laura was going to come with me. But she had to run to the loo, had an upset stomach. I waited to see if she was alright, but she said to go on without her.'

'And how is she today?'

'Fine, I think.'

'What a shame. I suppose you didn't manage to get out last night. You usually go out for a meal on Sunday night don't you?' I could see that Mother was probing with these questions.

'Oh, we went out last night. It was short lived whatever it was.'

I went to get the letter that had been in Jacob's bag from the sideboard drawer. Mother shook her head at me, a slight movement but enough to make me stop. I raised my eyebrow to her. She put her finger to her mouth then removed it. David hadn't noticed.

'David. Erica. You need to make sure that you never leave the boys alone like that. I don't know who took them. It was probably someone who thought they were doing you a favour, doing the right thing. But it could have been so much worse. It doesn't bear thinking about.'

David and I looked at each other. Of course Mother was right. We agreed that for football practice, one of us would stay during the session so there was no chance of being late and if we were honest about it, the supervision wasn't as strict as at school. They were volunteers after all. As for collecting from school or after visiting friends' houses, we would ring each other if there was any chance of being late.

David declined a cup of coffee, leaving for work.

'What was all that about Mum? Why didn't you want me to tell David about that letter?'

'Erica, don't you think it was odd that the first time David is late, someone was waiting to take the boys?'

'Well, yes.'

'And don't you think it even odder that Laura was suddenly poorly, which made David late, then was well enough to go out on the night?'

I didn't answer her, the impact of her questions hitting me like a brick. 'Mum, do you think Laura is involved in this?'

'Well, I've no proof obviously but it certainly is suspicious.'

The Book

Mother and I took the boys to school.

'Now remember, you only go home with Grandma, me or Daddy. No one else. Promise?'

'Yes Mommy,' they both said.

'Even if we're late, you wait with your teacher. One of us will come for you. NO ONE ELSE.'

'YES MOMMY,' they shouted back at me, laughing. For good measure, I informed their teachers of the incident and asked them to monitor who collected them, making sure that the staff understood that only David, Mother and I could take them.

Tea made and spiced ginger cake sliced, we headed to the dining-room. I had already decided that I needed to look again at what I had written in my Book of Shadows. I recorded everything as soon after a dream as I could, while it was fresh in my memory but like all dreams, they faded quickly. Mother and I sat in front of my book. It was almost full. I hadn't realised just how much I had put in there. We started to read from page one.

'Mary was right there at the beginning Erica.'

'You're right. She started it all, helping Catherine get Jack to come back. And she was there protecting Eugenie from Justin. And that was certainly by magic.'

We read all morning.

'Erica, look. Mary had a book that she was reading from when she was looking for a spell to help Eugenie. Where did she get that from?'

I tried to put myself back in that dream. Yes, Mary was looking through a large book, battered, with lots of pages, all hand-written, and bound in what looked like a leather cover.

'Well Mum, it was definitely an old book, and it looked a lot like my Book of Shadows. But surely, it wouldn't still be around would it? Mary must have died a long time ago.'

'Perhaps she left it to someone.'

'I don't know, but thinking about it, that book had been left to her. By the old lady who left her the cottage. Alice Bracebridge.'

'Even if she had left it to someone, why would they think we had it? We're not even related to her.'

The last few hours seemed positive, even though we didn't have any answers. At least we had an idea of which book they wanted from us. The image in my head was of a book that would qualify as a Book of Shadows. I didn't even know if that's what they were called back then but it was a book which definitely had spells in it and other advice and information.

We were pleased with what we had found so far but it was nowhere near enough. A week – that's what they had given us to give them the book. And we were no closer to knowing where the book was. Every time I stopped doing something, every time my mind had time to wander, the knots crept back in my stomach, tight enough to make me lean forward, hold my stomach to steady it.

'I think it's time to take a break. I'll make some lunch.'

'I don't think I could eat.'

'Erica, you will be ill if you just live on cake.' I followed her to the kitchen and watched her make sandwiches, ham and thinly sliced cucumber, a smear of mustard, on lightly buttered bread. There was no cake.

'Why would Jacob be so convinced that it was Annie?'

'Just mistaken, I suppose. Why do you ask?'

'Because Erica, he has known Annie since he was a little boy. It must have been a really good likeness for him to get mixed up.'

'That's a good point but I don't know what it means.'

We ate our lunch in silence, pondering on the unanswered questions.

We now knew that Mary had a book which could well be the book that they – whoever they were – wanted. We knew that Mary was definitely a witch. From my visions, there was nothing to suggest that Mary had married or had children. There was no mention of sisters or brothers, any other family at all. We knew she was close to Lucy, Eugenie's maid. We knew that she had friends still at the big house where Catherine and Eugenie had lived as children but no idea who. We knew that she was close to Eugenie and had helped her with the people living in the row.

'Mum, why would they want the wretched book in any way? What good is it to anyone?'

'I can only assume that the book is valuable. Perhaps it's worth money because it's rare due to its age.'

'I wonder if Fey would know. She asked about books didn't she?'

We decided to go to the shop, speak to Fey. We walked, to clear our heads, taking the path through the patch of grass. Birds lined up on the power cables, singing to each other, taking flight then bouncing the cables as they landed again.

We took Bruno with us; he was being neglected just lately, and he leapt out of the house, raring to go, disheartened when I reined him in. I didn't feel like running after him. There was nowhere to hide on this patch of worn out greenery, no bushes just the hard-edged walls of the surrounding houses.

'Erica, we seem to have a visitor.'

I looked up, saw someone dressed all in black coming towards us. 'I'm going to speak to him, find out what he's up to following me all the time.'

'I'm not sure that's the right thing to do. If he's the one who broke into my home, don't forget he assaulted me. He might be dangerous.'

'Don't worry Mum. We're out in the open, people can see what's happening and we've got Bruno.'

We kept on the path and he did the same. He slowed down, as he neared us.

'Be careful,' he said.

'Are you threatening me?'

'No, I'm warning you. They aren't your friends.'

His eyes looked over my shoulder. He stopped speaking and continued walking.

'Lovely dog,' he said, loudly, much louder than his previous words. I turned to see what had made him change his mind about talking to me. At the other end of the path, I spotted Dale, jogging towards us, in a hurry. I waved to him, and we waited for him to catch up with us.

'Hi,' he said. 'Are you calling in at the shop?'

'Is Fey in?'

'She should be. Can't stop, I'm running late.'

Mother and I watched him go.

'Now, that was very strange. All of it,' said Mother. 'Is our man in black scared of the people from the shop?'

'It did seem that way. Or perhaps he doesn't want people to see him talking to us, so there's no witnesses to his intimidation.'

'Did you notice Bruno didn't growl? His hackles weren't up. No worries at all.'

'I've always said this dog is a waste space.' The shop was busy today. A young mom buying rabbit food, an elderly lady asking for a tonic for her sickly goldfish, a teenager sniffing incense over at the witchy counter.

'Fey, the other day you mentioned family Bibles, old books. Are they valuable?'

'Yes.' Her tone was sharp. 'All that knowledge carefully recorded. Of course people would want them.'

'Fey.' Dale called her. 'I could do with some help here. Now.' I was surprised by Dale's tone. He was usually so polite to his boss. Fey drew in a deep breath, breathed out slowly.

'Excuse me,' she said and obediently walked to Dale's side.

'Come on Erica. Time to go or we will be late.' We left the shop, not speaking until we were well clear of the frontage.

'What was all that about?'

'I don't know, but this day just gets stranger.'

******

Dorothy sat at the table, her eyes not leaving her mother as she gathered ingredients on the polished wooden surface. Jars of dried seeds, small brown bottles, a wicker basket with fresh leaves still with traces of morning dew on them. Edna took a pestle and mortar, added small dark seeds, ground them to a powder.

'Poppy seeds are good for a cough. The seeds are only tiny, so if you grind them, they can be cooked in food, even cakes.' She tipped the powder into a jar. 'These are for Amy Eatwell.' Dorothy wrote a label in neat, clear writing – Amy Eatwell. Use in cooking for cough.

Edna stripped the fresh leaves from their stalk. 'This is feverfew. Made into a tisane, it helps with migraine headaches.' Dorothy prepared a label – make into tisane.

'Who is it for Mom?' She added the name to the label.

They worked steadily, fulfilling a list of orders. Every action was meticulous, each jar or bag labelled with necessary details. Dorothy wasn't just helping her mom, she was learning.

******

I realised I had lost myself for a while. The boys were eating their tea, their favourite cheesy beans on toast, and hadn't noticed. Mother had, and wanted to know what I'd seen. I added this latest bit of information to the Book of Shadows, reading out loud to Mother as I did so.

'It's odd Mum. Edna was a trained nurse, but she was making herbal remedies.'

'It does seem a little odd, but don't forget, Erica, many of our current medicines came from folk remedies. Aspirin was developed from willow bark that people used to make into tea. Digitalis for heart disease came from fox gloves. Of course, they are made synthetically nowadays but that's where they started.'

'I hadn't realised. I suppose Edna must have learned those skills when she stayed with Eugenie on the farm. She helped Mary if I remember right.'

'She must have seen how Mary's remedies worked first-hand, and decided to keep using them, alongside her medical training.'

****

The week passed. I was a wreck. I wasn't sleeping, my mind whirled round, trying to figure out what was going on and in the darker moments seeing images of my boys lying hurt in a ditch, dead even. Mother came down later than usual, her face haggard, showing her worry.

'What am I going to do Mum?'

'I don't know Erica. All we can do is tell them the truth. We don't know where the book is. We can't do more than that.'

'But what about the boys? I think we should tell the police.'

'That letter said not to tell them. And what good would they be in anyway? They weren't interested in the person who broke into your house, and they weren't interested in the one who broke into mine. And I was assaulted.'

'I'm going to phone the school. Tell them the boys are ill and can't go to school. At least that way I can keep them with me. I'm not going to let them out of my sight.'

'Say they have chicken-pox. They can be off with that for a couple of weeks. They can't go in as they would be contagious.'

I phoned the school. They didn't question what I told them. I told the boys it was the school holidays. Jacob looked at me puzzled.

'I thought there was another week to go.'

'You've got that mixed up, silly. The holiday starts today. And we're going to stay at Granny's for a few days.'

We packed our bags, and I wrapped up my Book of Shadows and took that with me as well. I needed to keep reading, see if I could get any clues. It was a bit of a squash with Bruno in the back as well as the boys and the bags. My book travelled on my lap, so it didn't get damaged.

On the journey, I gazed out of the window, watching trees spreading away in the distance, hills faded to grey in the sunshine.

'Mum, I know where the book went.' She glanced at me but turned her eyes back to the road.

A collection of hats

'Where?' Mother demanded as soon as we were indoors.

'Mary gave it to Edna. How else would Edna know so much about the herbal remedies? And Edna knew magic. She threw a bubble of light around Dorothy, Jack and Catherine in the bomb shelter. It kept them safe.'

'And if Edna had it, perhaps she gave it to Dorothy, when she,' Mother paused, 'well, when she no longer needed it.'

That makes sense, Mum. But where would it have gone from there?'

'I've no idea. It was such a tragic thing to happen.' Mother's eyes moistened, and I remembered that Dorothy and Mother had been close. Mother never really spoke about how her cousin died, and I suppose I was too young to think about asking. Mother discreetly wiped away the tear that had formed and was trickling down her cheek.

'Dorothy and Jeremy were such a lovely couple, and it was clear they loved children. When they married, everyone thought they would have a large family. They certainly had enough money to raise a football team if they wanted. Jeremy's father was a wealthy businessman, and Jeremy followed him into the family business.'

'I remember visiting Aunty Dorothy when I was little. It was always exciting. She had goodies stashed everywhere.'

'They were unable to have children, but they had money and the freedom to come and go. They loved exotic holidays, travelling to places most of us had never heard of. They went on holiday to

China. While they were there, Typhoon Nina struck. There was terrible rainfall, so we heard. A dam collapsed. Lots of people died; the area was devastated.'

'They both died?'

'Yes. Their bodies were never recovered. It happened just one year after Edna had passed away. Dorothy was only fifty.'

'How awful.'

We fell silent for a while, Mother busying herself with making the tea while I helped the boys carry their bags upstairs and left them to settle into what was to be their bedroom for the next week.

'What would have happened to her things Mum?'

'Hmm, let me think. My uncle Edwin it must have been, Dorothy's father, who sorted things out. I can remember he sent me a collection of hats. He said that I was the only person he knew who would get any use out of them. I have no idea what happened to the rest of her belongings.'

I took my Book of Shadows to the bedroom I always used when I stopped at Mother's. I placed it on the dressing table, opened the pages, and recorded the information about Edna and Dorothy. When I first started having dreams, they were about people far removed from me. Now they were about people close to me. I knew Dorothy. Her story entwined with mine. On one hand this was a puzzle to solve, with frightening consequences if we didn't get it right. On the other hand, it was the story of my family rolled out like a movie on the big screen.

I climbed into bed but couldn't sleep. Even though the boys were in the room next to mine, I was unable to rest. What if someone broke in and they were there with no one to protect them. I took my pillow and eiderdown, and settled down for another uncomfortable night on the floor.

****

I phoned David to let him know that I wasn't at home so he wouldn't be having the children this week. Mother had said I shouldn't tell him where we were. I could see her point, but David wasn't stupid and would work we were all at Mother's. He would know that I wasn't brave enough to take the boys and Bruno somewhere unknown for the week.

'There's something you're not telling me isn't there, Erica? It's not like you to pull the children out of school.'

'They're ill David.'

'Then they should be at home.'

I faltered. David had been alongside me since we met. We had shared everything, especially about the children. 'I'm scared David. Someone is trying to hurt the children. It wasn't someone trying to be helpful taking the children after football.'

'I'm coming straight over.'

As I was wondering how to tell Mother what I had done, she came into the living room.

'I'm going to speak to Patricia. If I was given some of Dorothy's things, then she probably was as well. She may remember more. I feel it would be best to go to see her face to face. She's not happy using phones, says they are for business only. Says conversations between friends should be sat next to each other. Bit behind the times that way, although I have some sympathy with her way of thinking. I shall head off now.'

The boys threw themselves at David when I opened the door for him.

'Daddy, Daddy.' Their excited cries made me wince once again at how they were affected by our separation.

David had bought a comic for each of the boys and a bag of dolly mixtures. The boys soon engrossed by these, David and I moved to the kitchen to talk, under the pretence of making lunch.

'David, I know you think my dreams are just fantasy and nonsense, but I need you to listen to me, before passing judgment.'

I told him about the threatening letter that had been left in Jacob's bag. How they wanted something by the end of the week. And how they made it clear that the boys would be their target if I didn't deliver. I reminded him about the man in black, and updated him with the strange behaviour and conversations.

I told him that we believed they were after an old book that had spells in it, that we thought it might have been passed to Dorothy.

'That's where Mother is. She's gone to visit Aunt Patricia to see if she knows anything.'

I didn't tell him all. Not at first. I held back our suspicions about Laura. So far, David had listened, wide eyed but no sign of disbelief on his face.

'There's something else David. Please don't be mad at me.' I took a deep breath. 'We think Laura might have something to do with it.' I explained why.

His stance changed. He straightened his back. Put his hands flat on the table.

'You are going too far Erica. Up till now I can almost believe what you're telling me. But to accuse Laura. That's ridiculous. Or is it jealousy?'

David stepped back from me, shaking his head. 'You're not right in the head. I've taken time out of work to listen to this?' He called the boys. 'I'm going to take them to the park. Let them run around for a bit. You can't keep them shut up indoors.'

'David, please be careful. Don't let them out of your sight.' The door slammed behind them. I had never felt so completely alone.

****

Mother returned with a bag of shopping and a smile on her face.

'Patricia remembers Uncle Edwin giving her some of Dorothy's belongings. A large box. Apparently there was a collection of handbags, some costume jewellery and there was something else at the bottom of the box, wrapped in tissue. Patricia said it was a leather handbag but never took a proper look at it because it was far too big for her. Never took it out of the box.'

'What? Do you think it could be the book?'

Well, it's a possibility.'

'Where is it? The box.'

'Now that is the next problem. Patricia doesn't know. When she and Geoffrey moved to this new place, they had to get rid of a lot of things. Downsizing, you see, ready for retirement. They wanted something they could manage easier.'

'Fair enough, but what did they do with it? Don't tell me she threw the box away.'

'Wendy handled the move for them. Patricia sorted out what she wanted to keep, and Wendy dealt with the rest. Wendy has always been good to her mother.'

'But Mum, you came in with a smile on your face.'

'I did. Hear me out. Patricia thinks all the boxes may have been placed in storage. Wendy was talking of sorting it out and selling what she could when she had a chance. And don't forget, Erica, it was only last year they moved.'

I could see why Mother was excited. There was a possibility that it was still stowed away, waiting for us to find it. A slim possibility, but nevertheless, it was the closest we had come so far to light of any sort at the end of the tunnel.

'What next Mum?'

'Patricia is contacting Wendy. Unfortunately, she's on holiday in Greece. Patricia said she would be back in two weeks and she'd ask her then. Don't panic,' said Mother, smiling even broader. 'I've persuaded Patricia that this is an appropriate time to use the phone.'

I was so excited, I gave Mother a hug.

'The boys are very quiet,' said Mother, a question in her eyes.

'They're with David.'

'We agreed not.'

'I know, I know.' I stopped her before she could say any more. 'I know what we said but I just had to tell him. He's their father. He has a right to know.'

'Very well,' she said. 'It's your decision.'

She went to the kitchen, clattering pans, pretending to start cooking dinner, although she probably was. I left her to it; Mother would calm down; cooking, providing for her family - it's what she did best.

On cue, David brought the boys home. 'I'll pick them up again tomorrow, after work. I'm not sure what's in your head, but you need to get help Erica. I'll do what I can to help with the boys, but will you please see a doctor. Talk to someone.'

****

The week was almost up. We weren't at home, and the boys weren't at school, so I was hoping that this would mean we were safe, but I knew that the man in black had been outside Mother's house. He was dangerous, of that I was certain, and he had an accomplice, whoever it was who had picked up the boys from football. And then there was Laura. David was adamant that she had nothing to do with it, but he would, he was infatuated with her.

I was still sleeping in the same room as the boys, not settling down to sleep till I had checked the doors and windows at least twice, making sure they were locked, looking out into the night, listening for any unfamiliar noises. I know that Mother was doing the same. Each day her face showed a lack of sleep that all her potions and lotions couldn't disguise.

I woke to the stillness of day shaking off the darkness of night. The low light through the curtains suggested that dawn was well on its way but not yet fully arrived. Something had disturbed me. Both boys were collapsed into their blankets as only children can be.

I rushed to the window, opened the curtains a slither, spotted a dark shape on the garden path. I couldn't tell who it was, but their

movement was considered, furtive. I realised what had woken me –
the gentle thump of a something falling from the letterbox.

Mother joined me downstairs, dishevelled and not quite
awake. We read the letter together.

ONE MORE DAY LEFT. DELIVER ON TIME. NO
POLICE. YOU KNOW WE CAN GET TO YOUR BOYS

'Mum. I'm scared. What do we do?'

'First things first, we leave here and find somewhere else to
stay.'

Who has them?

'Eileen, thanks so much for having us.' I couldn't remember ever being so glad to see Eileen. She hugged me, which I found most out of character given our usual fairly hostile relationship.

'Whatever we can do to help,' she said. 'Erica, I want to apologise for dismissing all this as nonsense.' Mother had told Eileen the whole story, from the faces in the bathroom floor, my dreams, the evidence that they were reliable history, the witchcraft issue, the break-ins, to the threats against my sons.

Bruno was pacing round, sniffing everything. I watched him leave a trail of black and tan doggy hair on her cream sofa, just after leaving muddy footprints on the cream carpet. Eileen followed my gaze.

'Perhaps we could make a bed for Bruno in the utility room.' Mother's suggestion gave us an easy way out of this problem, just like she resolved our differences when we were children. I caught Eileen's eye and we both smiled.

James showed the boys to the recreation room as they called it, the equivalent of David's front room at home but on a much grander scale. Jacob was instantly converted to staying here: large screen TV, Nintendo console, air hockey and a pinball machine with flashing lights that pinged when the balls hit them. Joe would follow Jacob anywhere.

For the first time in a week, I felt I could relax a little, let my guard down. I now saw the value of having a top-notch security system. Sleep in a comfy bed beckoned.

'Right,' said Mother. 'We are safe for now, but we can't stay here forever. We need to solve the problem. I'm afraid there's been a bit of bad news. Wendy did put the boxes in storage, but she managed to sell most of the items, including the book.'

I gasped. 'The book? It was a book? Was it our book?'

'Yes, it was definitely a book, old and bound in leather. Erica, I think we've found it. Except that Wendy sold it. She took it to a bookshop that sold first editions and rare books. She doesn't remember the name, but it was in Bridgnorth.'

'We're not going to find it in time are we?' I felt my stomach knotting inside. Progress and yet not. We still had to find it and we were running out of time. 'Who is doing this Mum? And why?'

James and Eileen asked to go through the details again, now that we were together, rather than the outline that Mother had given them over the phone. We agreed that the book must be valuable given its age but as Mother pointed out, Wendy had treated it as just something else she had sold rather than something she had made a fortune on.

'So if it's not the value of the book itself, it must be for the contents.' James looked at me hopefully.

I told him what I knew. Lists of ingredients for healing, how to do spells and records of magic. He wanted to know what the spells were for, what sort of magic. I was nervous to tell him, keeping an eye on his face for signs of laughter. Seeing none, I told him about Edna's protection spell, the spell used to bring Catherine and Eugenie into contact with each other again, the spell that Catherine used to bring Jack back to her from Canada. I told him about the magic used to kill Justin, and Douglas. I didn't know if that sort of thing would be in the book, but it stood a good chance.

'And you believe that these spells, this magic, actually worked?'

'Definitely. My dreams showed the magic being used and the outcomes. Other things in the dreams, we've proved to be true. I have to believe everything is.'

'This is powerful magic. I think it's what they are after. Imagine being able to have that control, that ability.' James was right. It was frightening when you looked at it like that. Eileen offered to drive me to Bridgnorth the next day, to see if we could locate the shop. I wasn't happy to leave the boys but as she pointed out, I was the only one who could identify the book.

My phone rang. David. He was furious. I hadn't told him where we were, and he had turned up to take the boys out. I apologised as I told him about the latest threat. Mother had crept to my shoulder, was listening to the conversation. She wrote on a scrap of paper – do not tell him where we are.

'David, I understand you want to see the boys. No David, please, you can't do that. I'm not having a breakdown. I don't care what Laura thinks. I'm not a danger to them. If you report that to the police, the boys will be taken away from us.'

Mother snatched the phone from my hand. Eileen walked me away, leaving Mother to do the talking. I heard her voice raised, angry, then calmer.

'You and Eileen can drop off me and the boys on your way out and David can meet us. I'll spend the afternoon with them, then you can pick me up afterwards. He's agreed he won't report you to the police as long as he can see them, make sure for himself that the boys are OK.'

****

The book was resting on a dark wood lectern, the stand supporting it carved in intricate patterns. It was open, the pages lying smoothly as if they were well read. The woman turned each page gently, avoiding damage to the fragile pages.

She brushed the escaping strands of red hair behind her ear with a deft movement born of frequent repetition. Reading glasses perched on the end of her nose.

A man stood behind her, rubbed her shoulders. She straightened her back further into his hands, stretching as if she had been sitting in the same position for a while, engrossed in her reading.

'Well Dorothy, are you going to become a witch?'

Dorothy smiled at him, unperturbed by his jesting question.

'There's so much here, for healing, advice on how to help people in all sorts of trouble, but there is also dark magic here, how to kill, how to harm people.'

'And do you think it's real?' Jeremy turned her towards him, cupping her face in his warm hands.

'I don't think,' she said, 'I know. It saved my life during the blitz.'

'So? Will you carry on this family tradition? Live up to your heritage?'

'No Jeremy. I have seen   the harm it can do. I know enough already to heal through my potions. I don't want the responsibility of having the power to harm within my grasp.'

'What will you do with the book? Burn it? Get rid of it?'

'I will keep it. It's come to me for safekeeping. I would have passed it on to our children when the time came. Our family history.'

He hugged her close to him, warding off the tears.

'We need a holiday, not just any holiday but a great holiday, as far away from here as we can get.'

****

We walked up and down the main street then moved on to the side streets. We found nothing that looked like a book shop. Eileen caught my arm, pulled me between cars across the street to the Post Office, where we were given directions to a small shop well away from the sight-seers out for the day, through an iron gate to a courtyard paved in red bricks. We had stepped into the past, a place that belonged in my visions.

A bell tinkled above us, jangled by the door as we opened it. It made me smile, reminded me of Fey's shop.

An elderly man looked up from under a white shock of hair, wire reading glasses resting on his bulbous nose, his cheeks red and pockmarked. He moved around the counter to greet us, his movements belying his apparent age.

'Good afternoon ladies. How may I help you?'

His forehead creased in a concentrated frown as he sought an answer to my question.

'Firstly, can I ask you to tell me something further about this book? For example, what am I likely to find written in its pages?'

I told him some of the less awkward things, in case his pleasant manner might change if he heard of the stranger things it contained.

'Yes Madam, I believe I know exactly which book you are looking for. While not wanting to be impertinent, could you tell me why you are seeking it, and why you thought to come to my shop looking for it.'

I gave him the simple explanation of my aunt moving to a new house and getting rid of things she no longer wanted.

'But if she didn't want it, why do you?'

Eileen gave a 'hmmmph' and looked sharply at him. She had no need to speak her annoyance.

'I am most sorry madam if you feel that I am inquisitive but well, I am curious. This book is unique, and I wouldn't like it to fall into the wrong hands.'

'Tell him Erica. It certainly sounds like your book.'

I explained how it had been in my family for a long time, and how it had come into our family from some very special people.

'And does the name Alice mean anything to you?'

'Of course, Alice Bracebridge. She was the first person I'm aware of who owned the book.'

He took a bunch of keys from his coat pocket, locked the door to the shop.

'Come this way,' he said, and led us through a narrow corridor to a back room. He used his keys to unlock a cupboard that reached almost to the ceiling. Dark wood shone as if it was polished lovingly every week.

He lifted up a large book and carried it to the table. The cover glowed softly in the dark room.

'I was so moved when this book came into my hands, simply because of its age. I decided to keep it, spent time restoring the leather, which had dried out. It was a labour of love, I knew I would never sell it.' He ran his hands over the cover. 'But when I read the contents, poring over the spidery faded writing, just getting used to one person's style of lettering, then having to decipher the next owner's, I realised I had something that few people will ever see, a record that few people would ever believe.'

My heart faltered. I needed that book and it seemed as if he was going to tell me he couldn't let it go.

His gaze drew from the book to my face, held my gaze.

'Your eyes tell me that you need this book. It holds great meaning for you.'

He carried the book to the shop counter. Eileen and I followed, thanking him profusely. He wrapped the book in layers of tissue, then placed it in a large paper bag.

'No charge,' he said 'but please, use it carefully. The magic in here is powerful.'

Eileen and I flew out of the courtyard, as excited as when we were young girls up to no good. I took out my phone to call Mother, tell her the good news. The phone rang in my hand.

'Erica, they're gone.' Mother's cry was of someone in mortal anguish. I couldn't speak, my stomach churned, my vision went hazy. I crumpled to the floor.

****

Four of us stood in the living-room, as the sun moved away from the windows in late afternoon, taking the brightness from the stark white walls.

'David and I took the children to the park. We were by the lake, feeding the ducks. Laura joined us. She said she was desperate for a coffee, asked the boys if they would like an ice-cream. Of course they did, but they didn't want to walk to the café. Joe wanted to feed the ducks. Laura said she couldn't carry everything by herself, insisted David needed to go with her.'

'I should have believed you.' I thought that was what he said. David was bent over, his head in his hands, his shoulders shaking, his voice faint.

'Just tell me, simply, what happened.' Frustration was pushing away my fear, making me angry.

'I was standing by the duck pond, watching the boys. A woman on a pushbike ran into me, knocked me off balance. I stumbled. A man helped me up. There was a lot of fuss and Erica, they were gone.'

Mother went to put her arms around me. I gently pushed her away.

'There's no time to be upset, Mum. What happened next?'

'David came back – without Laura.'

'David, where's Laura?' I already sensed what he was going to say.

'I don't know. She's gone.'

Mother and David both looked at me, waiting for me to say something, to do something, to take charge.

Eileen pointed to the book, its leather cover glinting in the dying sun.

'We have the book,' I said. 'They must know that by now.' The threatening letters had not mentioned how to get the book to them, only the deadline. If Laura was in it, they would know where we were. Our flight to Eileen's had not deterred them. The book gave us something to bargain with, something to offer them for the boys' safe return.

'Mum, did you hear anything when the boys went? Did they scream or call for help?'

'Nothing at all to tell me there was a problem.'

'They're with someone they know. Probably Laura.'

Eileen was stroking the book, moving her hands over the patterns. 'Erica, that man said there is powerful magic in this book. Is there anything you can do?'

'You mean, as in magic?' My heart gave a jump. I recalled that terrible dream where Douglas fell into the well. I wanted to stop something terrible happening, and that's what I did, although with consequences I didn't intend. Then I remembered Edna, protecting Dorothy when the bombs were dropping, hiding her in a bubble of shining light.

Eileen's hand was on the cover ready to turn the pages.

'No need,' I said, taking her place next to the book, taking strength from the women who had written their truths. Somewhere deep inside me anger and fear merged and writhed, pulsing, growing. I let it move through me, till my body throbbed, tingled to the ends of my fingers, the tips of my hair. I thought of my boys, saw their faces, felt the pain of their birth, their connection to me, of my flesh, of my blood. I placed my left hand on the book, raised my right hand into the air, reached out to Jacob, to Joe and wrapped them in glowing light, surrounded them in my love, safe.

Eileen stepped back, a shiver rolling down her spine. 'I'm pretty sure you just did magic. The air around you is shimmering.'

The power of the witch

My phone rang. An unknown number.

'Answer it,' hissed Mother.

'Hi, it's Fey. I hear you have a problem. What can I do to help?' I felt a weight lifted from me. Someone who knew me, understood what I was facing.

'They've got the boys. Have you any idea who has them?'

'Do you have the book?' I didn't ask how she knew; I was used to Fey knowing everything.

'Yes, but I don't know how to contact them to let them know.'

'I have an idea who it might be. There are some powerful witches out there, seekers of knowledge. I'll make enquiries.'

Mother made food, then cleared up the untouched plates. The kettle was continuously hot as we drank coffee after coffee to see us through the night. I dozed in the armchair – none of us left the comfort of the others.

****

Georgie watched the harsh lines fading from Nellie's face, as the thoughts that had raged at her for years fell away. Nellie was sleeping peacefully.

Georgie was not at peace. Everything had been taken from her family. What had they to be grateful for? And as for forgiveness, why should she forgive? Now she was losing Nellie, this woman who'd stepped in. Who she knew as her Nan. Who had filled the place where her mother should have been, where her real nan should have been. And what was Georgie left with? A baby who had arrived before Georgie was old enough to leave her own childhood.

Georgie cried, not knowing if she cried for her nan or cried for herself. She lifted her head from the rough hospital blanket, wiping her face with the back of her hand.

'I swear Nan, those that did harm to our family, those that used witchcraft against us, all those terrible things they did. I'm going to set things right. I don't know where their magic came from but I'm going to find the source of their magic, take it away from them. Everything that went wrong for us started with Eugenie. She abandoned her own flesh and blood. I want justice for you Nan, for our family. If it takes me a lifetime, I'll do it. That's my promise to you Nan. You're the only one who's truly loved me.'

Nellie moved her hand across the blanket, reaching for Georgie's. Their hands stayed clasped as the light through the metal framed windows faded. Georgie felt Nellie's hand go limp, listened as her breath came jagged and laboured. Felt her heart break as Nellie left her, her heart harden against those who had led them to this.

****

I sat upright, wide awake.

'It's Georgie.'

'Georgie?' Mother didn't have a trace of sleepiness in her, as if she had been awake, watching over me.

'Do you remember the twins, the ones that were separated after Frances abandoned them? Harrison went to live with Constance. Georgie stayed with Charlotte and Fredrick, and Nellie.

She blames our family for everything bad that happened to her family.' Tears slipped from my eyes.

'Why the tears?' asked Eileen.

'I just watched Nellie die. Georgie called her Nan. ' I wiped my eyes with the tissue David passed to me. 'Not her real grandmother. The woman who stepped into her life as there was no one else to take care of her. William's wife.'

Eileen's eyebrows knitted together. 'Is that good or bad?'

'William is the one that raped Eugenie. He was a nasty piece of work. John killed him, though Eugenie never knew.'

'Though what happened to his little boy was terrible, barbaric. Not forgiving him, but I can understand him being pushed to the edge.' Mother was thoughtful. 'Nellie's world must have fallen in pieces when little Robert was injured, when her man turned to drink. Looking through Georgie's eyes, Justin and Eugenie were the root of all her hardship. Georgie must have grown up with all that hatred behind her.'

'It doesn't really help us though, does it?' Eileen concentrated on the real problem. 'Even knowing who it is, doesn't tell us where the boys are.'

****

My fingers fumbled as I tried to answer my phone.

'Fey, do you have any news?'

'Yes, Dale made some calls. We know who it is. They've agreed to an exchange. Today. In the park, by the duck pond. They told me to tell you – no police, no games. Anything out of order and you won't see the boys again.'

She said to be there for eleven; it was ten-thirty. Time to go. I carried the book in my arms.

'Come on Mum. We need to leave.' She was in the kitchen, faffing about at I didn't know what.

As we neared the pond, David pointed to the far side. Jacob had his arm around Joe, holding him tight. Joe started to scream. 'Mommy, Mommy.' As he started to run to me, a woman took hold of his shoulder, stopping him. He screamed louder, the fear in his cries twisting my heart.

'Keep quiet,' the woman yelled. She raised her hand to strike him.

'Oh my God, it's Laura.' David sprang towards them. She brought her hand down fast. David wouldn't get there in time to stop her hurting Joe. Laura's hand stopped in mid-air, shaking as if she had encountered something hard. The shock threw her backwards. She fell to the floor. My protection spell was working.

'Run,' I yelled to the boys. As they ran towards David, other people rushed between them. Mrs Purple Hat grabbed at them, bounced back, disorientated. Dale almost got his hands on them, but his arms fled upwards as if startled by an electric shock.

'Told you,' whooped Eileen, 'your magic worked.'

The boys clung to my legs. Mother rushed over to pick up Joe. Eileen pulled Jacob towards her. I needed to deal with the people heading towards me. Laura was back on her feet, followed by Mrs Purple Hat, Dale at her side. Fey stepped into the open, brushing aside the bushes that had hidden her from view. I had trusted these people, thought they were helping me, looking out for me.

His words came back to me, the man in black. 'They are not friends.'

They dropped back to let Fey take the lead. She slowed as she neared me, her eyes glaring, glinting brilliant blue in the morning sun, the fading red of her hair shining bright. Her face was screwed up, distorted.

'Give me the book.' Her shriek echoed off the trees, penetrating my ears.

That would have been the simple answer. Yet I would never have known peace again. She had deceived me so totally, I could not trust her. The book would give her great power.

Fey's eyes turned from me, towards a dark clad figure striding across the grass.

'Don't do it Erica. Don't let her anywhere near that book.'

The man in black turned to Fey. 'Let it go Georgie. Everything they told you is wrong. Eugenie helped our family, not hurt us. She never used witchcraft to harm us.'

Fey stopped, stared at the man in black. He wrenched off his hat, his dark glasses. His red hair shone in the sunlight, his eyes flashed a brilliant blue.

She shook her head from side to side. 'You!' she screamed, realising he was her twin. 'She stole you from us, brainwashed you. Join me. Take the book. Just think what we can do with that power.'

'No Georgie, this has got to stop.' Harrison spoke softly, pleading.

'You traitor. Don't get in my way.' Fey turned in my direction, arms raised, pointing towards me.

'I wouldn't use magic on Erica if I were you.' Mother was at my side. In her hand was the gas lighter from Eileen's kitchen. She was holding it at the corner of the book in my arms. Small whisps of smoke started to rise from the corner of a page as it curled and browned.

Fey lowered her arms, whatever she had been about to throw at me forgotten amidst the threat to the precious book. Fey's face contorted, her body shook. Words I didn't recognise spewed from her mouth.

The book whisked out of my hands, torn away by a sudden gust of wind that put out the embryo flame. I was blinded by debris blowing in my face. Wind tore at the trees around us, their branches shuddering in the blast. A branch crashed to the ground; Mother dropped to the floor, grabbing her leg in pain.

Laura, Dale and Mrs Purple Hat chanted in unison, calling on the elements to help them. Harrison stretched his hands in front of them, heading them off, the air rippling in front of him, repelling those who came against him.

'Deal with Georgie,' he shouted to me. 'Send her evil back to her.'

I concentrated as I had when protecting the boys. All the anger, fear and sorrow that were held within me, I gave them their head, let them grow, take hold. I thought of Georgie, of the trauma she had suffered, of the hatred that had pushed to the core of her being. All that she was firing at me, I returned it to her, sending her hatred back to her.

The whirling wind around me changed course, surrounded Georgie. Leaves and sticks torn from bushes mixed in the maelstrom, pelting her skin. I watched David from the corner of my eye; he gathered up the boys, grabbed Mother's arm, pulled her from the ground where she had stumbled and led them away from the commotion. Eileen followed him, leaving just me and Georgie facing each other.

Harrison stood at my side, his opponents bound from harming us, their spite tied tight in invisible bonds.

'Let it go Georgie. It's time to move on. You can't carry on with your head full of revenge.'

She screamed, the sound chilling my skin. The storm around us increased in intensity. I struggled to reflect it back from where it came. The wind roared, deafening. A bench dragged its metal feet across the gravel, ducks took off from the pond, buffeted away. I heard creaking, my eyes raked across the sky to see where it was coming from.

Harrison saw it too. 'Run Erica, run.' He took my hand, pulling me after him. The tree crashed to the ground, crushing Georgie, its quivering branches a makeshift tomb.

The tips of the branches slashed at me, making me stagger, grazed but not harmed. We turned to look at the devastation behind us.

'Did I do that?' I felt myself weaving on my feet, nauseous.

'You reflected back to her what she was trying to do to you. She doubled her efforts, her hatred, when I joined you. She hadn't realised who I was till today.'

'Neither had I. I hadn't realised who Fey was either.' Did he know that I knew his story, and that of his family?

'I'm sorry for, well, for all of it.'

'It's all in the past. Your family took me in, gave me a good life. There is no need to apologise.'

'Then at least let me apologise for not believing you.'

Harrison smiled. 'And I am sorry for what Georgie tried to do to you, for what she has done to your family.'

Laura ran to the limp body trapped amidst the still quivering branches.

'Mother,' she cried, crawling into the leaves to put her arms round Georgie's lifeless body.

'Mother?'

'Yes. Georgie used her to take David away from you. Used a love spell. David became infatuated with Laura without knowing why, without any choice.'

'Harrison, will anyone else come after me?'

'These here won't. They've seen how powerful you are, what you are capable of. I can't guarantee that anyone else won't, not if they find out you have that book. Your mother had the right idea. Burn it.'

People were gathering at the fallen tree, an ambulance arrived, blue lights flashing, closely followed by a police car.

'You should go now Erica, take your family home. They have been through an ordeal they won't want to remember. I will take it from here. Enough people will tell of the freak whirlwind that toppled the tree.'

I gave him a hug, tears stinging my eyes. 'Thank you Harrison for your help. I should have listened to you sooner.'

He kissed my cheek. 'You are a powerful witch. You could have done this without me. You have a huge decision to make. To learn the craft or to let it go. Whatever you choose will be the right decision.'

'Can we meet to talk about all this? When things have settled down. There is so much I don't understand, and so much to learn.'

'When you are ready, I'll be there.'

He walked away, towards the milling people, no backward glance.

My family waited for me.

****

Mother was busy clearing up, ferrying the remains of beef-burgers and chicken legs from the garden to the kitchen. I followed with empty wine glasses and bottles.

David was putting two exhausted boys to bed. He would be a while. They were still nervous, found it difficult to settle to sleep. We had established a routine, bath with lavender oil, drops of ylang-ylang oil in a diffuser, two stories and tuck up with teddies. Daddy would stay till they were asleep.

We finished clearing the debris from the barbeque. It had been a good afternoon - sunshine and good company. Eileen and I had renewed the fun that we had always had when we were young, that somehow had got lost along the way through to adulthood. Mother had made peace with Patricia, renewed regular contact with her and Uncle Geoff. David, James, and Geoff had found plenty to talk about, vying for supremacy over the charcoal.

I took a last bottle of wine into the garden, poured a glass for me and for Mother.

'So what did Harrison tell you?'

'Well, he explained a lot that helped me understand the things that didn't make sense. Like the power of the magic that made David fall for Laura. David didn't stand a chance. It took all the little niggles and made them into mountains, then when Laura arrived he honestly couldn't help himself.'

I had been reassured by this, although I knew it would take a while for me to get past it – the thought of him exploring another woman's body creeped me out, no matter how strong the magic.

'And what about that strange business with the boys going off with the woman who looked like Annie?'

'That, apparently, was a glamour, where a witch can change her appearance, not physically, but so other people see her as different. The boys really thought it was Annie. We will probably never know who took them.'

'And the faces in the bathroom floor?'

'Harrison had been keeping an eye on Georgie, as he had realised she was unstable. She had tracked me down to this area, and had decided to open the shop as the best way to suck me in. It seemed strange how she sold a hotch-potch of everything I liked, but I just thought I was lucky she'd opened up. She had hoped to persuade me to hand over the book by becoming my friend.'

'Well that bit almost worked then, didn't it? We certainly thought she was a friend.'

'And it would have done the trick if Dorothy hadn't come to warn me. I would never have known the value of the book, or anything about the magic that saved us. The spirit world leapt in to warn us.'

Mum laughed. 'In that case, remember to check your bathroom floor daily. And the big question Erica – how come they were both witches? Where did it come from?'

'Harrison learned the craft from Constance who saw it as a good thing to be used to help people, protect them. But he doesn't know where Georgie got it from; just that she saw it as a weapon to control people, and to hurt them.'

One last question. Your sparkly red pen?'

'That wasn't actually magic. Harrison wanted to talk to me in a place where I might feel more comfortable and listen to him. He noticed my red pen, so looked in shops everywhere till he found one. Thought it might be a plausible reason to come to our home. Didn't work though, as David wouldn't let him in.'

David came into the garden, a smile on his face when he saw the wine. 'Did I hear my name mentioned?' He poured himself a glass, ruby red in the last of the sunshine.

He took a large gulp, put his glass on the table next to mine. He wrapped his arms around my shoulders, leant down to place a gentle kiss on my neck. I turned my face to demand a further kiss.

'I shall leave you to it,' said Mother, a chuckle in her voice.

David and I sat in the last of the evening light, comfortable in each other's company but with the fresh eyes of new lovers, the nervousness of building a new relationship.

As night spread its darkness, Mum returned with a large object wrapped in tissue under her arm.

'Sorry Erica, but we need to talk about this book. Harrison said to burn it.' She put the book on the table, placed the lighter next to it. 'Are you going to do what he advised?'

I held my hand above the book. I could feel warmth through its thin covering, its gentle pulsing calling me.

'Well,' said David, sitting next to me. 'Are you going to?'

I flicked my hand towards the book; a wisp of wind lifted the tissue, revealing the deep glowing red of the leather.

I shook my head, a smile creeping across my face.

'No.'

Author's note

This story is set in and around Birmingham, where I was born, grew up and still live. I love my city. Although much of the work is fictionalised – Lansdowne farm does not exist – events set in Birmingham are based in reality. Catherine's life with Jack was shaped by my mother's tales of her early life in the back-to-back houses in Nechells.

Mom's recollections of the war years gave me an insight into life when bombs were falling, although she always kept humour in her stories. She described the chamber pot balanced precariously on the edge of a blown out building. People were worried that it might be full and would fall on them as they walked past, never mind the rest of the building. The Peace Garden on Bath Row is still there, a reminder of the church that didn't make it.

And yes, we do say Mom in Birmingham, not Mum. This has even been noted in Parliament where a Birmingham MP, Jess Philips, requested that her use of the word 'mom' was recorded as such in House of Commons records, rather than 'corrected' to 'mum'.

Acknowledgements

My thanks to Bobbi and Ashley, and Jake Gordon for the time they have so freely given to read and provide great feedback that has made this story so much better than the original draft.

Thanks also to my grandmother, Beatrice Annis, who saw ghosts and laid out the dead. Sadly, I never met her; she died before I was born.

And many thanks to the faces in my bathroom floor.

Author bio

A long time pagan, Portland writes about topics she has an interest in. The Face in the Bathroom Floor follows the interconnected lives of witches over five generations. An early short story, How to Write a Spell Book, was published in the anthology, Words from the Cauldron, a collaboration by pagan writers to raise funds for a children's charity.

Following a stroke that left her unable to continue her previous occupation, Portland studied for a masters' degree in Creative Writing, with a plan to turn her scribbles into something more substantial. She is now a contributor to Witch magazine, with a regular slot entitled Words from a Witch's Journal. Portland also volunteers with the Pagan Federation UK, as Disability Liaison for the Midlands, writing a weekly blog exploring pagan life when you have a disability.

Portland has a butterfly mind combined with a lifetime love of learning something new. She is a qualified aromatherapist, makes jewellery, played the Djembe with a band, and morris danced with Beorma Morris, Birmingham's only border morris side, entertaining the somewhat bemused local inhabitants. She throws pretty good fancy dress parties too.

The Faces

For a long time I have looked and wondered at the faces in my bathroom floor, patterns that when you look at them in a certain light are definitely people. I am not the only one who can see them.

Have you ever seen faces in patterns? Share your experiences at www.portlandjones.com

Reviews

Before you go, can I ask a favour?

Reviews are so important to authors, especially to new authors like me. Can you spare a couple of minutes to leave a review? Hopefully, it will be a good one. Thanks for reading.

Printed in Great Britain
by Amazon

57890365R00163